DEDICATION

*Terror was a diminutive woman
named Alace Sweets. ~Todd Worthson*

To all the folks out there like me who don't fear
those loud bumps in the night. We know
embracing the darkness doesn't always mean what
society implies.

CONTENTS

ACKNOWLEDGMENTS

Writing and preparing a book for publishing is not entirely unlike raising a child: Not something one can do alone. It takes a village.

From editors and proofreaders, to critique partners—there's no way I could do this without their assistance.

So thank you, Hot Tree Editing. Headed up by Becky Johnson, this team of experts has always had the best interests of my stories in mind, and this one is no different. I'm quite pleased Alace and Owen's story evoked such visceral reactions from you. Your feedback and assistance is critical, and I do appreciate everything. Five years we've been doin' this thang, and I've never regretted the partnership.

Thank you, Mel Barber of Whiskey Jack Editing. You've taken my manuscript and polished it until it shines. Your comments and observations are always thought provoking, forcing me to dig just a little deeper for the right phrasing and words. Plus, those moments when I jar a personal reaction from you truly feeds my creative ego. Makes me kinda preeny.

To those authors whose opinions I lean upon, thank you. Cover guidance, book description review, comments on the story theme—each piece of advice offered matters so much to me. Chelsea, Kathleen, and Glenna, you guys are the bomb-dot-com, and I hope you understand how much your friendship means to me.

Megan and Kori, my favorite alpha readers—huge thanks just for putting up with me and all my "but how did it made you feel" inquiries in addition to the dozens of other questions I threw your way.

Finally, to the readers who've come to love my favorite little serial killer: Thank you. I hope you find this expansion into Alace's world worthy of your time. I certainly enjoyed bringing her back to life.

Woofully yours,
~ML

PROLOGUE

Wilderness area

The figure sat on the edge of a planting barrel in a wide field—unnaturally still except for the tick-tocking metronome of their head. Tipping back and forth, it kept perfect time to the a cappella song floating through the air. The setting sun granted the monstrosity a dark halo, the buzzed-close hair on their scalp an illusion lending an air of false divinity to the figure. That vision was disturbed when they drew a tattered and torn hairnet tight over their head. Uneven coils of hair stuck through the mesh in clumped tufts where the netting was pulled awry. Foot-long hanks of different shades of blonde were woven in here and there, trapped by twists of wire, no care given to where sharp ends lay. Blood-darkened metal stuck both out and in, the hair lank and swaying in bunches framing the angular face.

When the song ended, they lifted their trophy-adorned head, the straight blade of their nose angling towards the nearby line of trees. "Again." Rough as bitten nails on a chalkboard, their voice scraped out in a croak ragged with disuse. "Please?"

An audibly drawn-out, shuddering sigh was followed by an uncomplaining resumption of singing. Wrecked here and there by coughing, the tune wavered high and low, unanchored on any given octave, shattered tone mattering less than the strangely predictable cadence.

Face tipped towards the sky and greasy hair falling in a tattered curtain down its back, the figure joined in on a final verse. Whispered vocalization tumbled out over dry and cracked lips, the last note sustained on a smile as they attempted to harmonize with the other singer.

"Don't go." The plea seemed to come from the air. "Please."

"Oh, darlin'." The figure pushed to their feet. The too-tight clothing cinched around their chest and middle made a division of their form, joined as if awkwardly sewn together from dissimilar things. A "made" monster like Frankenstein's. The binding wasn't comfortable, but it didn't have to be. *It's what I need.* "I have to, you know that."

"Please."

Bending at the waist, the figure put their hands on the edges of the barrel and tipped it onto one edge. Carefully balanced thus, they rolled the barrel to a small, bare spot darkening the yard. Framed by fertile, thick grass that looked black in the deepening dusk, the emptiness was revealed to be a buried piece of metal mesh. Stained fingers threaded through the diamond-shaped openings, beds of the ripped nails blackened by dirt and excrement. The closer the barrel came to that tiny, one-foot square space, the tighter their grip was on the wire, until the fingers were stark white in the twilight.

"Please." No longer wafting through the air, the plea bled up from the space below ground, voice hoarsened from hours of singing. "Please. I'll be quiet. Or I'll sing whatever you want. Anything. I'll do anything. Please don't go. I'll do whatever you want."

"Move your fingers, darlin'."

"Please. Oh God, please."

The form shook its head, hair falling in tangled sheets around its face. "You know I can't do that. Now—" They rolled the barrel closer. "—move your fingers. Don't want to give you a pinch."

Before the barrel full of dirt and flowers settled into place, cutting off the waning daylight from the cage constructed of dirt and wire and tree roots and boards, the form caught sight of the face that went with the fingers. Only for a moment, but enough to see hair darker than night, matted skull-tight to the prisoner's head. An eye tinged with yellow stared up—the green iris a startling clarity and brilliance incongruous in contrast. Plump lips looked nearly purple next to the blanched white skin of its face. Their gazes locked for a moment; then even that was cut off by the bottom of the barrel settling into place.

SEEKING WORTHY PURSUITS

Alace Sweets, #2

MariaLisa deMora

Edited by Hot Tree Editing

Proofreading by Whiskey Jack Editing

First Published 2020

ISBN 13: 978-1-946738-60-8

Chapter One

"All rise."

Well accustomed to the trappings of his courtroom, the Honorable Judge Todd Worthson swept out of the back rooms and up the steps to the Bench, ear tuned to the murmur of the spectators. He settled and leaned forwards, holding his hand out towards his bailiff for paperwork from the first case on his daily calendar.

"You may be seated."

Deputy Marshall had worked with Todd for several years, and they were in tune with one another, so Todd had learned to notice when Marshall did anything out of the ordinary. Today, his tone was significantly more formal than normal, and the difference tweaked Todd's attention.

"Anything I need to know, Marshall?" Todd accepted the folder without looking at it, staring at the deputy instead. Marshall's eyes cut to the folder and back to Todd, and he nodded towards the front of the courtroom. One of today's defendants had to be someone Todd knew. Typically, his bailiff would have brought it to his attention in chambers, unless he'd learned the details too late. *Great.*

Setting his jaw, he straightened and rested the folder in its accustomed place, then flipped it open. A picture stared up at him. Long, dark hair scraped back from a face that was gorgeous when it wasn't fixed in an expression of defiant anger, the woman was thin, the symmetry of features broken by sharp lines of cheekbones and nose.

He sighed, then angled his gaze up and across the room to where she was seated at the counsel table with her lawyer. She was staring at him, and even from this distance her brilliant blue eyes were captivating. *Son of a bitch.*

He flipped the folder closed, leaned forwards and motioned to both lawyers, silently asking they approach the Bench. "Gentlemen." He sighed again. "We are going to have a postponement." As expected, both men's eyes stayed on him, waiting. All of the attorneys who regularly appeared in his courtroom knew he didn't tolerate dramatic statements, and arguing with him without knowing the why would be a misstep neither would be willing to take. "I need to recuse myself." The prosecutor glanced over his shoulder to where the defendant sat alone. "I suspect you know why, but I'll make it clear for the record." Todd looked at his court reporter with a wry smile she returned, fingers moving on her machine. "I have a personal knowledge of the defendant." Both lawyers smirked, and he took it without comment, knowing he would be the topic of the day at the bars after court.

With a dismissive gesture, he sat back and stated, again for the record, "In the matter of the *State versus Temple*, I must recuse myself from the case, as I have a personal knowledge of the defendant, Madison Temple." He glanced at the folder, picked up his pen, and wrote a note on a sheet of paper affixed for that use. "There will be a one-week continuance as the court seeks audience for the case before another judge."

He gathered up the folder and handed it to Deputy Marshall, accepting the next case folder in exchange. He opened it and studied the information while the various lawyers and parties shuffled around, Maddy's lawyer making way for the next defendant's legal team. He glanced up in time to watch her ass sway out the door in her knee-length skirt, sensible heels elongating her legs in an attractive but understated way. He sighed again.

***

"Why didn't you call me?" Todd's words came out harsher than he intended, his tone more abrasive. "Shit, I'm sorry, Maddy. It just was a blindside, seeing you in my courtroom today." Ignoring the people bustling past his chambers, he reached out and cupped a palm on each shoulder, noting she'd lost weight in the couple of weeks since he'd seen her last. "You could have called, though."

"I know." She stood firm, chin up. "I didn't think it would go that far. I expected a hallway conversation and then for him to drop the charges." She shrugged and he gave her a squeeze. "Like he always does."

"You can't keep harassing him like this. He's a state employee, and there's always a chance of him picking up the phone and calling in a favor." Todd closed the door and took a step towards her, knowing from her stance that she'd resist being pulled into his embrace but that she'd gladly take it if the first move showed his need for her. He scooted close to align their bodies and wrapped his arms around her, neck bent to press his cheek to the top of her head. "There's no evidence he had anything to do with it."

"It" referred to her twin sister's disappearance three months ago.

"It" was the reason Maddy had been in the courtroom today, because she believed her sister's boyfriend knew more than he'd told the police—any of the three dozen times she'd caused him to be questioned.

"It" was also the reason Maddy wasn't in Todd's bed full-time as a live-in girlfriend.

"He did. Or he knows something." The words were hissed softly, muffled by his shirt. She'd buried her face in his shoulder, and her arms crept around his waist. She was reluctant to grant herself comfort, not knowing how her sister fared. Her dreams had given him that knowledge, an insight of which he suspected Maddy wasn't even aware. "I *know* it. I feel it in my gut."

Todd's eyes closed, and he focused on the woman in his arms, trying to communicate his care and a desire to see her healthy and whole through the contact. *If I could hold her together with my heart alone, I would.* "You can't keep this up, sweetheart."

"I'm not going to give up on Mackie." Her ferocity and loyalty, two traits he found attractive, were even more evident in Maddy's fight to find out what had happened to her sister.

"No one's saying to give up. I'm saying you need to let the cops do their job." Todd didn't have any dealings with the police in the Utah county where Makenzie had disappeared, but he knew enough cops in general to be certain of what he was saying. "He's already been cleared, honey."

"He was the last one to see her." *Alive*. The unspoken word hung in the air at the end of Maddy's sentence. "He admits that much. But he knows more. I feel it in my gut."

I feel it in my gut.

He'd heard that phrase recently, spoken by someone who had made a life's study out of paying attention to those indefinable details that the unconscious mind noted as odd.

"I have a friend who locates…people." *Understatement.* "Why don't I make a call or two tonight or tomorrow, see what it'll take to get this case in front of them?" Mentally slamming his head against a wall, he was immediately sure his impulsive offer would become a regret in the near future.

Maddy stumbled in her haste to pull back, blue eyes shining up at him. "*Please*. Anything we can do." In the face of her heartfelt plea, he had no answer other than a nod. Her arms were tight around his neck when she broke down, her "thank you" mixed with sobs.

Todd would do anything to keep this kind of pain from her, hated that Maddy was hurting like this. Even if Mackie was dead, as he expected she was, once Maddy knew for certain, that's when she could move on. Would give herself permission to begin to heal. She'd be stuck in this agonizing limbo until then, in every aspect of her life.

Now, he just had to convince his friend to talk about the job that would need doing to settle this case. This meant that first thing, he'd be making a call to the only person he knew who hunted people.

Alace Sweets.

CHAPTER TWO

Wilderness area

"Hey." The request was muted, weak and thin. "Can I have some water?" Silence lay thick on the clearing, the area so quiet just a faint hum of machinery could be heard in the distance. "Are you there?"

From inside the sunken cell, the overhead opening created an illusion. From far away, along the farthest wall, perhaps, it appeared no larger than a postage stamp. Sometimes the prisoner manufactured makeshift telescopes by cupping shaking hands together, creating the visual impression it was even farther away. *With distance comes perspective.*

Closer to the opening, the view expanded, growing until it stretched horizon to horizon. It revealed an entire world out there. Within sight, but entirely out of reach.

"Please?"

This plea was no more successful in garnering a response than previous questions. Fingers wound through the web of metal covering the opening, tightened, and pulled hard. The scrape from their body dragging along the dirt floor was loud, echoing in the space. When the prisoner's face pressed at the opening, the sharp edges of metal scratched the exposed cheek, grooved marks appearing in taut skin.

"Hey."

Silence.

From far away came the sound of a helicopter, buzzing along its way. The idea of working, of existing in the open air and interacting with other people, nearly caused a retreat. Fingers were forced tighter, the grip fiercer as a skim of blood made the wire slippery, hard to hold.

"Hello."

Louder this time, making a demand of the air because there was a sudden terror of being alone. Before, the fear had always been of the figure seen at the edges of vision. The form that gave sustenance…or withheld. Subject to their whims as untrackable as weather patterns. Running cold one day and hot the next.

Now the fear was a forced aloneness, the captor's hiding of self. Denial of company. Those few hours in any given sun-span that kept everything in balance. *If they can't hear me, then I can't be heard. I'll be alone.* Far worse than the threatened destruction of existence was the loss of being.

"Please. I'll do anything."

Maybe the time was right. Perhaps that particular breakpoint was what the figure needed. It didn't matter in the end, because following the words came a rush of footfalls, grass crunching loudly under each. A thud, then the outline of a head appeared, blocking out much of the waning light. Spittle rained down, dotting the fingers and cheek, creating tiny circles of distortion in the covering of dirt. "What do you want?" Screaming, over and over, demanding an answer to a question the form in the pit could not answer openly.

Everything would gain me nothing.

"What do you want? What? What?" The figure moved, sunshine glinting off the shiny dome of its head, dark hair shorn close to the skull. That was the first indication that this wasn't the same person, not inside, not where it counted. This wasn't the one who spoke softly, calling the prisoner "darlin'" and careful of injury. This was the angry one, the one who dripped liquid fire through the grate, making an impossible-to-pass circle around the meal bucket. The bucket retrieved on schedule, unemptied. This was the one who would maim for pleasure. "What do you want?"

Fast as it could be accomplished, the figure fell away from the mesh, hands shoving in tandem with heels to push away from the opening—creating distance that was as grand an illusion as the view through the opening. All the angry one would need do was lift the trapdoor. Locked into place from the outside, camouflaged by dirt and grass, it could be opened and then the entire range of anger would be unleashed.

Nowhere to hide.

A softly whispered word, one only, the best defense was a tiny offense. "Nothing."

There was no guarantee the kind one would return tomorrow with water. If not, it wasn't the first time of going without. There was no guarantee the angry one would stay, either. While challenging, that emotion was at least predictable. Worst-case scenario would be the third one would show. Back against the dirt wall, the prisoner closed eyes strained from holding them wide in the darkness. The welcome relief of darkness giving a false security, one where dreams were allowed.

Maybe I'll die tomorrow.

CHAPTER THREE

Todd

"Eric, may I speak with Alace?" From the pause on the line, Todd knew his request read as not only odd enough to be noted but—since the silence carried an oppressive heaviness—also unwelcome.

Eric Ward was Todd's best friend. A relationship earned on the high school football field as well-matched rivals and then honed through the years of college and beyond, their professions causing their lives to continually intersect. Eric was a prosecutor, Todd a judge. Their friendship was something the county court system had to work around, but to have a friend like Eric, Todd was more than willing to put up with the occasional grousing from the other two judges.

"Why?" A single word clipped and bubbling with anger told Todd he was not wrong. Eric was protective of his wife, and with good reason. Her job was unusual, and that oddness was the very reason Todd was on the phone right now.

He didn't try to hide his tension. Now wasn't the time to lie or joke. The only way Eric would grant his request was if Todd laid it out. He just had to do it while following the ruse Alace had carefully crafted over the past months. Allowing his voice to expose all the unease he felt, he said, "I have an idea for a story."

Alace had changed her life when she met Eric. Changed Eric's life, too, but hers had gone through perhaps the greatest metamorphosis. These days, the people in town knew her as a writer. Through the months her cover had held firm, and Todd knew, from evenings spent listening to Eric talk, she'd even had to turn down reporter-requested interviews about her job.

Her fake job.

Her real one, the shadow job that shouldn't have to exist, was why he was calling. He broke the silence Eric had let grow, expanding on the premise of a story idea. "I'd like to run it by her, see if she thinks it's worth pursuing."

"I'll call you back." The sound coming through the phone assumed the distinct tonelessness that indicated the connection had dropped or been disconnected without a goodbye. With a wry grin, he guessed the latter.

"Okay. I can do this." Todd ran his hand through his hair and leaned his car seat back a few inches, prepared to wait however long it took to get a return call. The only thing on his agenda for the remainder of the day was a trip to the grocery store. It could wait. He huffed out tension with a humorless laugh. *Waiting on the pleasure of a killer. Some judge I am.* His phone buzzed immediately, even before he'd had a chance to settle completely, and when he looked, it was to see a text from a number that wasn't in his contacts.

Go home.

That was it, the sum total of the instructions he assumed were from Alace. He scowled and raised the phone to punch Eric's number again, but the call died before it connected, a malfunction of the device. A moment later a second text buzzed his phone.

Go home, Todd.

His phone no longer had a signal. In this location, the message about searching for service was unusual enough to note. He'd held entire conference calls parked in this same p ace, with nary a staticky pause. He studied that message a moment longer and then tossed the useless phone to the center console. Moving by rote, he yanked the gearshift into reverse, slung his arm over the back of the seat to twist and look out the window as he backed out of his space. *Clearly, I'm going home right now.*

The drive was unremarkable, he encountered only limited traffic and the lights on his route cooperated for once. With his thumb pressing firmly on the garage door controller, he scarcely had to pause before he pulled into the structure. The door rose smoothly, late afternoon light slanting through the opening. A rectangle of darkness yawned ahead of him, and he startled when he realized the interior door stood open. He exited the parked car and, with the engine ticking its slow cooldown in the background, he tapped the button wired to the wall next to the door, the light slowly muting as the lowering barrier shut it outside, trapping him in.

Briefcase in hand, Todd stalked into the kitchen, not quite surprised to see a figure already seated in a chair at the table. Turned sideways, Alace had propped her feet on an adjacent chair, ankles tidily crossed, socks visible on her shoeless feet an indication of either the length of time she'd been present or how involved she expected the conversation to be.

"That didn't take long." Alace's tone held no amusement, even as teasing as those words sounded on the surface. "Must mean this is an important interruption in my day."

"It is." Eyes on Alace, he bent to place the briefcase on the floor next to the side table, where he followed the next step in his normal routine by emptying his pants pockets into the bowl kept there for that purpose. He patted one front pocket, trying to decide what was missing from the pile of belongings.

"You left it in the car." Alace's shoulders shifted slightly as she adjusted her hands across her middle, fingers threading together in a pose of relaxation he didn't believe for a moment.

His phone. That's what was unaccounted for, left behind because it wasn't functioning. Todd nodded, then dipped his head to stare at his fingers working the clasp on the old-fashioned watch worn on his right wrist. "How do you know I left it in the car?"

"Because that's where it pinged when I turned it back on." A small device rested on the table next to her. Thin, it was barely the length of an adult man's finger. She tipped her head that direction. "Tools of the trade, ya know. You missed a call. Should check on that later."

Watch carefully positioned on the surface next to the bowl, face angled towards the ceiling, cradled by a fold in the band, Todd ran out of things to occupy his hands and turned, giving Alace his full attention. He firmed his resolve and said, "I need to talk to you."

Her arms spread, fingers flared out, palms facing him, she gave him an obvious opening. He just wasn't sure how to begin. What had seemed so clear in the car, muffled by the buffering voice of his friend, was muddled now that he was directly within reach of her. *Wow*, he marveled. *I'm frightened of Alace.*

"You should be afraid, Todd."

His heart stuttered and sweat gathered along his spine, heat held in with the covering from his suit jacket, not yet removed.

"Right now—" She broke off as she lifted her feet from the chair, swinging them to dangle over the floor.

Todd found himself studying every movement as if she were a viper about to strike, no matter she was fifteen feet away and seated.

"I'm looking for a reason to allow you to threaten my world." One elbow landed on the tabletop as her tiny chin nestled into her propping palm.

Compared to him, all parts of her were tiny. *Size doesn't matter here, not with Alace.* For all he'd initiated the meeting, had started this game, she held all the cards.

"You need to be a hundred percent certain you want this conversation to move forwards. If you don't, just say so. Say so and then we can talk about what I should get Eric for his birthday next month. You're his best friend, and I rely on your lifelong insights into the surface things he enjoys. Easy breezy, we'll have ourselves a real quick chat full of pleasantries, and I'll be out of your hair before you even know it, thanking you for your gracious hospitality."

The legs of her chair screeched across the floor as it was pushed backwards, her feet gaining firm purchase on the tiles when she sat forwards, balancing on the edge of the seat.

Small didn't mean weak. Alace's visible musculature was defined; each line of her body revealed a tension like the coiled power of a tiger about to spring.

She lifted a hand. "If you aren't a hundred percent, and we start down this path, I hope you know your indecision provides absolutely zero reason for me to turn back." Her hand formed an "O" as she spoke, finger and thumb meeting in a circle. Her chin lifted, and he was pinned in place with her gaze, the flat stare as disturbing as anything he'd ever experienced. "Approaching me is like leaping from a cliff. Once that first step is made, the only direction is down."

Silence ruled for minutes, each tick of the kitchen clock marking another inch towards no return. He'd shown her his fear; the air reeked of it, fabric under his arms sodden. Maddy's eyes flashed through his thoughts, that brilliance dimmed by her sorrow, the absolute worst of it the not knowing. Mackie deserved to be found, to be saved if she could be, and celebrated in a way that gave closure if the journey turned out to be recovery instead of rescue.

Todd pulled in a deep, deep breath, lungs and ribs aching as he drew more in than comfortable. Then he nodded, toed his shoes off, and sock-footed made his unsteady way to the chair opposite where Alace still sat. Actions clumsy, his limbs unaccustomedly ungainly and slow, and if he'd eaten or drank since walking through the door, he would wonder if he'd been drugged.

"It's the adrenaline crash. Want me to get you some juice?" Alace matched actions to words and was up and around the table in a moment. "I know just the thing." She passed behind him with a touch to his shoulder in a move that had every nerve in his body blaring an alarm again. Todd twisted and watched as she confidently made her way to the refrigerator, and without looking or seeking, put her hand on a can of sparkling juice he used as the light mixer Maddy preferred with her cocktails. Alace popped the top one-handed, bumping the refrigerator door closed with a hip as she reached for one of the glasses stacked in the dish strainer. "Give you a little boost right here. Like I said, just the thing." She was beside him an instant later, half-filled glass deposited on the table, can cradled in one hand as she returned to her seat. She lifted the can, drank deeply, and winked at him. "See? No poison."

"God." He stared at her, the façade of the sweet girl Eric loved and cherished pulled entirely away, exposing the driven professional underneath. His mind still tried to shy away from the idea of that profession. "Am I that transparent?" Ignoring his still-jangling nerves, he lifted the glass and took a drink, not surprised to find it cold and sweet, and exactly what he needed to wet his Sahara-worthy dry mouth.

"No. You actually gave good poker face. The things you could control, you did, very well." She shrugged, drank from the can again and set it to the side. The empty rattle of metal on wood said she'd drained it dry. He took another drink, the bottom edge of the glass clattering against the table as he set it down. "It's the involuntary reactions that matter most to me, and I've made a study of cataloging those. Micro-expressions, heart rates, skin changes—they all mean different things, and I've learned to speak their languages." She quirked an eyebrow at him, and he instantly wondered if that expression meant something different in Alace-speak than it did his, where it usually preceded a clever quip. "It's nice I can put you at ease, Todd. I like the fact you don't look much past the face value of things. For instance—" She leaned in slightly, elbow and hand returning to their previous positions, her chin propped lightly on the edge of her palm. "It never would cross your mind that the poison could have already been in the glass, and me drinking the rest of the can of juice a ploy to earn your trust and compliance, so you'd in essence drug yourself by following typical social mores and taking a sympathetic drink."

Concrete settled into his lungs, his body crying for another breath he couldn't take.

Alace's hand tipped, and she rubbed the edge across her bottom lip, as if to chase away a stray drop that dared remain. "I didn't, of course. You're Eric's best friend." Voice rising in a sweet, girlish lilt, she asked, "Why would I do that?"

Todd didn't blink, didn't look away, frozen in the knowledge that she could have. He was an intelligent man, prided himself on his ability to quickly assimilate details of a case, dredging up obscure rulings and precedent at will. He enjoyed pastimes that allowed him to flex his mind, worked at staying sharp. Yet he had the feeling Alace was so far out of his league he couldn't even see the starting line from where he stood. *Hell, she probably already knows why she's here.*

"I had to recuse myself from a case today." He blinked, lids dragging painfully over dry eyes, and he blinked quickly a few more times, reflexively swiping away the wetness flooding his vision. She moved and he paused, watching. One finger tapped the device that still rested on the table, and he heard a high-pitched whine, almost a mosquito's drone, but only for an instant. "What'd you do?"

Both elbows on the table now, Alace balanced her chin on the heels of her hands. Her head tipped the slightest amount to one side, a corner of her mouth twitching. Once. She didn't say anything, or shift position again, just stared at him.

Shaking off his unease, Todd glanced at the device, surprised to see a dim, pulsing red ring of light around the edges of the screen. He deliberately decided to set that aside and closed his eyes as he continued. "Madison Temple is a good friend of mine." *Did I put too much emphasis on "good"? Not enough?* He squinted against the light in the kitchen, waning now as the sun settled towards the horizon outside. "Her sister went missing a few months ago. Maddy's convinced that Mackie's boyfriend knows something. He was the last known person to see her. Maddy can't let it go, and she keeps harassing him. He puts up with it for a while, then has charges brought against her. The case today was one of those. Maddy told me she has a gut feeling about him." He stopped when Alace's pupils flared slightly, waiting.

Alace hummed softly. "Mmmm. I get it. It might not be what she thinks, that would more likely be her desperate desire to find her sister tacking itself to some aspect of his personality she doesn't even know she finds offensive. But once the gut's involved, it's all bets off whether a person can let it go, set it aside, and move on." Alace sat back in the chair, gaze steady as she stared at Todd. "What does your gut say about the boyfriend?"

He was shaking his head before she finished speaking. "I don't know enough to make a considered judgement. He's from Utah, where Mackie was living with him. I've met the man twice, more than a year ago. Both were at social functions where I was more concerned with appearances than I was about what I thought about Maddy's sister's boyfriend."

"That's honest, at least." The corner of her mouth pulled sideways into what might have been the beginning of a grin. "You are kinda preeny." He stared, not sure how to take her statement, and after a moment she burst into laughter. He found himself smiling at her, then looked more closely at her face. The laughter came from her throat, her mouth moved with it, lips curving up, but her eyes stayed focused, that flat stare still in place. His smile dropped away, and that was the moment the corners of her eyes crinkled, echoing the amusement still coming from her mouth. "That's an improvement, Todd. You really should be better at this, you know? You're surrounded by such rich opportunity every single day, and it burns a little to know you've been ignoring the lessons right in front of you."

"I don't know what to say." Didn't know what not to say was more like it, not wanting her to take offense at anything, not now that it seemed she might be open to looking for Mackie. "I'm preeny?"

"Masculine peacock, strutting around at parties like that. Silks and suedes covering your finely honed muscles that aren't for strength but pursued for how they help you fill out a suit. Hair trimmed and styled, hundred-dollar products used to plaster it in place, pristine teeth peeping out from behind unchapped lips." She shrugged and sighed. "Preeny." Her lips pursed. "I bet this Madison is pretty. You'd go for a petite woman, not because she'd be easy to overpower but because she gives you something to protect. Caveman tendencies are natural, at least to some extent. I bet she fits right in the curve of your arm, because then it's comfortable for everyone. You, her, the people watching how well you go together. A pretty picture manufactured by careful packaging."

"It's not like that. I liked Maddy as a friend first. We slipped into a relationship naturally, building on years of conversations and experiences. She's pretty, I can't deny that, and to try would be a lie. And yes, she fits me, but that's more because we've gotten comfortable with each other, so being with her is as easy as breathing." He shook his head. "I won't argue with your evaluation of me, because that's your opinion and has only as much effect as I allow. My job means when I'm out and about, I'm in the public eye. But I didn't become a judge on the strength of my looks or how well I fill out a suit, silk or not. So the fact you seem to have a demeaning estimation of me as a person doesn't matter to me for anything other than what it might mean for my friendship with Eric, and what it could mean for Maddy and Mackie. I hope you won't dismiss Mackie's disappearance out of hand because of dislike for me."

"I don't dislike you." Alace's head tipped the other direction this time, and he wondered if there was any pattern to her physical tells, if he could discern her real intent by analyzing the physicality she displayed within a conversation. "I didn't say that. I said you were preeny, and you asked what that meant to me. I didn't say I didn't like it about you."

"I'm confused." Should he let this slide, move past it and see if he could steer the conversation back to Mackie? No, it would bother him if he didn't know. He'd be considering every word around her, overthinking his wardrobe choices, and that lack of comfort would lead to avoidance, which would eventually mean not hanging out with Eric. "You catalogue me as 'preeny,' but it's not necessarily a bad thing. It's just another detail to tick on your mental list when you think about Eric's friend Todd?"

"Pretty much. Preeny isn't an insult; it's an observation. I've met preeny guys before, and pairing that trait with a dozen others can help give a rounded view of an individual." The device on the table vibrated and she glanced down at it, brows pulling together. "What kind of car does Maddy drive?"

"A yellow—"

Alace was moving before he finished. She tapped the device, the red ring disappeared, and when she stepped out from behind the table, she was clad in soundless, rubber-soled boots he hadn't noticed on the floor. *Where did she—* "I'll be in touch." A hand gripped his shoulder as she passed, the whisper drifting aimlessly, still wafting through the air as he turned to find an empty kitchen, Alace having disappeared up the hallway to his bedroom.

"Alace." His call was met with silence; not even the air moved behind her.

The doorbell trilled, and he startled to his feet, chair sliding out behind him until it crashed into the barstools next to the breakfast bar. A distinctive click of a key, this from the front door just as he saw a shadow pass through the backyard, shimmering through the twilight and the sheer curtains.

"Todd?" Maddy. *Of course.* "Are you home?"

"Yeah, I'm in the kitchen." He glanced at the table, gathered the juice can, and dropped it into the empty glass, making a paired set that masked the reality of two people sitting here only moments ago. "Come on in, join me. How'd it go?"

She paused in the doorway, and he scanned her down and up, then down again. The reality of Alace's observations hit him like the soft punch of a pillow. Maddy did fit him, effortlessly. And she was gorgeous, even with dark circles under her eyes giving silent testimony of her sleepless nights. Slim-hipped, perfectly proportioned. He opened his arms and she walked into them, willing to ask for comfort now they were alone behind closed doors, and he wasn't arguing with her about how to manage her grief and fears.

"You didn't answer your phone." Her voice was muffled against his chest, the pressure of her lips a benediction. She turned her head, cheek resting above his heart. "So I took a chance you'd be home."

"I forgot it in the car." Cradling her close, he laid his cheek on top of her head, mapping her comfort by the cadence of her breaths. "I'm glad you came over."

Todd eased her into discussion of their evening possibilities, keeping up the comfortable cadence until dinner was ordered online and delivered, served from the packages lined up along the edge of the kitchen countertop. Sometime later he made another aborted attempt to pull his phone out and gave in to her laughing separation from his hold, her hands shoving at his butt as he rose from the couch.

"Go get it already. You're making me antsy with how much you miss that thing."

At the doorway, he glanced back, catching her giving him a look filled with sad fondness, as if she mourned along with him all the missed opportunities to have this tiny bit of normality and comfort. Since Mackie's disappearance, most of Maddy's evenings were spent making calls and posting pictures online in groups and on boards, engaging tipsters in the forums built around that kind of activity. "I'll be right back."

Maddy lifted her chin and smiled, even that so sad it tore another piece off his already tattered heart. "I'll be right here, Todd."

Phone retrieved, he closed the car door, darkness falling in the enclosed garage. Tapping on the phone's screen, he woke it and unlocked the device, finding the service connectivity restored. He saw the missed call from Maddy, but the previous texts were gone, as was any indication he'd received contact from an unknown device. The only thing remaining from his afternoon pursuits was an addition to his photo roll, a book cover of a popular mystery written by local celebrity Alace Sweets.

The image on the cover was of a falling-down farmhouse, a sinister half-covered well partially in view behind the structure. The title was *On the Case*.

CHAPTER FOUR

Alace

Hunched over the desk positioned in a corner of the room she'd claimed as an office, Alace ran fingers through her hair, idly straightening it strand by strand until it fell in a comfortable flow behind her ears and down the back of her neck. On the surface in front of her were two tablets, each showing news articles. Different papers, different locations, different decades—but otherwise so much alike they were eerie in resemblance.

Idaho, twelve years ago: a blight covering more than three years in which thirteen girls and women went missing from towns over a swath of geography that framed the edges of nearly a half-million acres of national forest.

One reporter had drawn correlations between them, even though the local police had claimed no such connections and publicly refuted the reporter, called his article fearmongering. Repudiated by the authorities, the reporter's sources were hounded in ways untraceable and had eventually recanted their stories, memories claimed muddier with time than initially thought.

She flicked that article to the side, surfacing the one directly behind it on the tablet. Idaho, two years ago: sunken areas in a series of forest clearings surveyed by a drone enthusiast revealed strangely similar features too regular to be natural. Curiosity piqued, a forest ranger had followed up on the report, traipsing into the woods thinking he'd hone his orienteering skills if nothing else. His visit had turned up a partial skeleton, human, discovered when his boot sank to the ankle along the edge of the environmental artifact. He swore to the reporter, not the one who'd written the original article, that when he'd pulled his foot out of the hole the hand had been gripping the sole, as if trying to reach sunlight.

Six skeletons were discovered in that single, sunken-in grave. All had been identified as coming from the pool of missing.

When the drone operator had reminded the authorities of the other clearings with similar peculiarities, they'd panicked and closed the forest for two weeks.

Eventually many of the missing had been located.

The original reporter had dropped from the grid by then, perhaps never knowing his suspicions proved founded in fact.

She pulled the other tablet closer, neck bent as she read an article printed in a sensationalist rag two months ago, a month after Makenzie Temple was reported missing by her boyfriend—that report a detail Alace noted Todd had left out of his brief recounting of the story as he knew it.

Eleven girls and women missing from towns and villages surrounding a broad swath of national forest in the great state of Utah. That forest abutted and extended north beyond the Idaho state line, creating a conjoined section of wilderness as rugged and remote as anything any other state could boast.

Eleven individual disappearances, with more than half chalked up to the walkaway wife syndrome. The others were tagged as troubled kids, runaway material, a covering brush of excuses to hide the fact the local authorities hadn't tried too terribly hard to find them. *Easy way out.* She twirled a strand of hair in front of her ear, reading through the article a second time.

One deliberately placed fingertip to the tablet flicked that image away, and she tapped a couple of times to locate the one she wanted to see next. A topographic map of the area, darker greens indicating heavily wooded areas versus the lighter color of a section ravaged by forest fire two decades ago. Replanted, but those efforts took years to see the culmination of the dream. She enlarged the view, going close enough to read road names on the high-resolution image. Broad sections without roads crisscrossing, without communities trespassing on the isolation. There were a number of widely spaced clearings bisected by a named trail, lightly hiked.

Another flick against the tablet and she again rooted for the next thing, a web page filled with video streams. Some live wildlife cams, but most were recorded drone flyovers. A tap, another tap, and suddenly a video took up the screen, the rolling circle indicating file buffering glaring up at her. It resolved into a close-up of grass and weeds, the edge of some hard surface the drone launched from, that edge turning into a square diminishing in size as the device took to the air. No narration, but the person who posted had provided longitude and latitude for the location, and a tiny compass swung in the corner of the camera view. Oriented north, the drone flew over an enormous sea of green, trees covering the surface as far as the camera view stretched. Occasionally she could make out the dark brown of the path below, through small breaks in the canopy.

The drone paused and spun, compass now pointing east as the tiny camera took off again, darting away from the path. Ahead the tree line dipped, and the drone skimmed the tops as it flew into a clearing. It traversed the space side to side, in a uniform path, the intent of the exercise counting the number of surviving seedlings planted the previous year. To one side of the clearing, the drone hovered in place, the view sweeping side to side, surveying a space roughly eighteen feet square where the seedlings were gone. Disappeared as if never planted. But in the center, incongruous in its placement, was an old, wooden half barrel. The contents were dead, dried and withered in the merciless high-altitude sunshine. The drone lifted and turned, and Alace's hand darted forward, freezing the video. She spent a moment staring at the screen, then carefully rewound it to the moment just before it began to rise. On the far side of the planter was a small rectangle of dying grass. Not dead, not like whatever the flowers had been inside the half-rotted barrel. But dying, as if from lack of nutrient. Yellowed and short, stunted when compared to the vegetation nearby.

"Alace?" Eric's voice drifted up the stairs, curling around her like a comfortable and well-known blanket. "You coming down for supper?"

Alace blinked at the tablets, glanced up at the computer screens filled with biographies of the twenty-four dead and missing women, some more rightly labeled girls, not yet out of their teens, and sighed.

"Yeah, be right there."

She thumbed the off switches for each tablet, ensuring they shut down completely as she considered her options. Discovery of the video footage wasn't a breakthrough, not really. One piece of video wasn't worth a trip, wasn't worth sending one of her operatives to check things out. If she found more, however, that could tip the scales.

She sat straight in the chair, reached for the computer keyboard, and dragged it towards her. With the keyboard balanced precariously on top of the overlapping tablets, she typed furiously, writing up an analyst request for a job board accessible only via a myriad of security protocols. Disposable email created to field responses, she double-checked the stated parameters and clicked the button to post.

Deftly composing a message, she carefully considered her words. She hadn't gone out on a gig herself since dealing with the betrayal of her former handler. A shiver worked through her muscles, leaving the hair on the back of her neck standing on end. *A lifetime ago, seems like.* Refocused on the task at hand, she reminded herself that unlike the gigs he'd produced for her to work, this wasn't a for-profit job, wasn't even a job yet, not really, and she didn't want to set off a separate line of investigation yet. Mentally delving through her options, she picked Owen, her most dependable hunter. Owen Marcus was an ex-military intelligence, ex-rogue government asset who had spent formative time in Central America, developing a hot hatred for human traffickers.

Message sent, she tried to find any chinks in her half-formed plan.

With a shake of her head and fingers repeating well-known patterns, she quickly exited the server, then the mask server, then the dummy server, finally back to the surface of her vast security network.

Louder than before, Eric called out again. "Alace? Supper, baby."

Her lower leg tingled as she unfolded it from underneath her, preparing for the moment she'd finished shutting down and could stand. "Coming," she called over her shoulder, timing herself for the next forty-five seconds, toes wiggling and stretching. Unplugging the biometric scanner from the back of the desktop computer, she stood and lifted her arms overhead, arching backwards with a groan. Scanner deposited in the wall safe next to the window, she thudded the heavy mirror back into place against the wall, covering the camouflaged safe door.

Exactly on time, she exited the room, leaving the door canted open behind her.

Nothing to see here, folks.

CHAPTER FIVE

Alace

"I don't know how long I'll be gone." She stared down at the backpack under her hands, balanced on the edge of the bed. There was a small stack of clothing to shove inside, and then she'd be packed to leave. She didn't move, couldn't, not without Eric's permission, and he was willfully silent from his stance in the center of the open doorway.

She imagined his soulful eyes, dark with emotion, already worried about her.

Alace's nerves reminded her how long it had been since she'd worked a gig herself. Once she'd made the important mental switch from being the immediate and present arm of justice and revenge to the one developing the plans, detailing what needed to happen and matching those demands against available skill sets, it wasn't a line she had wanted to cross.

This one is different.

Not only because Todd had brought it to her but also because the sheer scope of the possible victim count left her staggered. The Idaho police hadn't made the connections she had, even with the available information right in front of them. They'd attributed the deaths to a variety of individuals, and in one case even claimed a bear attack the cause because of gnaw marks on rib bones recovered from a pile of brush about twenty feet from what Alace knew was another burial spot. They hadn't bothered to bring sonar equipment in, hadn't given much thought to what else might be waiting under the sod.

I've got the benefit of experience. She did, too. A serial killer looked at disposal locations differently from investigators. She could tell at a glance that the carefully squared off areas weren't graves. Those were sloppier, rounded edges, shallow—or deep enough to upend a corpse into. What the police had misidentified as graves were used for a very different purpose. Somehow, and she wasn't certain how yet, the killer had created the rudimentary equivalent of a livestock holding pen. He'd kept his captives alive, played with them probably, then killed them or allowed them to die through inaction—thirst, starvation, or exposure culling them. Same result any way she looked at it. Except for the large cluster of skeletons found together. Those victims had been abandoned. The coroner reports had corroborated her thoughts, his timeline putting the deaths of all six women very close together.

If she was right—and her hunches were telling her she was dead on the mark with this one—the drone footage in Utah was of the same kind of holding pens. The one where she'd found the dying rectangle was likely a trap door to access the cage. Undoubtedly the half barrel had a purpose, too; she just hadn't come up with a valid idea yet.

Over the past two days, the other five videos identified by her freelancer had revealed the same setup, all within about five hundred square acres. A fairly limited area, given the size of the forest itself.

The tipping point this morning had come when her system alerted her to another missing woman report. Nearly a week ago, Nyla Davison had left home for work at a bakery in a nearby town, never got to work, and never came home. Her car had eventually been discovered parked in the stall of a car wash, locked, keys inside, her phone and purse neatly tucked in front of the driver seat.

Another disappearance and no response yet from Owen. He was between gigs and owed her nothing, so if he had decided to fade into the woodwork completely, she couldn't blame him. A courtesy call would have been nice, but even that, if it meant balancing his mental health against her wondering and worrying, she'd pick him every time. Fact remained that he hadn't called, and her system had pinged. That was why she had to go. If the killer, and there was no doubt in her mind there was a killer, a singularity to be clarified at a later point, but only a human would hunt other humans in this way. If the killer had taken a new victim, it likely meant they'd reached a point where a previous captive was expendable, or already expired.

"I've got to go."

"So you said, beloved." Her peripheral vision caught sight of Eric stalking towards her. The fluid sway of his hips, the length of stride, the way his arms swung loose at his sides—he was coming for her. Alace stood straight and closed her eyes, head tilted back and to the side. She was inviting him in, making herself vulnerable in a way he wouldn't mistake. "Tell me what you want."

His demand was an echo of her words, spoken so many times against the skin of his neck, his chest, his cock. Her way of confirming consent, even when it was known, a way to check in with him and make sure they were on the same page. He wasn't sure she'd accept him now, in this moment, and the idea of Eric not knowing she'd want him struck her as absurd.

"I want you to love me." His scent rolled over her, known, familiar, cherished. Dark with sugary undertones, he smelled just like he always tasted, and Alace turned. She lifted her chin higher, making up for their height difference. "Love me, Eric."

Voice low, vibrating with emotion, he told her, "I do."

His words doubled in her head to a recitation of the tender vows she'd never expected to earn, and her breath hitched painfully in her chest. The ring on her finger sat heavily against her knuckle, a token of forever love she'd have to remove in a few minutes. Leaving it behind—not because it didn't matter, but because it mattered too much to risk out in her shadowy world.

Eric's fingers slipped up her neck and around the back of her head, cupping the curve of her skull. His other hand landed on her side, a firm touch skimming along the bottom of her breasts from one stiffened thumb. "I will always love you. Forever, Alace. You're mine."

His breaths caressed her lips an instant before his mouth covered hers. She opened, immersed immediately in the taste of him, whiskey dark and chocolate sweet, remembered tastes imprinted on her psyche until they were synonymous with... *"Eric."*

Blood pounded between her legs, a thumping throb she never tired of experiencing, drawn to life only by him and his expert handling of her body, her senses, her love of him.

"Baby." *Fucking, fucking Eric*. He knew what that word did to her, still. No matter how often he pulled it out of hiding, it tripped her up every time, a velvet snare deftly applied by a master trapper. His mouth slipped along her jaw, nipping and kissing each inch of flesh he touched. "Alace, baby. Tell me where you're going." Eric's soft plea was sweetly cajoling, the subdued demand rubbing her nerves the wrong way, because they didn't have a relationship where she hid anything from him, not these days. His voice carried hints of sadness lined with a trust she didn't know she deserved.

"I found a pattern." Alace's palms danced across his chest, mapping each dip and divot, the stacked rows of his muscles hot underneath her touch. She measured her words in the same way, lips careful of her secret, which if he'd known would have disrupted everything. Instead, she gave him a solid truth, immutable and sound. "None of the guys are right for this one."

With a groan, he took her mouth again, making love to it. Their breaths mingled as they parted in tiny instants to sip at the air, panting hard. "Beloved." His murmur touched her like it did every time, carrying his love to her like a blanket, wrapping her in the safe knowledge that he was hers and she was his. Paired by fate, partnered by strength of will, and promised by vows. Not the ones spoken in front of his family and friends, but the ones muttered under the covers, cradled in each other's arms. He held her now, tender care in each movement as he stripped her clothing from her, uncovering her like a prized treasure. She flew through the air carried by his steady arms and then was pressed deep into their bed by his chest as he stretched out over her. She let her hands roam, discarding his clothing with help, cherishing the intimacy of their soft laughter at the difficulties removing jeans with a rigid cock trying to tear through the zipper closure. Caressing his skin with fingertips and lips, she worshipped him in the ways she knew he loved best.

When he pressed inside, head thrown back on a groan, she bit and tongued the underside of his jaw, finding the mapped and well-known sensitive spots that made him quiver and then drive deeper inside with every quaking movement. Each kiss pulled another groan, each groan tempted her to explore farther, and each new section of skin so abused earned her a rocking thrust and a vow of devotion and love.

Then he got into the swing of things, and her husband's dirty mouth came out to play.

"So fuckin' hot, baby. I don't know how you don't burn me right up. Hot and tight. Lord, God, so tight. Love to feel you wrapped around me like this. Love to feel you under me, feel me in you knowing you want this too."

"I do," she promised, hips rising to meet each downward plunge he gave her, pelvis angled to take him deeper. She lifted her knees, cocking them alongside his hips, and folded her lower legs over his ass, ankles hooked so she could draw herself tight to him. This position initiated more rocking than thrusting, and he swiveled and twisted against her, grinding against her clit with every pass of his hips. "I do, always and forever, my Eric."

"You're gonna come home to me, baby. Love you, love on you. God, how I love you. You're gonna come home." His mouth attacked the side of her neck between each breathy statement, the crisp scrape of his whiskers a brand on her skin as his hot lips and hotter tongue blazed a path up to her ear. "Love you so much, Alace. Mine. Always my Alace."

The end came in an unavoidable rush, the climb up the backside of the wave, paddling hard to reach the peak and then freefalling, rushing through the splashing whitewater along the face of the wave, tumbling into the churning wash at the end. Body thrown this way and that by the force of her orgasm tied to his, pounded into the mattress until his back arched as she writhed underneath him. *My lover. My husband.*

"My Eric."

CHAPTER SIX

Alace

She took a moment to settle the straps of her backpack into place, stroking up and underneath them with her thumbs, straightening out any last wrinkles in her shirt as she surveyed the parking area. Only two other cars shared the lot with her raggedy old beater, and she studied them closely. One was newer, a fresh covering of bugs on the headlights that spoke of regular washing and maintenance, marking this as a special trip. Not a speck of rust on fenders or wheels. Whoever owned this lived in a nice neighborhood with gated access, based on the tag she saw affixed to the inside of the windshield. Parked right next to the trailhead, the HOA-discreet, innocuous-in-color-and-form vehicle said a lot about the owner.

The other occupant had parked farther away than she had, nearly the opposite corner to the road entrance and the beginning of the trail. Covered in dust, even that revealed details, because intermingled with the various layers were handprints on the rear fenders and trunk lid, dust aging the marks and telling her that while the vehicle did move, it didn't go far or fast, because none of the sharp lines of fingers and palm were distorted by swirls that would be left behind with speed. The door handle on the driver side was shiny, the most frequently touched surface on the car. Unlike the other car, this one had few bugs scattered on lights or windshield, which reinforced her instincts this had to be a near-local resident. The sameness of the dirt and dust told of roads repeatedly traveled, probably between where they lived and here, time and again.

Alace smoothed under the straps a final time, pulling tight and clipping the chest strap to anchor them in place. Her vehicle keys were hidden in a fake rock she'd brought for that purpose, a disposable key safe most people wouldn't look at twice, tucked in next to her tire as it was. Mental map fixed, she set out on the trail, pacing herself. Even with taking frequent breaks she found herself huffing harder than she'd expected, and mentally put more frequent interval training on her list of things to change in her life once she got home.

She was on one of these breaks, perched on a pile of rocks just off the trail, when she heard traffic coming. She had made it far enough into the woods there were no car noises, no nearby highways or roads curling along the edges of the tree line. A helicopter had flown over about an hour before, and she'd tracked it from horizon to horizon, noting the DNR symbol on the side.

Whoever was approaching from the trailhead direction wasn't trying to mask their travel. Steady footfalls were punctuated with quiet metallic clinks, most likely a water bottle swinging against a clasp.

Pack positioned between her feet, Alace stared up the trail as she set the snack of homemade trail mix to the side, freeing her hands. *Just in case.*

Owen Marcus strolled into view.

She blinked. When she'd left the car, she'd checked a final time and the system had shown a view of the information she'd sent him but no response, just a logged access that didn't tell her anything other than he'd maybe, perhaps, seen the material. She didn't have an identity set up for him, hadn't shared hers, had given the barest skeleton of data intended to provide the foundation for a more detailed brief to be provided later, when and if he accepted the gig.

Unlike her former handler, she'd opted to meet each of her hunters at least once, wanting to get to know them as more than images on a screen or names in a database. Her gut, which she still trusted more than anything else, hyper-heuristic algorithms aside, meant she'd made decisions about her associates based on those meetings. Eliminating several candidates along the way, but also creating solid relationships with the ones accepted.

Owen had become one of her initial favorites, with that place in her estimation not changing through the months they'd worked together, albeit remotely. Trust was such a two-way street; she couldn't be his handler without believing he'd tell her if something was right, or wrong. Him showing here, now, without directive or request, smacked of a disrespect and lack of trust she wouldn't stomach. Not couldn't, because as her various personas through the years proved, she could swallow a metric ton of shit when she had to. Like when it suited her needs, advanced her agenda, or was a tactic used to gain access to a mark. But not here, on a gig she didn't want to be on. As if her body were scalding, she yanked her palm from her belly, where it had gone without her permission.

Head held high, she didn't verbalize any of the thoughts whizzing through her head, simply sat on the rocks and waited as he approached, pace slowing to a crawl as he neared. Owen stopped while still on the trail, framed by the two trees she'd stepped between to gain her perch, and didn't say a word to her. Careful of her balance, she fluidly brought her legs up into a loose lotus position. Still without acknowledging him other than her relentless gaze.

Finally, fucking *fucking* finally, he ducked his square chin, giving her a view of his tousled dark hair when he slipped off his cap, fingers raking through and causing strands to stand on end. It was such an aw-shucks move and fit his non-working personality so well she couldn't help it, the laugh breaking free like a bark. Owen peeked at her from under his pronounced brow, gaze now worried instead of steady. It took another moment of silence between them before he risked a greeting. When it came, the single word was low and quiet, his throaty tones conveying hesitance. "Hey."

"Should I be pissed right now?" By asking the question, she was giving him a stated benefit of the doubt that he could choose to use or discard, depending on how much he valued the partnership they'd built so far. "Would you be, in my shoes?"

Another aw-shucks duck of his head, full bottom lip gone white from the pressure as it was pulled between his teeth, then Owen nodded. "Yeah, you've every right to be pissed at me. I shoulda told you I was headed this way. Days ago, I shoulda told you. I got sucked into research, and when a new element came to light, all I could think about was getting here and seeing if I could fix it. It felt wrong and I needed to fix it."

That gut thing again. An instinctive reaction to something out of alignment in the universe. She had a feeling Owen was as sensitive to it as she was.

During their interview, he hadn't talked overmuch about his time in Central America, the government work he'd done in countries stretching from Colombia to Guatemala, with missions forced down his throat by a vow he still tried his best to honor. He just had gotten stuck on the fact that there could be domestic enemies who factored in foreign lands.

She'd had to dig deep to find reports on his last assignment. They'd been hidden behind black-smeared redacted statements, file names referenced in other reports, with a final single word giving her the knowledge where to look next: Cosmic.

It was a level of security clearance typically only associated with NATO briefings, so with that info in her pocket, she'd crafted a series of tiny queries. Set free on the darknet, the resulting ripples and threads identified deeper currents that had eventually led her to a full, complete rendition of the cataclysmic outcome of his final officially approved mission.

Owen had inserted without issue, transported himself to the correct placement. The operation's stated intent had been to take out a local threat. A foreign national who held too much power in that restrictive government and had enough closet skeletons on file for other persons of interest that the target had become a distinct liability.

At the compound, lying on his belly atop a low building that gave him the correct height and angle to take the planned shot, Owen had allowed his gaze to stray. Had seen acts happening in an adjoining building she suspected still haunted his dreams. He'd expertly disassembled his weapon, found his way to the inner sanctum via a lone window facing where he'd previously been poised to strike, and instead of eliminating, had interrogated the target. At length. Thoroughly.

Then Owen had razed the compound, leaving only dust and rubble in his wake. Personally escorting a group of more than forty children to a nearby village where fully half of them were greeted with upraised hands of thanks, parents' knees hitting the dirt as they expressed gratitude for the out-of-the-blue salvation of their children rendered by one lone Norte Americano. The other half were welcomed home within days, as Owen had made his way through the region, returning each child to their family, ensuring that where he could, they were mourning no more.

He'd been well aware of just how far he'd gone past what was sanctioned, and the report stated when he arrived at the extraction point two weeks late, he'd calmly laid his weapons on the ground, took a knee nearby, and patiently waited for his arrest.

The authorities hadn't known what to do with a warrior turned vigilante.

They couldn't praise him for the carried-out execution, even if he'd ultimately concluded that portion of his mission successfully. He'd caused a near-nuclear political incident, deviated from orders in ways he'd known were proscribed, and then expressed no remorse.

His consistent response, recorded in page after page of testimony, was "I'd do it again. I couldn't live with myself if I'd left those children behind."

The military might not have known what to do with Owen.

But Alace did.

"Yes, you should have told me." Alace tipped her head to the side, indicating a nearby boulder that would make companion seat for her position. She adjusted to face it as Owen followed her wordless instructions and made his way through the brambles. He did a quick sweep, probably for snakes, as she had done before seating herself. "But you didn't. If you had, I would have told you I got the same ping."

"The disappearance." His eyes narrowed as he stared at her. "Claudia Amanda Nelson, sixteen, sophomore in the local high school, now considered a runaway."

Alace studied him. "Nyla Davison, twenty-eight, unskilled bakery assistant, missing person."

Owen's nostrils flared, and the skin over his carotid jumped, trembling at a faster rate than before.

Tension in every muscle, he leaned forwards. "Thirteen."

"When did your Nelson girl go missing?" Alace hauled her backpack up, dug through a side pocket to find her tablet. Retrieving that and a black rectangle, she placed the bag back on the ground. Turning both devices on, she arranged the satellite Wi-Fi hotspot, angling the built-in antenna towards the southern horizon. She glanced up at Owen, who was watching her with a grin. "What?"

"Not often I get to see the boss lady in action. Just lockin' this info away for future consideration." He brought his phone out and entered a combination of pass phrase and his thumbprint to unlock it, then appeared to access a local file. By then Alace had connected to the satellite data and was engaging the security on her servers holding information for this gig. Owen continued, "Claudia Nelson was seen walking into school yesterday before school started and attended three of her morning classes. She ditched the fourth one, not for the first time. There were no eyes on her for lunch, or the afternoon. When she didn't get home in time to babysit her little sister so Mom could go to work, her mom started calling friends. Early morning, life as usual. First three classes, no one noticed anything out of the norm. But then she just dropped out of sight. Nothing at all after a camera picked her up headed down a side hallway to a lesser used bathroom. Her books and backpack were stored in her locker, which wasn't normal, according to her friends. That's the only thing out of place, Alace. Her mom finally got the cops involved about midnight last night. That's when I got my alert."

As he spoke, Alace scanned the information she'd already read through at least once. She'd left yesterday evening, the drive a solid ten hours from home in good weather. It had taken her twelve, so she'd been on the road when the report for the Nelsen girl—*Claudia*, she reminded herself it was okay to personalize the victims—would have hit her radar. Quickly reciting the details about Nyla Davison, she shook her head. "Why didn't you pick up on this one, Owen?"

"She's older than any of the other missing. Means she's outside my parameters for the search." He shrugged. "That'll teach me to believe a madman would stay with what's expected."

"Thirteen," she echoed his earlier statement. "Same number as Idaho." She shivered, the wind having picked up slightly. The forest was alive around them, filled with the sounds of small animals, insects, and the constant scraping of wood against wood, branches moving with the breeze and rubbing across their neighbors. "I still don't have a solid handle on why the killer abandoned their killing fields there."

"Did we ever get a good timeline on the deaths? I know we're talking about half a dozen counties, with all kinds of different paperwork requirements, but even estimations might tell us something." He sat straight, scanning the area, head on a swivel out of instinct, not because anything in their vicinity alerted him. Owen was simply vigilant, all the time. "Just from the pictures, I had a feeling that the largest grouping, that pod of six, I think that was his first. Something happened, either it got out of hand, or it was too hard to get the outcome he wanted, and he abandoned them."

Alace looked up from the tablet to stare at him.

He shrugged and angled his face away, either embarrassed or playing at an act. "What?"

"That's the same feeling I had after I studied the info for a while. Gimme a sec." She glanced back at the tablet, navigated to a different folder on a different server, and took the time to make her patient way through three levels of pass phrase security to get to the blind keystroke key she preferred. "Here." She maximized the document and turned the tablet towards him, waiting as Owen stood and made his way to her pile of rocks. "Look at the dates as I've got them lined up here. That group is identified by P6." She appreciated the fact he didn't reach out to take the device, because she likely wouldn't have given it up, but he didn't know that. Glancing around him, she saw he had brought his backpack with him, gripped in one hand, but angled to where she couldn't easily reach for it. *Maybe he would understand.* She'd always been a jealous owner of the tools that allowed her to not only do her job but do it well and survive in the end. He might be, too.

"Yeah, yeah. See that?" His finger hovered over the surface of the tablet, and his head bobbed in a staccato reaction to what she'd already discovered. "Six dead in that one pod, but two of them outlived the other four by days. Maybe more than a week. They'd been taken at around the same time, and there was no evidence of cannibalism, which means the two that lived longer must have fended off the other four for resources. Those four were slightly younger, maybe easier to intimidate. The two teamed up together." His head shot up and he stared at her, eyes round, whites showing in a broad circle edging the dark iris. "Did you see the pictures? Those two were at opposite ends of their pod."

"Holding pen, that's what I call what they were in. Yeah, I saw the positioning. At first I thought it was in avoidance of the dead in their midst, but now that you've laid things out, I wonder if it was more than that." Alace withdrew the tablet, minimized the document, and found the image she was looking for a moment later. She angled the device so they both could see. "The one built a barricade from the corpses to keep the other one at bay. That's the only thing that makes sense."

"I can see that." Owen nodded and sighed. "Humans are the most vicious animals."

"So you think the two women in that pen first banded together against our abductor? They were all starving, but it would have been slow. Water, though. Dehydration is a fast killer. Maybe they knew the odds, or saw something happening, maybe to one of the younger ones in their pen. So they changed the game, made it so it wasn't enjoyable, or interesting? Then when the kidnapper's attention turned elsewhere and there wasn't any more food or water coming their way, they created a divided society?"

"Yeah, in a bigass nutshell, that's what I think." Owen flashed her a quick smile, but his face quickly set back into somber lines as it faded. "Control, and lots of it. That's what this guy wants."

"Why are you so stuck on the killer being male?" Alace angled her head back, staring up into Owen's eyes. She affected a cold, flat demeanor, feeling that place in her gut settle, all unease leaving her, steady ripples of anticipation the only thing building. He knew her background, all of it. One of the things Alace had insisted on with the hunters she pulled into her circle. There was no danger to her in them knowing her history, and she'd felt the need to force feed the information in order to level the playing field. Most of the ones in their line of work, and she included herself in this mix, harbored a thick thread of narcissism. Playing judge, jury, and executioner fostered that personality flaw, and while she might not still be in the game like she had been, she certainly wanted to be top dog in the house she was building. Alace fought a smile when she saw the moment Owen realized what he had been implying, those quiet insinuations that women couldn't, wouldn't be the same kind of monsters men were. She was a silent but present contradiction to that stance, and he knew it.

"Seventeen percent are female. Eighty-three are male. Those odds are overwhelmingly in my favor. No offense to the boss lady, but you're pretty much an anomaly." She marked his tight, small smile, more a contraction of the muscles at the corners of his mouth than a lifting; it was a slip in his good old boy mask. She also marked his language, pulling her exercise of her skill set into the present, when, for all Owen knew and all she'd suggested, it had been left behind when she folded herself into Eric's life. "And I don't care what that database says. It's only as good and thorough as the killers who've been caught. Means there's a wealth of data not present, and that's not an absence I can map. Not like a void I can see. You're a mystery to more than just me."

"Let's keep it that way." She scanned the forest, noting how the shadows had lengthened, marking time as it slipped away while they sat and talked. "We're in agreement that the grouping of six corpses was probably the killer's initial efforts. The existence of such a collection indicates whoever they are, they had a span of time not just to abduct so many, but to keep them alive for at least nine months." The initial disappearance marked the start date to that section of the killer's spree, and the tentative date of death in the reports put a pin in the outer ring of continued involvement in what had become a failed experiment. "You think the killer stayed to watch, or not?"

"You think that portal was for viewing and not a privy pot?" Owen straightened, hands drifting across his torso for a few seconds, a private dance of reassurance Alace knew well, but she didn't empathize enough to not use the unconscious action as a way to map where Owen's weapons were. "You think he watched."

"I'm sure of it." Each of the pens in Idaho had been constructed with two egress points. One was a trapdoor large enough to get a body through, and one was a too-small-to-exit round or square hole in the center of the ceiling built from a mix of wood and wire. The reports indicated they were all common to commercial shipping pallets, easily obtainable anywhere. *That hole, though.* "Trust me, they watch. But did he or she stay after disengaging from the prisoners, or was it not a failure at all, but an involuntary abandonment?"

"Outside influences matter." Owen went quiet, and Alace gave him the space to run through whatever scenario he had in his head. "Huh. What's the intervals of those first thirteen again?"

She rattled off the dates, letting him fill in the months between.

Silence descended around them as he mulled things over. Alace threw another handful of trail mix into her mouth, the crunching as loud in her head as she imagined Owen's thoughts were in his.

Chin lifting, he pulled in a ragged breath, head turning as he scanned the area around them.

"This dude's military or something like it."

CHAPTER SEVEN

Owen

"Why do you say that?"

Alace's question wasn't a surprise. It was the same exact thing he'd have asked in her place.

The first time he'd met her, finding the truth of their similarities had been disquieting. Knowing up front the openly acknowledged measure of what she'd done, the acts for which she'd claimed responsibility, Owen had been half expecting a hulking monster schlumping along, some twisty-tortured frumpy woman with crazy eyes whom he wouldn't be leaving alive when he was done with the meet.

So far off the mark.

Not movie star elegant—though if you saw images of those women out shopping with no makeup artist at their elbow, it was questionable whether even movie stars lived up to the false reputation promoters and movie producers fostered—but still, Alace ranked up there if a body was inclined to measure things in numbers. Memorably gorgeous. But something that had struck him with greater impact than her beauty was the intelligence he'd recognized in her eyes.

Alace Sweets wasn't an angry person; she'd never been in biz for the thrills. Owen expected she still dreamed of her kills, and not in a held-breath excitement way. He'd bet money her dreams were more like his, where there was always one more person to save, someone out of reach, an illusory failure that crippled in the nightmares that visited him with disquieting regularity.

So to have gone into that meeting with one expectation, he'd been dumbfounded at how wrong he'd been. Their paths up to the point where their journeys converged might have been very different—his an average raising in a comfortably situated Midwest family, hers birthed from violence in a town shattered by economic woes—but somehow they'd found themselves at the same fork in the road, and both had chosen to take the far less traveled and more bloody one.

"The breaks." He surveyed the area, marking the things that were the same as well as any differences since his last scan. A darkness at the base of a tree hadn't shifted or changed with the setting sun; different angles of the rays were now shining off the scales, revealing a coiled snake. "They're staggered in what feels like a deployment cadence. Other than that first pod, that first group. But he could have been home for longer for some reason. Injury, extended furlough, legal inquiry. All kinds of reasons he could have been sent back out of cycle. Legal would make sense, if he can't keep it together while embedded or deployed. Or maybe that pod represented extreme frustration at being taken out of action. Hard to say for sure without more data."

"Yeah, but there are other occupations that entertain the same kind of in-and-out tempo when it comes to home life. Truck driver, offshore rigger, boat laborer. That's off the top of my head." She looked down at the tablet and fiddled with things, as comfortable in his presence here in the remote woods of a national park as she had been in that diner months ago. *Is it confidence or true trust?* Only time would tell. She snorted. "We're in Utah. Perhaps it's a missionary?"

"Oh, add religion in the mix and that's a recipe for confusion." He scanned the area and abruptly decided he didn't like how he was looming over her. He took a step back, crouching to rest one knee on the ground. "The intervals, though, do you see it?" *Why am I asking for confirmation?* He was used to working alone, sorting out the details provided by whoever was processing the orders from on high, but the final interpretation had always been his. "I have a guy I can reach out to, get him sorting through deployment orders for service personnel living in this area."

"Already done," she said, sounding distracted. "It's a large geo target, but the dates are immutable, so it builds a decent framework to bolster our question." She looked up, and without missing a beat, asked him, "What is it that disquiets you about me being here right now?"

"What?" A stalling tactic, because he'd heard her clearly. She knew what he was doing, too, telegraphing her knowledge with a tiny eyeroll and a delicate snort. "I don't tandem things. I expected to come up and run some recon, hike out, and report back what a boots-on-the-ground view looked like. Drones are great, but unless they're hired and self-directed, footage is subject to the original purpose. Can't get a full picture from video alone. Maybe a little bit of me wanted to make the boss lady proud, doing the unexpected. Above and beyond." Might as well be completely honest; he'd already opened up far more than intended. His next breath drew sandpaper up his dry throat. "You and me, we're more alike than even I'd expected, and you showing up here makes sense, because you had the same thoughts I did. But we looked at different data sets and still came to the same conclusion. So you being here chasing something I didn't see means there could be even more I didn't see. It's not necessarily you that's torquing me over; it's all"—he made a vague gesture with his hand, winding up resting his wrist on the knee that jutted upward—"that."

"So it's not because my count exceeds yours?"

Hell, how would she know he'd found out that tidbit, unless she knew he'd dug deeper into her than she might want a person to do? "Does it?" Keeping his tone casually light, he tried to sell idle disbelief. "I'm not too sure about your assumptions."

Her kill count was huge, when reckoned against these kinds of missions. His was far larger if the total from the first compound were included. In an instant, the smell of dust swept around him, heat from a central American sun shining down on his shoulders, holding him in place as the rattling rap-rap-rap of small arms fire sounded in the distance. Ignoring the swirl of anxiety that accompanied the skim of sweat covering his body, Owen waited it out and kept his eyes on Alace. As long as she didn't fade, he was still *here.*

Shifting position subtly, Alace abandoned the ease and relaxation of the half lotus she'd been in since he'd stalked into the clearing around her rock pile. Tension sang through her muscles, and the edges of her boots dug into the rock, ready to support a solid muscular flex if she needed to react to something.

Tongue poking a tent from the inside of his cheek, he blew out a long, slow, silent stream of air, centering himself in a different, yet still so similar way.

"Counts don't bother me," he said finally, deliberately pushing his shoulders down and back, opening himself physically, hoping she'd see the vulnerable position as it was meant. Trust. *I trust you,*

Alace. He shouldn't, but then again, she shouldn't trust him either, and yet, she apparently did.

"Me, either." Her lips were still full and rosy, not pressed thin and white like his had to be. The only place she carried visible tension was directly in front of her ears; the muscles anchoring her jaw had pulled taut. Alace gave him a smile that, like the others he'd seen from her, didn't even come close to reaching her eyes, then slowly tipped her head down and studied the tablet. "Did you finish answering my question about why you think it's a man?"

He ran their conversation back through his head, spending the moment wondering at her question before realizing the why of it. A dry chuckle escaped his lips and he saw her mouth curl, still directed down at the tablet. She'd re-asked a question from before he'd nearly lost himself to a flashback, undoubtedly to put him back in the more recent mindset and not the reeling vulnerability he always felt after his memories swamped him.

"Statistics don't lie." He shrugged. "But anomalies exist." He spread a hand, palm up, creating an unbalanced scale. "Guesswork and conjecture only take us so far. There's no DNA, no sequencing, no physical evidence to point to who the killer is. One of us will be right, and one will be wrong, and the crux of the needing to know is being able to predict behavior based on an immutable facet of the killer's personality and existence. With both of us, and taking different mental approaches, we'll cover all angles regardless."

"That we will." Her head lifted, and she stared into his eyes. "You cool, Owen? Really cool? Me being here, me disagreeing with you? All that jazz?"

"Yeah, Alace." This too was honesty. "I'm cool with you. I'm cool with you leading, as long as you don't get me dead."

"I'll try to keep that in mind." She placed the tablet and satellite Wi-Fi into a cushioning sleeve, and then into the backpack, followed that by wrapping up her snack and putting that into a smaller bag that clipped on the outside of her pack. "Ready to get rolling?"

Owen pushed upright, adjusting his pack instinctively, settling the weight against his back. "Yes, ma'am."

"Owen." She stood, her hand drifting down before jerking to the strap of her pack. She lifted and slung it over her shoulders, giving it the same shoulder roll he'd done to place the straps comfortably. "Don't ma'am me."

"Yes," the following word hovered on his lips for a long moment but had Alace's squinty-eyed stare to keep it at bay. He finally released a breath and caved, giving her only one word.

"Alace."

CHAPTER EIGHT

Alace

Owen made for a great trailblazer. Walking ahead, being taller and broader, he successfully cleared the trail of briars that had made the leap across the space, as well as the plethora of spiderwebs spanning the gaps between the trees on either side. He just wasn't very happy about it.

Alace grinned down at the toes of her boots as he burst into curses again, arms moving to sweep webbing from his face and head. As amusing as he was, something about his responses was off, but she wasn't yet sure what it was.

"Hey, Owen." She waited for him to turn, and without lifting her head, offered him the object in her left hand. "Doubles as a web gatherer."

The rough walking stick was yanked from her grip without a word, and a moment later, she heard his footsteps moving away. More walking and less stamping, which would be good for a lot of reasons. Alace chanced a glance up to see he had the thick piece of wood held like a scepter in front of him, the end whirling in a smooth figure-eight pattern. She let him get another few feet ahead before she stirred herself and followed.

They'd traveled nearly five more miles before she believed she had the truth of it.

"Smooth footfalls for a dozen steps, then a forced clumsiness. Your gracelessness reveals you." He was silent, as he'd been since they'd left the unexpected meeting spot, with the exception of his growling arguments with the spiderwebs. "Why do you pretend you've no woodcraft at all?"

She stopped walking when Owen did, kept her chin raised to meet his eyes as he turned to face her. For an instant—a fragment of a fraction of a second— Alace saw every piece of herself in his gaze. Flat, cold, with blunted affect and lacking empathy. Entirely familiar, and just as thoroughly disturbing. She'd understood logically, but recognizing and *knowing* were different in practice. The woods harbored at least two killers today, and, if they were lucky in their pursuit, perhaps three.

The moment he decided to be truthful was marked by a soundless sigh, a minuscule lowering of his shoulders, hands relaxing their grip on the wooden cudgel she'd willingly put in his reach. She'd picked up another piece of wood along the way, and if he chose to use the one he possessed as a whirling bludgeon, she'd match him move for move.

"Habit, to create the illusion of a lower level of skill." Owen blinked, the movement as fraught with intent as if he'd shrugged. "Upper hand stuff."

"You pretend to be a stumbling babe in the woods, and if they'd bought the act, when needed you can easily shift to the true skilled huntsman and would succeed in catching any adversary off guard." She let the top of her head tip oh so slightly to the side, knowing he'd read it as loud as any flashing billboard. "I get it, probably more than you know. But why now, with me?" He opened his mouth and she flung up a hand, stop-signing his lie. "Not a habit. That is a deliberately activated skill. Why, Owen?"

"Trust doesn't happen easily." A bird cried a short distance away, the echoing ritak-ritak bleeding through the air. "I could talk to you every day on the phone, on the computer, and truly believe that you'd have my back when I'm out on an op. But in person, I still can't trust you when we're walking side by side. Not completely. And that is more than habit, you're right. It's a trained reaction based on personal experience. Give me time, Alace. If we work together often enough, or have enough success, maybe you'll retrain my instincts."

"Well, at least you're honest." She shuffled her feet, then used the end of her impromptu walking stick to point at the trail stretching out ahead of them. "Let's keep going. We're within a mile of the clearing." Owen nodded, and she bit back a laugh at how relieved he looked. "And Owen?" He glanced at her, a little of that ease leaving him when he nodded in acknowledgement of her silent question. "Stop pretending to be a bull in a china shop, would ya?"

"I'll try, boss lady." He moved a dozen soundless strides up the trail, nimbly ducking under a hanging branch instead of walking through it. "I'll try."

She had gained to only a few steps behind him when she hit the first spiderweb.

"Asshole."

CHAPTER NINE

Owen

Setting up camp that night was a revelation in how competitive Owen's boss was in real life. During their many remotely conducted conversations, he'd gotten the impression that she was firmly secure in her skills without being at all arrogant. Even their single face-to-face had been extremely collegial. Belatedly, he realized that was because, at the time, they'd been discussing projects and missions that *he'd* be working, and she'd likely been subtly evaluating his abilities. Not disclosing hers. Not at all, really.

Alace Sweets was a master at their craft.

Earlier in the day, he'd felt clumsy as a toddler when she'd called him on his instinctive reaction to hide his skills. He hadn't lied when he'd told her it was a trust thing, had probably given her more truth today than any single person had garnered from him in half a decade. Having her at his back on the trail had been nerve-wracking—an unsettling creepy-crawly sensation slithering up his spine every instant she wasn't in view, hidden behind his shoulders. So he'd constructed dozens of opportunities to catch glimpses of her, even from the corner of his eye, to put his nerves to rest for the span of a breath at the most.

By the time they'd found the first clearing, he'd given up any pretense of hiding his unease, Alace's knowing gaze on him every time he wrenched his head around to look at her.

It wasn't until they'd walked directly into the broad clearing that he'd breathed deeply. Then that capability had been stripped away as he'd watched her work the area, stunned by her rapid assessment and ability to pinpoint things the drone hadn't come close to revealing.

"Look." Alace didn't indicate which direction she meant, or at what, but since she was crouched and bent sideways, her cheek perpendicular to the ground, it wasn't hard to discern. "I count six depressions that might be something."

Owen crouched where he stood, not wanting to get close to her again. The hair on the back of his neck had barely lain down from their time on the trail. Allowing his eyes to slightly unfocus and drifting his gaze from left to right across the clearing, he saw what she meant. There were many more dips and contours to the earth than the six she'd pointed out, but those six had a regularity, a symmetry that confounded natural origin.

He held his breath and then allowed it to seep from his lungs so gradually it didn't disturb a blade of grass, exactly as he would if he were perched in a high-hide, scope trained on a target a thousand yards away. And he let himself see.

"There's an access next to each of them." Without standing, without shifting, even if his calf muscles were starting to twitch with the sudden and strained stillness after so many hours of activity, he counted what he saw again. "Maybe one access that doesn't have a paired holding area." Keeping his eyes on the spot, he pushed off the ground, and without sparing a glance for Alace, something he wouldn't have believed possible even minutes ago, he strode across the clearing to the small, square patch of prairie grass and weeds that had captured his attention.

Alace hit the ground with a knee at the same time as Owen, and he darted his gaze up at her, finding a ferocious expression on her face. He pointed along the side just in front of her, finger a scant inch away from the shorter grasses edging the square. "Just there," he said, and bent close, using all his senses to try to suss out any kind of trap. "No wires, no smell, organic or chemical."

Her hand appeared just in front of his face, and Owen jerked back as her fingers dug into the dirt. "Overgrowth says it's not been disturbed in a while. Maybe weeks, with the lack of rain in the area." Alace bent over, half her hand disappearing into what had looked like solid soil a moment ago. "Still loose enough to feel—" She cut off and he watched her as, with eyes closed in concentration, she grunted and strained, the muscles in her arms bunching. "It's not budging. There's a wooden platform."

"Hinge side? If it's not a set-in-place cover, it might be rigged to swing?" He crouch-walked along one edge to the far corner and delved into the loosened earth there. "Let me see if I can do any better on this end."

She rocked back on a heel, elbow to her bent knee as she stared at his hands. "Go, go, he-man."

"Not a he-man." He got a solid grip and adjusted his stance, grunting as he heaved with as little luck as Alace had found. But it felt like the resistance was uneven, so he shifted farther around and dug in again, feeling his way along the sawn edges of the wooden platform covered with inches of dirt and foliage. "But I might have found—" Much as Alace had, he cut off and heaved, grunting when his end of the square lifted a couple of inches. "Maybe."

Before he could ask for help, Alace was beside him, working her way along the edge to the other corner. "On three."

"One," he counted them down until they made their joint effort, the platform rising with startling ease once the matting of roots was torn free. He gave another shove, and the entire thing went over backwards, settling at an angle as whatever held on the other end stayed firm. Owen glanced into the hole and startled backwards, certain for an instant they'd found a body. "Holy shit."

"That's interesting." Alace's words were muttered under her breath, tone wry.

"The fact we found something I can't describe?" His gaze jittered, uncertain where to come to a rest. A yellow wig, clothing, landscaping half barrel, buckets stacked inside each other and resting on their sides, a box that looked to contain canned meat. Phone in hand, he snapped a series of photos, stepping around the opening so he could document each side. "What the fuck is this?"

"More interesting that you can't describe it. Reinforces my assumptions that your past roles have been more solution than investigative." The movement in the corner of his eye resolved to Alace reaching down with the stick he hadn't realized she still had. She stirred the clothing, using the wooden tip to flip folds back until a button-down shirt and pair of overalls could be recognized. "Not a bad thing, but this?" She sat up and he looked at her, shocked to find a smile he could only call joyous stretching her lips. "This is a gold mine to me. It's a stash, which means

it's personal, and the contents will tell us so much about our mark you won't believe. I'm going to dissect this, and it'll be a while. Since none of the others are freshly disturbed, let's leave them alone for now, give me a chance to see what I can find from what our killer left behind."

He stood and took a step back, ceding her the scene in a way she couldn't miss. Glancing up at the sky, he noted the angle of the sun and nodded. "I'll find a camp spot adjacent to the clearing."

"Coffee would be welcome. Makes me somewhat less murdery." She angled her neck to stare up at him, the flat gaze back again, reminding him of exactly who this woman was. Unable to determine if she was joking, he felt a sudden relief when Alace looked back down into the pit, head tilted to one side. "I've got a hammock, so I don't need flat or open."

"Roger that." He thumbed towards their backpacks, left at the opening to the clearing. "You want me to leave your pack, or am I good to haul it to where we camp?"

The return of that dispassionate regard hit him like a punch to the solar plexus. "Don't open it."

"No, ma'am. Wouldn't think of it." He sketched a salute and turned to walk towards the wall of trees, scanning as he went.

"Owen." Twisting back to look at her, he was surprised to see a grin back on her face, those eyes that had been so cold only moments before now shining with amusement. She reminded him of her earlier demand. "Don't ma'am me."

"Yes, Alace."

As he prepared their dinner, a freeze-dried meal of meat and pasta rehydrated in a pan of boiling water over a lightweight camp stove, she'd first busied herself with one of the tablets, and then with gathering deadfall branches to lay wood for a small fire, and stacked some to the side.

She'd brought the contents of the pit back to the camp with her, which told him exactly how this was going down. Up until then, he hadn't been certain she wouldn't involve the local law, which in this case would be the rangers, but her casual disturbing of the scene said the gleaning of clues was all up to them.

If she'd let him get a look, it'd be up to them.

Right now, it appeared it was entirely up to her.

By the time the meal was finished and cleanup complete, light rays speared through the canopy at steep angles, slanting sideways in long shoots of light. Like Alace, he had brought a hammock in his pack, and he levered himself into the strung fabric, the slight sway as he settled not unwelcome. Easy and comfortable. If he shut out the sounds of his companion, this could be any hunting or camping trip.

Except it wasn't.

The newly missing victims they were looking for had to be here, in this forest. He felt it in his gut. The timing they'd discovered, the victims already located, the new killing field they'd been to today—it all stacked up in his mind. *Can't go on gut alone.* Certainly not with Alace dogging his heels. He'd not heard her theories on the field yet, she'd been so immersed in the contents of that damn pit. After setting up the basics of camp, he'd returned and walked the area, using a system of markers to identify the holding pens and their access hatches. While he hadn't opened any of them without her express approval, he'd used a bladed tool to slice through the interwoven matting of roots holding the access hatches closed. Each of the larger depressions had a strange artifact, a round impression as if something heavy had sat in one place for a long time. The circumference of the circle was approximately the same as the half barrel they'd found. *But why? Why would the killer have risked notice from casual hikers passing by with something that would stand out in the wilderness? What had been the purpose of placing the tub on top of the holding pen?* He shook his head. Not knowing the why was something he'd had to come to grips with a long time ago, because every mission had those kinds of questions. The why was insanity at work, nothing more and nothing less.

Movement across the campsite had him opening his eyes and glancing towards Alace. She was stringing her hammock now, having spent the past two hours hunched over on the ground.

"Your turn." With Alace's back to him, the meaning of her words wasn't immediately clear. When he didn't move or respond, she glanced over her shoulder at him. "See what you can figure out from what we've got."

"Gonna let me put my brain to work? Cool, boss lady." Owen rolled out of the hammock at the same time she sat back in hers. Immediately she paled, lips pressing into a hard slash, and he saw the muscles of her throat working as she swallowed several times. All symptoms of nausea. *Wonder what she found in the pit of treasures that would cause that kind of reaction.* He didn't mention his observations, instead going to his backpack to gather what he needed before walking to where she had the items laid out on a lightweight tarp.

He studied the layout, then pulled out his phone and consulted the photos he'd taken of the undisturbed pit. After first taking pictures of how Alace had left the cache, he quickly moved things around to how the killer had left them. Donning earbuds, he searched for an appropriate playlist before settling on the ground beside the tarp.

Snapping a fresh set of nitrile gloves on each hand, Owen acknowledged to himself it was not to preserve the evidence so much as he didn't want any of that crazy fucker's DNA attaching itself to him. *Serial killer cooties,* he thought with a quiet snort of amusement. He quickly went through the clothing, finding multiple versions of identical shirts and leggings, some more stretched and worn than the others. The flannel shirt and single pair of overalls were both larger sizes than the fitness wear, so maybe that was for the killer while the lighter-weight items were for the victims. He pulled up the reports on the known victims. Quickly annoyed by the small screen, he jackknifed to his feet and retrieved his tablet, folding back down into the same impression in the dirt, minimizing the footprint of his involvement here. Another thing he and Alace had in common, he saw, because she had just the single impression on the other side of the tarp, no matter the number of times she'd gotten to her feet in the time she'd spent delving through the items.

None of the previous victims had been discovered in anything resembling the stretchy fabric. While each of them had at least one article of clothing on or near them, those items could be tracked back to their own closet. So maybe the tights and shirts were for something else. Maybe the killer had the victims perform somehow, forcing them to don a costume. *Not enough data.* He moved on, not allowing himself to dwell on the contradictory items. Obsessing on the clothing wouldn't help him learn anything more than he already had.

The wig gave him the heebie-jeebies, but he'd never tell Alace that fact. Homemade in the extreme, it held uneven clumps of hair pulled through a hairnet and held in place with tiny twists of wire. The hair wasn't synthetic; he could see skin tags on the ends of some strands, and as he carefully turned the net inside out, he found larger chunks of scalp on the longer, thicker locks of hair. The edges of that tissue had been excised, straight edges revealed even through the curled and wavy dried pieces of flesh. The killer had scalped some of his victims, but not wholesale. *In pieces.* Owen swallowed hard, thinking that Alace's nausea was understandable. *Except she's a serial killer, too.* He shook off the thoughts, focusing again on the items in front of him. A quick review of the incident reports for the previous victims showed no mention of scalping. *Except...*

He switched reports, looking at the very first statements. *One.* One of the victims had been too decomposed for the authorities to say it had been mechanical rather than rodent activity, not with the lesser tools at their disposal, but they definitely mentioned damage to the scalp of at least one of the women.

With that knowledge bolstering him, Owen reviewed each article in detail again, finding two more mentions of damage to the skin and scalp. Each of the three women had been blonde, with hair of varying lengths when they disappeared.

He laid the tablet down, picking the wig back up and studying each hank of hair individually. Now that he knew what he was looking for, he could easily see the different colors, variances in shading, even as faded as some of the hair looked to be. *Creepy as hell.*

Setting the wig aside, he stared at the rest of the cache. There was a length of leather under the overalls, a crude lacing through holes punched on either end. *A garrote?* The whole thing was awkward if so. He knew from personal experience. Owen had always preferred a simple thin wire with handles that gave room to loop through and pull tight. *Easy to use, disguise, and discard.* A piece of leather like this, the length spoke to a distance maintained between the killer and target. *Erotic asphyxiation?* He shook his head. Another area where he'd never know exactly. Each item allowed an educated guess at best. Idly running the leather through his fingers, he found two areas where the edges curled in, as if from a constant pressure. He knew that pattern of wear, the tantalizing thought just out of reach until he shifted in place, the cinching of his belt pulling tight at his sides helping identify the random thought. *Ah.* He set it aside, resting it on top of the overalls, remembering that Alace had it placed by itself in her layout. *Belt. Gotcha.*

Nothing else was of much interest. The preserved meat hadn't expired, and without a key for the manufacturer information stamped into the container, he couldn't know if it had been purchased locally or from farther away and transported. The wooden half barrel was a garden-variety yard adornment. Treated wood to protect against rot, circled by a dull metal band near the top, staves held in place with screws. The bottom wasn't any different, nothing of note there. *Except...*

He tipped the wooden structure upside down and got close, angling his head so his cheek was perpendicular to the surface, much as Alace had done in the field earlier today. There were weathered scratches across the grain of the wood. Multiple lines of impressions, laid into the surface four at a time. Suddenly he realized what those mysterious markings were on top of the holding pens. He'd bet money that each was an access port, too small to exit through, or perhaps barred somehow, but a threat-free window or opening so the killer could watch his victims. *Fuck.* It was one thing to think maybe the killer forced them to dress in spandex for a performance and another to find a possible validation in that theory.

He left the barrel as it was and went back to the rest of the stash.

The small glass bowl and a spoon could have been used to feed the captives, but as Owen lifted them to look at the bottom of the bowl, he caught a faint whiff of diesel fuel. A study of the spoon confirmed it was discolored about halfway up the stem. He glanced across the tarp, not seeing what he expected. On his feet again, he stifled a groan as he stretched and looked at the fading light. He'd been hunched over the items long enough for his hike-stressed muscles to stiffen up slightly. Without a word to Alace, he took off at a trot through the woods and into the field, angling directly towards the pit. The covering lifted with little effort this time, and he heaved it open. Jumping down into the pit, he crouched and scoured the corners, finally seeing the tiny pieces of white he'd expected. They were the crumpled remains of Styrofoam. When he stood, Alace was right there, head cocked to the side as she stared at what he held. He flinched when she reached out, and at her narrowed gaze, he deposited them into her hand.

She looked at them for a moment, then him, and then off towards the camp, as if she could see the items laid out on the tarp. "Homemade napalm?"

Owen nodded.

Alace turned on her heel and stalked away, back rigid, shoulders back.

Oh, she's pissed. He shivered as he climbed out of the pit and reseated the hatch in place, one eye always on her retreating form. A pissed Alace wasn't something he knew how to deal with.

He took his time returning to the camp, spending the brief walk turning over in his mind what he knew from his study of the cache. The killer dressed to fit his fantasy on site, which included clothing himself like a hillbilly in flannel and bib overalls. Overalls with a belt didn't make sense, but that was the only thing the leather strap could be. The wig was both camouflage and trophy, built as it was from the scalps and heads of victims. It bugged Owen that it seemed to contain reminders of only three women, but maybe the killer was going for a certain look. It was at odds with the hillbilly clothing. He shook his head. *I can't expect everything to make sense right off the bat*. The food stash was self-evident, no real explanation needed—portable, with a long shelf life, it was the bare minimum to extend, not sustain life. He hadn't looked closely at the buckets, but the brown staining along the rim of one marked it as a probable toilet, the others likely transports or water containers.

The napalm didn't fit. Neither did the exercise wear.

Stopping in the strip of land where the natural grasses failed to thrive, a ten-foot line demarking the end of the clearing and the beginning of where the trees owned the land, he stood in that place that was neither this nor that, and pulled out his phone.

The undisturbed cache. Napalm equipment rested inside the buckets, laid on their side, the brown staining of the top bucket in the stack extending down the inside, proving his theory about its usage.

Utilitarian, they were grouped by function. The half barrel filled in a corner of the pit, food in an opposite corner. The clothing was all in a single stack resting on what looked to be a large, flat box he didn't remember seeing.

He flipped ahead in the photos to the ones he'd taken of Alace's arrangement. Her stacks were arranged as clothing, strap to the side, food with the bowl and spoon, and buckets beside the half barrel. The box wasn't in the picture.

The chill of the shadows made him shiver, and he glanced up to see the sun balancing at the edge of the earth, brilliance shining through the trees in streams divided by those immovable sentinels. They'd lose the light in minutes.

He finished covering the distance to camp with long strides. Fists on his hips, he scanned the contents of the tarp, verifying the absence of the box before he looked at Alace, stretched out in her hammock, the top edges curling in so he could scarcely make out her face.

"What was in the box?"

"What's the leather for?"

Tit for tat? Really? He bit, letting her set the hook of promised information against his desire to know. "Belt. Weird as hell buckling system with those laces, but I think it's a belt." She was silent, and he took in three slow breaths before the steady glint of her eyes was interrupted by a blink.

"Flower seeds. Full packets as well as empty ones. What do you think about the buckets?"

Buckets? They had a clear usage in his mind. Three total, one was a toilet, the other two for storage or transport. He gave her the bare minimum to count as an answer. "Functional usage, nothing special." He thought about the half barrel, remembering the gritty feel of the interior wood against the tips of his fingers. "Was the half barrel used as a planter?" The round impressions on each pit where the killer rested the barrel, they made more sense if there was soil inside, weighting it heavily.

"Maybe." She was quick with that answer. Too quick, which meant he'd missed something about the barrel. *Dammit.* "Napalm?"

Owen jerked his chin up in acknowledgement. "The glass bowl smelled like diesel, probably because it was never washed. Diesel evaporates but leaves a residue. What's up with the spandex leggings and tanks?"

"Layering." Alace shifted slightly, the hammock gently swaying back and forth. "You look at the wig?" The swaying became more pronounced as she sat upright, then flung her legs over the side and dug her toes into the dirt, stopping the motion. Her lips were again a strained line, clamped tightly together. Almost as if she were fighting nausea, and not for the first time.

"I did. You match the vics with the samples?" Her head moved as she turned her flat gaze on him. *That'd be a no.* He gave her the names of the ones he suspected. "Weird how he doesn't harvest from each of them. If it was a trophy, I'd expect it to be multicolored with dozens of different lengths." She came out of the hammock and toed into her camp shoes, then wordlessly walked off into the trees.

Owen stared after her. *Guess sharing time's over.* "Good talk," he muttered.

Snug under his covers, thirty minutes later he watched her return to the darkened campsite. She bent over her backpack, then approached the stack of wood she'd placed in a crude fire ring and crouched. A flickering light accompanied the quiet click of a lighter, and she quickly set the kindling afire. The well-known sounds of burning wood filled the air, the crackling advancement of destruction sending streams of cinders to the ground as it tore out of control.

Owen blinked and reality reasserted itself.

The tiny flames crept along the kindling slowly, not at all the conflagration he'd seen in his mind. He shifted and turned, putting his back to the fire as he tried to ignore it. The sounds were unceasing, working their way into his ears no matter how hard he tried to cover them, how tightly he clamped his fists to the sides of his head.

"Owen, you okay?"

Oh, no. She didn't get to trigger him and then act all concerned. Without filtering his words, he flung that worry back at her, using false care as a toxin. "Are you okay, Alace?"

She stripped his anger away with a single word. "No."

Awkward in the hammock now, he threw himself into contorted positions to turn and face her. "What?"

"I keep feeling sick." That gaze settled on him, the dancing light from the fire giving her expression an uncertain cast he never expected to see on her face. "I was going to tell you in the morning, talk through what your plans would be for the rest of your investigation before I headed back to the parking lot."

At her statement, something in his chest settled, not even having announced it was awry. From her earlier reaction, he knew when he'd shown up without warning she'd felt threatened and he'd lost a certain measure of her trust. When he'd explained he didn't quite trust her, he'd lost a little of her consideration for him. When he'd matched her in reviewing the cache, he'd earned a tiny bit of her ire. All of those had been weighing on him, consuming energy as he turned it over and over, trying to find a way to win it all back.

By her telling him she would be leaving this mission up to him, it was like she'd pushed a reset button, returning to him everything he thought he'd lost.

Her stare was tangible, pressing heavily on him and demanding he answer her earlier question. Owen gave in to the inevitable, approaching it from an angle where he wouldn't have to admit to weakness. That simply felt too dangerous around her.

"I was down in Colombia. I took out my mark on target and within the timeframe demanded. Did my job, you know? But, before I could get the proof required, the jefe's men set fire to the compound." He paused and swallowed, beating back the remembered taste of ash on the wind. "Without evacuating it." Another pause, this longer, hoping she'd give him an indication she understood. "I don't like fire much."

Their gazes locked and she nodded. Then she leaned forwards very deliberately, never looking away as she stirred the fire with a stick, causing sparks to shoot high in the air, giving the flames more life so they flared and danced, knowingly filling the space between them with the thing that most frightened him.

And that, my friends, is Alace Sweets in a nutshell, he thought.

***

Alace

Squinting through the opening of the hammock, Alace was treated to the changing brilliance of the stars, followed by the first rosy tints of the sky announcing the sun's imminent arrival. She didn't bother checking the time. It didn't matter here.

Owen still slept, which should be no surprise given the length of time it had taken for him to surrender to his exhaustion the previous evening. The man had tried valiantly to remain still, but even a softly cleared throat and the huff of a frustrated sigh had betrayed his lack of slumber. She'd fallen asleep before him, and now she was up before him, which was fine.

The rolling in her stomach hadn't yet begun, but from the acid in her mouth, it wouldn't be long. Better to wrestle her way out of the hammock now, before it became a desperate sprint to gain privacy.

The moment she inclined her torso off the hammock, the nausea hit, instinctive swallowing keeping things at bay as she extricated herself from the fabric. She made it three running strides into the trees before her stomach betrayed her. The retching seemed to be unending, a running undulation of her body in reaction to the tiny being now growing in her middle.

A baby.

Eric would be pleased. There was no doubt in her mind about his reaction at least. They might not have been a couple for long, but the connection was solid, his faith in her unwavering. He accepted her as she was, no trying to change her or adjust things to fit into his life before. He'd willingly taken on all of her, and she'd be forever grateful.

A child limited her in ways she hadn't considered. Finding the spotting in her panties the previous day had shocked her, a seeming betrayal by a body that had never let her down before. This nausea, morning sickness by her reckoning that didn't restrict itself to the actual morning, was another. An uncontrollable reaction that was not only uncomfortable but made her furious.

I should apologize to Owen, she thought, as she evaluated the receding wave of nausea. Done for now, but likely to resurface if she didn't get something light in her stomach. Most of her anger yesterday hadn't been because of him, even if he'd wound up the target. She wouldn't, but even considering the apology was a step away from where she would have been standing a year ago.

Wood striking wood behind her was worthy of a glance, and she watched Owen stack sticks into a log cabin square, a less intricate arrangement than she'd used last night but perfectly serviceable for a small, morning fire. He struck flint on steel, the muscles and tendons in his jaw standing out in relief, pulled tight. The story he'd shared ran through her head, and she imagined the memories he had to ruthlessly suppress to be able to kindle a fire. Saliva pooled behind her teeth, and she spat it to the ground with a thrust of her tongue. A swipe of the back of her hand across her lips was all the cleanup needed; she'd managed to bend over far enough to not even spatter on her bare toes. She retreated to her pack and grabbed her toiletries, slipping her camp shoes on before going deeper into the woods to take care of the rest of her business.

By the time she returned to their camp, the dry wood was burning brightly, a welcome warmth already radiating from the fire.

Owen grunted at her. Fully dressed, he hunched over his pack as he returned various items to their normal storage spots. Their joint food bags had already been retrieved from where they'd hung them in a tree, and his camp stove was ready with a capsule of fuel, waiting on something to cook.

Alace grabbed her food bag and took out four packets of oatmeal, then a full package of jerky. She could afford to be generous since she had only a day's trek to return to her car. "Here." She thrust the food towards him with an unneeded explanation. "Your pan's bigger." Another reach to her pack, and she returned with a water container. He was staring up at her, the look on his face bland and blank, hiding any emotion he felt towards her offerings. She decided to add in a personal plea. For a man like Owen, a born caregiver who hadn't yet realized why he did the things he was driven to do, it would be something he couldn't ignore. "Feed me."

Their positions didn't change. Still, a sense of static electricity built up along her skin, standing hair on end all over her body. Then he broke it with an easy smile, lines close to the corners of his mouth rounding in an echo that said he smiled all the time. It took a moment to reach his eyes though, and she watched with interest as he consciously engaged the muscles there, curving his eyes over rising cheeks. If she didn't know better, didn't know him as the consummate actor he was, she could believe her request had tripped his trigger into happyland.

The tension in his shoulders and arms put the lie to that. He took the food and water from her hands, and she was aware how carefully he handled the items, ensuring he didn't touch her in the process. *Fear.* She breathed deeply, catching a whiff of more than unwashed body, the acrid stench of stress-sweat confirming her thoughts.

"Nausea isn't any worse, but I'm still going to leave you to it today." Moving deliberately, she turned her back to Owen, ignoring the prickle of gooseflesh all along her arms. She might trust him intellectually, knowing in her head that she wasn't his mark, but her body protested allowing a threat to be this close and unobserved. The survival instincts she'd spent decades honing exploded with a klaxon blare of warning. If he'd noticed her reaction, she didn't see it when she turned around, angling to sit in the hammock, stilling the swinging movement with her feet against the ground.

"Okay." His apparent focus fixed firmly on the pan of cooking oatmeal, he had fingers and knife flying as he minced pieces of jerky into the mixture. "Anything in particular you'd advise me to watch for?"

"Another six miles or so there's a second field to the north of the trail. You'll have to bushwhack for half a mile or more to get to it. I marked it on the map in your packet. It's a pretty big file, so you should download the update before I go, use my connection." An involuntary tensing of the muscles near his eyes. Something in what she'd said was unwelcome. Reviewing her statement, she thought she found the reason. The question was whether she should address it directly or beat around the bush. A flash of her dreams last night rolled through her head, the wash of red across her mind's eye stark and jarring. *Direct it is.*

"The download doesn't include any tracking scripting." An aborted glance towards her highlighted how correct her guess had been. "Owen." With harsh emphasis on both syllables of his name, she leaned forwards slightly and waited impatiently until he lifted his gaze and looked directly at her. "My old handler used trackers on me without my knowledge. It ruined the relationship." An understatement if ever there was one, and for a moment, her memories swept in from that night not long in the past when she'd confronted that handler—the man she'd thought her friend: Regg—the finality of smoke rising in the distance, reflected as a dwindling column in the rearview mirror of her gig-worthy junker. "I value your contributions too much to risk setting us down that kind of path. I've been upfront with you about what tracking elements I've included in any items provided or software required to do your job. You can trust me." It always came down to such a simple, single concept. Trust, the confidence that what another person did, or said, or offered was the truth. *Faith*. "And I believe I can trust you."

Owen's gaze was unwavering, locked on her face, but she noted his hands didn't slow, the knife flashing and moving in motions of unadulterated confidence. "Okay, boss lady." He blinked, and the slant of his shoulders changed, lowering the slightest amount, a signal that whatever else he was going to say, he was just a bit more comfortable with her at least. "Ma'am."

Alace didn't try to hide her smile of relief.

That didn't stop her from drawing the knife from her ankle sheath and flicking it towards him, tang driving into the ground inches from the sole of his boot, handle quivering in place. "I think my knife's sharper. Give it a try."

Without missing a beat, he rested his open blade on his thigh and plucked hers from its resting place, giving the double-edged knife a cursory swipe against his jeans before he went back to mincing jerky into the oatmeal. "I'd say they're about the same." Finished with the preparations, he tested the edge of the metal with the pad of his thumb, raking it sideways. Then, quick as a thought, he flicked the blade back her direction, the tang once again sinking into the earth with a thud, handle quivering. If she were to measure it, she suspected it was the exact distance from her boot that it had been from his. "Thanks for the loan."

Alace sat up and retrieved the knife, wiping it carefully before replacing it in the sheath. Just the movement made her stomach do a slow roll, and she wished for the ability to control her body as easily as she did her weapons, mentally rolling her eyes at the idea. If she'd learned anything over the years working gigs like this, it was to control what you could and manage the fallout of the rest. She'd just gotten accustomed to being more in control than not.

Her gaze fell to the objects from the killer's cache, hidden under a swath of tarp they'd flipped over to protect the items from the overnight dew. She didn't know if she could blame the barely there pregnancy for her mental lapses yesterday. Missing the belt wasn't a big deal, but the wig? Not paying attention to the specific victims was a blunder of epic proportions. She'd lain awake for a long time last night going over each piece of evidence. There was something about the wig that kept bubbling up, coming close to focus but never quite getting there.

A mug appeared in front of her and Alace jerked backwards, the hammock swaying. Owen had gotten close, inside her defenses, without even a twinge from her radar. He stared at her, an expression of the same surprise she was feeling etched on his face. Wordlessly she accepted the oatmeal and settled herself. It smelled good, the combination of complex carbohydrates and protein undercut with something sweet. Lifting a loaded spoonful to her mouth, she delicately touched the tip of her tongue to the food, tasting apples and cinnamon.

At her question, communicated with a look, he laughed in response, this time the involvement of his eyes immediate, signaling true amusement. "I added my own oatmeal to the mix. I've got a sweet tooth like nobody's business, and on hikes like this, it helps if I indulge early in the day."

Alace allowed one eyebrow to lift, mentally marking the preference to include in her file for Owen.

They ate in silence, neither allowing the spoons to clink against the mug sides or bottoms, but when she handed hers back, his hand out in an unspoken demand, she saw Owen's mug was as scraped bare as hers. He cleaned up and then set himself to tidying the few items left out after making breakfast. Alace stood, stretching before she took down her hammock. "I'm going to take the wig back with me. I don't think I'd get anything from the rest of it; the items are too common for them to provide much in the way of location."

"Agreed. Something's off with it, but I can't put my finger on what's tweaking my head." His overly communicative response pulled her attention and she saw he was otherwise occupied, having unpacked most of his backpack, and was looking through things with a thoroughness that surprised her. Then he shocked her again by verbally acknowledging the same thing she'd been thinking when she offered the food. "Since you're going back, if you have more jerky or other protein, that'd be welcome. I didn't pack for more than a couple of nights, and if I stay longer, I risk running short. I can hunt if needed, but carcass disposal on federal lands is always dicey. No reason to chance it."

She nodded as she bent to her pack and dug, coming up with two more bags of jerky and a handful of protein-rich bars in addition to two freeze-dried meals. She picked up the satellite Wi-Fi and balanced it in her hand, finally deciding having the ability to communicate with him long term was far more critical than the chance of her needing to connect before she could get into normal coverage range. It was her turn to startle him, walking up behind him and waiting, staring down at his dark head bent studiously over his pack. He froze in place when she cleared her throat. She held the items out and said, "Take these." Owen lifted a hand without looking back, accepting the items.

"Thanks." No telling inflection in his tone, but from the tension straining his muscles, keeping his unprotected back towards her was taking all his focus, evidenced by how the hand with the new foodstuffs didn't move, lying on his thigh where it had dropped.

She backed away, then returned to her pack, stowed the hammock and food sack, and packed the wig into an emptied bag. She wrapped the brittle hair around the mesh, protecting the wire ends as best she could. Packed, and water supply checked, Alace turned to face him. Everything about this in-person partnership had been strained, harder than it should have been because of who they were. *What we are.* When he stood and faced her, she studied his expression, seeing the same stress on his face that she felt inside.

"It'll take me most of a day to get home." More if she didn't push herself, but she didn't offer that up. Showing weakness in his presence felt like letting a wild animal sniff an open wound. A risk that had no purpose and a wise woman would say wasn't worth taking. *So wise.* "You get a hit on something, go ahead and upload it, don't wait for me to ask. Once we're done in this area, I'll sort out how best to call it in. We'll get those girls home to their families." When they'd gone through the remaining areas Owen had marked yesterday, they'd had the unwelcome but expected appearance of two decaying bodies. *Only two. Could have been worse.* He dipped his chin once, clenched muscles holding it firm. Neither of them had been happy leaving the discovered bodies lying in their cages, but it was the best way to protect them from additional damage. Of the pits discovered, only those two had shown signs of usage, which had become a point of confusion for Alace. Why had the killer abandoned this field, or *was* it abandoned? Did the monster move between different clearings? Would this become a repeat location at some point in the future? Nothing in the workup on the killer indicated anything along those lines, but something she'd learned in all her years was that people were unpredictable in the best of circumstances.

This was far from the best.

Alace swept Owen with a glance. With his rigid stillness everywhere else, the restless movement of his fingers surprised her, a slow stroking along one edge of his pack's shoulder straps. Down, and then back to the same place, followed by a side-to-side brush as if checking something. As if checking to ensure nothing had changed. She shifted to one side and caught a glint of something metallic in that place, and in the split second she allowed her attention to remain on it, saw a loop of wire.

That's why he was so quick to reclassify the leather as a belt instead of a garrote.

One mystery solved, she locked gazes with him, giving him her best do-not-fuck-with-me stare. "Keep me in the loop." At the edge of her vision, she saw his fingers stutter in their movement, returning to where the choking wire was before completing the normal full sweep down the strap. Now, to ensure he knew she'd seen, something he'd wonder about if she didn't, eventually deciding her words would have been a coincidence. Instead this would reinforce all the reasons to fear her. *Trust only goes so far.* "So to speak."

"Yes." He hesitated, and she thought he'd retreat to the honorific she'd forbidden in an effort to invoke humor. Or, he might use the role acknowledgement he'd settled on a while ago, ending each check-in call with that damned "boss lady." Owen surprised her instead, something she was coming to understand might become the norm in their relationship. "Alace. Travel safely."

Hefting her pack, she settled the straps on her shoulders, never letting their locked gazes drop even for a moment. "You as well."

A turn and dozen strides had her at the tree line, and she followed the edge of the clearing around to the closest point to the trail, exiting there and making her way to the cleared and flattened path. The only time she paused on her way back to the lot and her car was to scoop up a piece of wood. Then, makeshift hiking staff and sometime web clearer in hand, Alace walked out of the wilderness.

CHAPTER TEN

Owen

Briefly tracking Alace as she made her way through the woods, Owen stood staring at the last place he'd glimpsed movement as she walked out of sight. That had been the single most surreal moment of his life. Even more than standing in front of the officers of the courts-martial, unofficial though they were, and listening to them formally ending his military career.

Alace's nearly playful toss of the knife had signaled a change in their relationship, afterwards cemented by the way they'd both relaxed their environmental awareness enough to be taken by surprise. Then she'd exhibited his worth in her eyes, isolating herself until she got back to civilization as she offered him a connection to the world via the Wi-Fi. His fingertips teased the tiny wire loops. Threaded through the cording along the edge of the strap, it was easily removed and prepared, needing only two tiny sticks to create handles. When someone like them learned about a hidden tool, the instinct was to protect that knowledge, knowing t left the other person exposed by being even slightly in the dark. That she hadn't, had woven it into a casual comment instead, settled him.

Alace Sweets is pregnant.

The idea was still a ot to unpack, but it was the only thing to fit all the facts. He'd bet money she hadn't told her husband yet. *Alace Sweets is married.* Owen never planned on meeting the man, but having seen pictures of Eric with Alace that showed clear evidence of highly protective body language, Owen knew if she had informed him of the baby, there wouldn't have been a field trip of this sort in Alace's future, near or far. He hoped she got back to her car safely but would never have insulted her by asking if she wanted company.

It took only a couple of minutes to return the cache to the pit. He restacked things into their original positions, lacking only the wig to complete the collection. Back at camp, he hefted his pack and angled through the woods away from the field, intending to rejoin the trail farther along instead of retracing their tracks from yesterday.

The terrain changed and the incline grew steeply as he hiked along, ducking under low-hanging branches and avoiding spiderwebs. Once he hit that connection point, it was only about six klicks to the next location. Given the difficulty of the terrain, without pushing himself, he wasn't going to break any world records getting there. *No biggie.* When he judged he was getting close, Owen pulled out his phone and brought up the map he'd downloaded during breakfast.

A rocky outcropping seemed a good landmark, and he slogged onwards, only stopping when he stood in front of the corresponding cliff rising to the west of the trail. Consulting the map again, he oriented himself using his compass and observed the topography, getting a good sense for what lay between where he stood and the open clearing Alace wanted him to check out.

Bending at the waist to balance his pack, he scooped up a thick stick and struck out, bushwhacking as Alace called it. This route wasn't traveled, wasn't an official trail, but halfway to the clearing, he stumbled on something that was a good deal more defined than he'd expected. Owen hesitated before putting a boot on the worn groove threading through the vegetation thriving in the shade of the tree canopy. Crouching, he angled his head to stare both directions along the path, identifying half a dozen animal tracks before he found what he'd been looking for. There was a distinct bootheel, followed by another, about half a stride beyond. They weren't crisp, the impressions' edges rounded by the light breezes that played at this elevation. But they were there, and light as they were, the footprints would have been washed away by even a drizzle, which meant they'd been made recently, since—if memory served—this region had seen a torrential deluge about two weeks ago, part of a cold front sweeping in from Canada.

Staying to the underbrush, he paralleled the trail, identifying and noting each indication of manmade tracks. They were even, not struggling or stumbling, and not overly deep. When he found a pair of tracks, they were consistently about two-thirds to a full length of his normal hiking stride, which spoke to the lesser height of the person.

The trail meandered north at an angle away from what his compass said should be a direct line to the clearing. It was following the path of least resistance, circumventing a broad thicket of brambles, wicked sharp thorns driving him to take his first step on the path. Owen felt exposed, and he'd only taken a couple of strides before he crouched low, head swiveling to cover the trail ahead and behind, peering through the vegetation on either side. His advancement continued that way, slower than he would have liked, but he catered to the short fuse of his nerves, trusting those senses he'd finely honed to keep him safe.

Once past the brambles, he opted to remain on the path, keeping his steps to the hummocks of grass as much as he could, leaving little impression behind to mark his passage. Something about this trail had him spooked, and his mind kept pulling up images of that wig, blood-tipped twists of wire holding the hanks of hair in place. Something moved in the brush off to his left and Owen was prone instantly, watching as a doe stepped into view. She scented the air, head swiveling much as his had been, tick-tocking back and forth.

With a sigh, he pushed up to his knees, surprised to see the deer stare at him without any attempt to flee. It was only when he rose to his full height that she leapt sideways and was away, tail flagging alarm as she ran. Owen expected his alert to fade after that, his nerves validated by the presence of another living, breathing being. He was wrong. The farther he went on the path, the tighter things inside him wound. It was worse than having Alace at his back yesterday. This was an oppressive feeling of dread, very much like…

Stopping abruptly, he allowed his mind to follow that errant thought, because this did feel familiar in a bad way, like he was reliving something he'd rather not. Not in a flashback, because these woods weren't anything like the jungles of Central America. Still, this felt way too much like one mission he'd taken that hadn't turned out as expected, and instead of settling into his hide to track the movements of his target, he'd stumbled into a valley decimated by death, the entire village wiped out.

The wind shifted, and he caught a whiff of what might be rotting vegetation or something much darker.

Off the trail again, he worked his way through the woods, orienteering skills keeping him on point. Just over an hour later, he paused at the edge of the clearing, seeing where the trail dissected the trees to his north by about a quarter of a mile, picking up on the far side of the opening and disappearing into the woods there, turning back into a true animal track tunneled underneath the vegetation.

That path only earned the most glancing of attention, his full focus on the clearing and what he saw there. If he imagined the open swath of land as a clockface, then sitting at two o'clock, about midway through the sweep of the hand, was the artifact.

Incongruous and out of place, there was a half barrel.

CHAPTER ELEVEN

Alace

Even in dreams the landscape never changed. Alace raced through the trees, chasing the disappearing point of the long-abandoned tracks. Red. Everywhere she looked, red.

She jerked as she woke, head angled uncomfortably against the passenger door of the car. Sitting up with a yawn, she tried to rub the twinges of pain from her neck, groaning as she dug deep into the complaining muscles.

A look at her phone said she'd slept an hour or less, and another jaw-cracking yawn said she'd come down on the lesser side of that equation. Gulping a few swallows from her bottle of water, she shook her head, trying to dislodge the lingering cobwebs of sleep. Squinting out the windows into the dark, she could make out the hulking outlines of the same trucks parked ahead and behind her as when she'd stopped, fatigue overcoming her desire to be home. The on-ramp had been a safer bet than a rest area, and tucked in between the semis as she was, it felt like her parking spot was even more protected.

Shuffling back behind the wheel, she took another drink as she buckled and prepared to roll out. A peek at her phone showed she had signal for the first time since she'd started the trip home, and she opened the normal text app to find three messages from Eric, his messages colored in ascending levels of concern.

Thumbs flying across the screen, she sent what she hoped was a reassuring text just saying she was headed home and would be there within a couple of hours. His response came before she could change apps, and she smiled at the bossy and demanding, **Call me.**

"I'm fine." She led with that when he answered, even before a greeting. "I stopped for a nap because I was tired, but I'll be home soon."

"You're okay? You were quiet for a long time, Alace." The worry in his voice tore at her chest, opening tiny wounds that she'd caused him to worry. "Are you too tired to drive? Should you get a hotel?"

"I'm good. I promise, Eric. I'm ready to be home. With you." Alace's lips curled because her voice was pitchy and soft, the love that filled her evident in every word. *Such a sap.* It made her inordinately happy to feel this way, because she knew he returned the love. Unreservedly. "Want me to wake you when I get there? We could have happy sexy times." *Unless I'm spotting again.* Her brain was unhelpful at the moment, shoving that thought front and center, because during her speedy hike back to the car, she'd found evidence of blood each time she'd gone to the bathroom.

"Just come home to me, Alace. I'll be waiting." He didn't say goodbye, and knew she wouldn't either, finishing with a husky, "See you soon," before disconnecting.

With a sigh, she thumbed back to the text string, sending him a heart emoji, the only one she ever used, and only with him. Words were less likely to be misunderstood, and all of her messages had direct consequences if the other party got it wrong.

Another flick of her thumb took her to the secure log-in app that got her into her outer network, and another two-factor authentication got her into the next ring, where her email lived. Nothing of note there, all things that could wait until she was home and in her office. A different anonymous VPN connection took her to a page with a single, blinking cursor. She typed in the pass phrase, slow and deliberate in her exhaustion, because at this level in her network a single failed log-in resulted in a self-destruct sequence she couldn't back out of.

Of the five folders in view, four were in their normal state. Each displayed a different color indicating what stage the hunt was in, and waiting communications were highlighted by a hovering number. Four held zeros, but one, the one she'd set up for Owen with this hunt, showed he'd uploaded three new items, requesting a read-receipt for each.

She glanced around at the darkened on-ramp again, watching as headlights in her rearview showed a large vehicle just turning off the local road and onto the highway. The semi was still gaining speed as it rolled by, but the wind of its passage rocked the car.

She touched the folder. Two images and one document. The images were still resolving, not fully downloaded, so she tapped the document to open it.

Timestamped at twelve hours after she'd left him on the trail, it was a succinct description of another killing field. He couldn't have had time to investigate all the pits yet, but it appeared one had drawn his attention from the moment he'd stepped foot into the field. The body inside hadn't been dead more than a couple of weeks. He'd tentatively identified her as a woman taken around three months ago, one of three women who had disappeared over the course of a six-week period. That was three confirmed bodies for this killer, sixteen if she believed it was the same one who had gone inactive in Idaho. *Sixteen, then.*

Alace sucked air between her teeth, forcing down the anger at herself for abandoning the hunt when she had. Owen was competent, and he was the absolute best she had for this particular gig. He was already invested in the victims, which meant he wouldn't stop hunting. Even if she were to wave him off at this point, he'd ignore her. She knew that as a fact, because it was what she would have done.

He'd found another cache, and the itemized list was very similar to what they'd gone through earlier. The differences included significantly more food and a stock of supplies to make the napalm instead of just the implements. Alace finished reading and typed her response, waiting for the document to save and upload before she exited it.

Good work. Doc everything. Pics are good.

Recommend not exploring other pens. *Highly* recommend. Leave no trace works in our favor here.

The now-downloaded images included one of the inside of the cache, and just as the list of items had been similar, even the arrangement in the soil-walled square was the same. The only thing not present was a crafted wig, and Alace wondered if the one packed in her bag was the killer's only trophy. *Why would it have been at the dead field instead of the active one? Maybe our killer is reactivating the field?*

The other image chilled her blood, and Alace stared at it for a moment before she reopened the document, typing in another block of text before saving and exiting.

The barrel. What's with that? Now there's two of them. To what purpose? Why a planter? It's a hell of a signature, and nothing that was noted in Idaho. Two planters but one trophy? It doesn't make sense. I think we missed something there. Give me your thoughts.

In an image taken from across the clearing, the half barrel stood alone as a mute witness to the death that had come to pass underneath it. It covered the small, square access point, same as the ones Owen had identified in the pits they'd found. To have found two of these planters, these heavy garden accessories, hauled in over long distances across uncertain terrain meant they held greater significance than Alace had attributed to them. *Another mistake.* She wondered how Regg had done it, that unwelcome thought circling not for the first time. He'd always seemed so absolutely certain of anything he'd told her. He'd also been a habitual liar, and not just for the sake of the gigs they worked together. *Regg isn't me.*

The phone in her hand chimed, startling her. Almost as if he knew she'd delayed, Eric sent her a two-word text. Alace disconnected from her private network, withdrawing as carefully as she'd inserted herself, wary of the traps she'd set. Then she buckled up, fingers given permission to glide across her belly for an instant, and pulled onto the on-ramp, angling the nose of the car into traffic and towards home. The message circled her thoughts, warming her in indescribable ways.

Come home.

***

She'd scarcely parked the car before Eric was at her door, yanking it open with one hand, his other reaching for her face, palm cupping her cheek. Alace smiled up at her husband as she unbuckled and grabbed her phone by feel. The rest of her things could wait for the morning.

"Welcome home, beloved."

The simple sound of his voice soothed her, well-known tones smoothing around well-known words, a greeting and declaration in one, echoes of their meeting and the instant inferno between them.

She stood and was scooped into his arms, one large hand supporting her ass while she settled her legs around his waist. The solid clunk of the car door signaled with finality the ending of her life as she knew it. At some point in the last two hours of the trek home, Alace had come to a point of acceptance. Now, in the driveway of their home, middle of the night arrivals setting schedules askew, she whispered the prologue to their changing lives in his ear. "I have something to tell you."

Eric never missed a lick, his stride unfaltering until the house door closed behind them, and even then his motion was to soothe her, a hand skating up her spine to grip the back of her neck, urging her to rest against his shoulder. "Tell me, beloved." That word again, that fucking, fucking word that tore her breath from her chest because it meant so much. His thighs jostled her ass as he tackled climbing the stairs still holding her. Thick and strong, like everything else about Eric. He was solid, capable, unswaying in his love for and belief in her.

Alace was wordless, adrift, uncertain how to best frame the news. Not uncertain of the reaction, never. Eric wanted it all, just as Alace did. Telling him about the baby wouldn't rock his boat, no. She smiled into his neck, taking in a deep breath of everything that was Eric. Worried about her, he was still dressed from work, his shirt—which would have been crisp this morning—now molded to his shoulders and held the notes of his cologne along with that earthy scent that meant Eric to her mind.

"I reek." Truth. Even after only two days in the woods, the efforts expended had been more than enough to start the beginning of a true hiker's funk. "Shower with me?" His hum was an agreement that vibrated through her bones, the always-appreciated sound of Eric happy and content, simply because she was here with him.

"Be my pleasure, baby." And that was Eric aroused, moving from the echoes of Querida and beloved to baby. She had enjoyed mapping the reasons for his pet names, finding the provocation of each a shining example of the depth of feelings this man was capable of. They were made for each other, truly, because as much as she loved him, he returned the emotion. With a devotion that was covetous and always growing, she hadn't yet come to an ending for how she felt about him.

In the bathroom attached to their bedroom, she skated down his front as he slowly released her, reaching for the floor with the edges of her boots. It was the work of moments to find her footing so she could roll back up and onto her toes, arms wrapping around his neck as she drew him down for a kiss. Eyes dipping closed, she relished the sensation of roughened silk as his tongue drifted side to side across the seam of her lips, asking for entrance. That mother-may-I move was one of her favorites, and she granted it, as she always did, as hungry for the taste of him as she was the feel.

Their hands were busy as they kissed, untucking and unfastening, fabric shoved out of the way as touch ruled the day. Suit pants joined hiking boots on the floor, her grungy and dirty clothing mixed with his starkly clean items. It didn't matter how much they might not appear to match—as he lifted Alace again, nothing between them, giving her some skin-on-skin therapy a la Eric—they fit together like puzzle pieces created for that exact purpose.

Steamy water pelted the sides of the shower enclosure as he backed under the water, testing the temperature with his own skin before turning to place Alace directly under the stream. She moaned as, with a physical release, strained muscles began giving up their clenching, tight hold. Eric's palm slipped up her back and settled between her shoulders, pressing with a steady pressure. Alace went with his suggestion, settling her cheek against his chest, head tucked underneath his chin. His cock bounced once against her, but Eric didn't move to take things in hand, seemingly content to hold her, a stark contrast from the kisses and touches he'd treated her to as they'd undressed.

"Eric?" She held there, keeping the rest of her words trapped behind her teeth, waiting at the tip of her tongue for his answering hum, that rumbling response that made her shudder with need, clenching muscles around a frustrating emptiness. She stayed in place, soaking up heat from two sides, wet steam drawing that relaxed feeling into her muscles, and the furnace that was Eric against her front, solid and wide, wet and slippery but so stable all at once. "I got the feeling we were going to fuck, but now this seems like a cuddlefest instead. Is everything okay?"

"I took the garbage out while you were gone."

What was he talking about? *Why would the trash matter?* He didn't give her anything more, didn't fill in the spaces between what he'd said and what he meant, making her sort through her pre-trip preparations.

"Something we need to talk about, Alace?"

Gruff and rumbly, his whispered words didn't roll through the shower so much as they settled on her skin. The pregnancy test, wadded in a handful of toilet paper, but if it had been dislodged from that weak camouflage, unmistakable in name or that damn giant plus sign in the plastic window of the pee stick.

"I'm pregnant." The way his arms tightened around her could mean anything. Maybe it was grief at losing their couplehood too quickly, or maybe a counter-revulsion at the idea, holding her close before he thrust her away. She reminded herself of her certainty over the past few days that he'd be excited, that it would be something he'd welcome, a change in their relationship status that would make him preen and cluck like a rooster, crowing about his virility.

"*Beloved.*" The vibrating emotion in the one word—still with the one-word thing, it made her crazy sometimes—put all her fears to rest. Arching backwards in his arms, she lifted her chin to see wet shining in his eyes, heated gaze fixed on her face. "The test, it is reliable?"

Alace folded her arms around his neck, tilting her head back to wet her hair in the shower stream, closing her eyes against the naked joy in his expression. "Yeah. Plus there's my boobs being sensitive, and the on-and-off nausea. So—" She released her hold with one hand to scrub at her scalp, twisting and reaching for the shampoo from her perch at his waist, as if this were an everyday thing for them. Puddling a little of the gel into her palm, she replaced the bottle and then spread the shampoo across both palms, transferring it to her hair and scalp with efficient movements. "Plus I'm late, as in I don't remember my period last month at all, which was why I thought to take the test."

Eric's cock thudded against her ass.

Lids shut tightly against the threat of stinging suds, she arched just the tiniest bit more, pushing her breasts up and into the air. A moment passed; then he groaned and shifted, and heat covered one mound as his tongue wrapped around her nipple on a hard, deep suck. Moving slower, she finished shampooing her hair and leaned back to rinse, Eric's movements timed with each thrust of her fingers through her hair. Halfway through the rinse cycle, he shifted to the other breast, treating it to the same attentive suckles, adding a stinging nip to the tightly drawn bud.

Palms slicking her hair back, she straightened and met his mouth halfway, tongues tangling in that delicious slide he'd perfected, knowing it drove her nuts. Teeth to her bottom lip, he nipped and sucked, then laved across the blood-plumped flesh, chasing away the sting.

She wiggled, unlocking her ankles as she propped her knees on his hips, toes tucking along the front of his thighs. "Put me down." The insistent press of his hard cock hit her differently in this position, slotting lengthwise between her lips, flanged head of his cock riding up past her entrance. "Let me finish washing up."

"Beloved." His arms tightened, and she halted her preparations to dismount, looking into his face. The intense expression was still evident, the reality of what she'd admitted not having taken any time to settle in. "We're pregnant."

"We are." She loved the fact he'd taken ownership of the condition in such a way, making it clear this was about as far from unhappy as he could be. His arms loosened, and she slipped down his wet skin to stand on tiptoes, his rigid cock trapped between her legs a prop she was reluctant to release. "Are we ready for this?" She arched her back, dragging her hips backwards an inch or two—not enough to lose contact, but just a tease—then forwards, retaining her body's hold on his. Again, this slide easier, wetter. Her hands on his shoulders helped keep the stretched position, while his palms cupping her hips steadied her. Eric would never let her fall. Another thrust and pull, a tip of her hips with the slippery wetness nearly putting the head of his cock where she wanted it.

"We are." His promise was as steady as he was, firm and ringed about with belief that would hold no matter what. "Now, finish up in here so we can go to bed. Cuddlefest is over. Time for the main attraction."

Gaze on his face, she smiled and reached where a fresh washrag waited, draped over the inside handle of the door, his predictable preparation. Stepping back, she wet it in the water and squeezed a dollop of gel on the fabric, ready to scrub the dirt from her face.

"Alace."

Eric's terrified tone didn't make sense, yanking every ounce of Alace's attention. Eric stood cupping his cock, chin tipped far down as he stared at his rapidly wilting erection. It was smeared with red, diluting in the splatter from the shower, but not washing away fast enough to be denied. "Alace?"

She shoved the damp and soapy rag between her legs, pulling it out to see more red, so much red, bright and brilliant, and instantly agonizing. Her chest seized in a rough cramp. This wasn't spotting, not even close. This was the bloodied aftermath of something brutal and probably meant the end of a dream she hadn't realized she'd longed for.

Eric yanked the cloth from her hands and dropped it as he pulled the shower door open, his other hand turning off the water. A towel wrapped around her, shoulders to knees, and he draped a smaller one over her head. Eric wrestled his way into his clothing, skin still wet and tangling the fabric around his legs as he cursed. She stood unmoving, gasping for breath as she became aware of a trickling heat that wound its way down the inside of her thighs. Alace trembled at the knowledge. It was a loss that continued, no matter how she clenched and tightened, unable to hold back what felt like a flood.

He disappeared, something she hardly had time to process before he returned, a camisole with a shelf bra and pair of panties in hand. He was on his knees in front of her when she saw the fabric of his pants going dark in splotches. Those would dry with white rings, those droplets of water, so saturated with salt from her stinging eyes. Frozen as she was, she couldn't help him, couldn't force her limbs to move. Gently but with urgency, he dried her skin, and the guttural cry that escaped him when he saw the smears between her legs wracked her with pain. Pad wedged in the gusset of her panties, he pulled shorts manufactured from thin air up her legs, then lifted her against his bare chest and ran down the stairs.

Fifteen minutes later, they were standing in the waiting room of the local ER, and Eric was shouting for help as Alace clung to him.

***

She choked on the pill Eric handed her, swallowing half a glass of water to finally force it down.

He sat on the edge of their bed and leaned across her onto a propped arm, his gaze fixed on her face, that intensity she'd seen in the shower back in his expression. There was an uncomfortable sensation in the pit of her stomach she couldn't blame on the pill, a crawling underneath her skin driven by his pain and fear.

Alace knew Eric loved her. Knew it down to her toes scrunched in the sheets, making tiny divots in the mattress underneath. Knew it to the tips of her fingers, clenching and unclenching the fabric of the scrubs he'd worn home, arms firmly not in a stranglehold around his shoulders, letting him set the distance between them. If he needed it, she'd give it, even if her everything demanded she be held tightly right now. She knew it in her heart, where so many secrets were safely stored. But the determination he'd exhibited when things were falling apart, that told of an unexpected depth of love she hadn't yet explored.

She shifted and released him, masking her immediate desire to burrow against him by impatiently shoving at the pillow, pushing it into a more comfortable sitting position. He didn't say anything, didn't have to, the words of the doctor still fresh and painful enough to keep her bound to this bed without any kind of restraints. Just her fear and Eric's love.

"Not a miscarriage." She repeated what the doctor told them and watched the minuscule tension between Eric's brows become more pronounced. "Just a serious warning."

Alace had put the pregnancy at risk with her strenuous activity. A thing so much more tenuous and fragile in the first weeks and months than she'd known, and the doctor had shaken his head when she told him about the forced hike, not calling it that, of course. Just describing the terrain as challenging, minimizing the pace and distance as merely formidable.

"Bed rest." Eric dipped his head, crowding closer as he traced along her cheek with the tip of his nose. "That's gonna kill you. I'll have to figure out a way to get you through this."

Oh God. He'd gone from making this a them to just *her*, that fast.

After hours in the ER, the relief present in Eric's eyes had been overwhelming when he'd heard the doctor's words, calming them with statistics about early pregnancy and spotting. Being granted the chance to watch that fear and relief give way to an enraptured joy when they saw the rapid fluttering movement on the ultrasound monitor had filled her with shame. Having gone from the high of the thrill and excitement of his unfettered happiness at the idea of the pregnancy, to the lows of that terror-filled ride to the

ER had slammed the knowledge home that she'd caused this. *I did this. Nearly took this from him, from us.* Razor-sharp thoughts circled through her head. *As selfish and single-minded as I am, how can I hope to be a mother worth having the name?*

"I didn't mean to do anything to hurt it." Alace dipped her chin, looking away, bending her knees in turn so the covers seen beyond Eric's arm looked like a marching army was underneath. Teeth to her lip, she braced for his fear to turn to anger. Maybe even wanted him to rage, because then she could better soak up the responsibility. *It's all on me.* "I wouldn't, Eric."

"*Beloved.*" Her neck twisted at the word, wrenching her head to one side, face angled away, unwilling to brave his anger. "Alace, baby. Look at me." Strong yet gentle, his fingers gripped her chin, pulling her face back into alignment with where she presumed his was. With her eyes squeezed shut, she couldn't see, didn't want to see, wouldn't stand to see. He shook her gently, side to side. "Alace, look at me."

"I don't want to." Honesty wasn't her go-to, but with Eric, she knew nothing else would do.

"What are you afraid of?" Quiet and calm, he was close enough to send puffs of heated air across her cheek with each word. "Hmmm?"

Her whisper was clogged with tears. "I didn't know it would happen."

"I know that, beloved. My beloved. How were either of us to know, hmmm?" He'd pinned her against the mattress, his hips on one side, arm on the other, body hovering over hers as he leaned in. Dry heat touched her cheek, his lips skating along her jawline towards her ear, where they pressed a gentle kiss. "The doctor said for the moment everything is okay. Said about a quarter of women who encounter this have spotting with no other problems. And now we know, hmmm? Now we know, and we'll work together to make things as okay as we can." *We*, he was saying *we* again, and her heart gave a tiny leap that brought more stinging salt to her eyes. She blinked, wanting to believe everything Eric was saying. "I love you, Alace. We'll figure this out."

Her stomach rolled again, and Alace must have failed to keep her composure at the acrid taste because he quirked an eyebrow at her, corner of his mouth pulled to the side. "My stomach's pissed." She shook her head. "I ate granola bars and protein packs yesterday, then with everything last night and this morning—everything that happened in between came before food, and now there's that damn horse pill." Eric's expression hovered between angry and concerned, with the empathy eventually winning. "It's nearly dinnertime. I should probably eat something."

"Then I'll feed you. Feed my baby." Something shifted in his face, a lightness around his eyes, and she knew in this instant that the phrase had forever changed for him. "Any special requests?" His face drifted closer to hers, his fingers still trapping her chin. Not that she would have tried to avoid his kiss, the touch of his lips on hers something she'd been craving, fearing the loss if he blamed her for the stupid, selfish actions that had caused the spotting. His mouth glided across hers, dropping tender pecks at each corner. "I can cook or call something for delivery." The glint in his eye promised an argument if she tried for anything other than those options, limiting selections to the ones that could come to her.

"I'd eat eggs and bacon if you wanted to do breakfast for dinner, or anything without tomato sauce from that Italian place." She shrugged and allowed her palm to slip up his arm, curling around the back of his neck as she boldly tugged him closer. She had to clear her throat twice before she could croak out her request. "Hug first?" Eric's arms folded around her in an instant, lifting her from the pillows to be cradled against his chest again, legs draped over his lap. She burrowed her face against his neck, holding her breath to keep the rogue sobs at bay. It took minutes in which he patiently held her, his grip renewing around her waist and shoulders, his hands playing a symphony of touch along her arms and back, where each soft caress felt like a promise of faithfulness and fidelity to her. A pledge he'd spoken many times, had written into their marriage vows, and had delivered again in dozens of loving IOUs. The offering of more he'd kissed into her lips, pressed into her flesh as he loved on her, and scored into her mind with each day that passed.

"I've got you, Alace." He tipped his head to rest against hers, cocooning her close. "We're okay. No matter what, baby. Beloved. We're always okay."

"I love you." At his pleased inrush of air, she silently swore an oath to say those words often and with meaning. An immediate repeat wouldn't go amiss, because maybe, just maybe, Eric was as wretched as her at the idea of losing any part of the other. Until it had been nearly torn away, she hadn't yet cherished the idea of holding a tiny bit of Eric inside her. Hadn't paid enough attention to the miracle in action, had seen it as a distraction and encumbrance. *Never a nuisance, not ever again.* She wouldn't take any part of having Eric in her life for granted, and she needed him to understand. "I love you."

"As I do you, beloved. As I do you." He hummed softly, then relaxed his arms to a lighter hold, no longer squeezing the life out of her ribs as he'd been threatening to do. "I'll go find food." Another hum. When he spoke again, his voice dipped a register, vibrating with the exposed emotions. "Feed both my babies."

He pulled away and she let him go, staring up at him, unsure if he'd allow her request. *The hell with wondering,* she thought. *Just ask.* "My pack's out in the beater. Can you bring it up here to me?"

Not even a wrinkle of his brow as he agreed. "I'll bring it up after I sort food. Just the backpack?" Alace nodded. "Okay, back in a minute." He paused at the door, one hand resting on the wooden frame, knuckles tapping a nervous cadence so lightly it hardly disturbed the air. "Stay in bed."

"I will," she reassured, holding her smile in, wanting him to see how seriously she took the doctor's warnings. "I'll still be right here when you get back."

CHAPTER TWELVE

Owen

Tablet balanced on his knees, his thumbs tapped out a beat much faster than his heartrate. Anxiety rocked him more than the just-finished five-klick section of trail that sported a greater-than-challenging grade along most of it.

The unassuming surface of the tablet reflected the overhead sun. In between the masking gleam, it also displayed the fact that, other than the initial responses, there'd been zero new activity in the folder. That made it nearly a full day with no new notes, documents, or information—it was as if Alace had dropped him out into the wilderness and then immediately transformed what had begun feeling very much like a partnership he could value into a wasteland instead.

Alace's first note had been an admonishment to leave no trace, which had matched what he'd already done at the time. After realizing that clearing was more or less a still-active scene for the killer, Owen had verified no living captives, then taken time and care in retracing his steps, returning everything to the exact place and position it had been found.

Her second note, time stamped only minutes after the first, was a surprise. Less a directive and more thinking-out-loud comments, she'd plucked at his thought processes with her musing statements. She wasn't wrong in her assessment, because given the remote location and the sheer weight of the half barrel, the idea the killer had one per field felt hugely significant in some way.

He just had no idea what that way was at this point.

Owen discarded the things he felt were too obvious. This killer's motivational triggers were further in the past than a horticulture class in college. The dressing up a certain way to fit a part that only existed in the killer's mind, the carefully prepared pits—and Owen had calculated the time needed to complete even one pit, much less the number they were looking at now, and the facts indicated it would be no less than four days' hard work each to peel back the layers of vegetation and earth, excavate the pit sized from four feet square to an eight-by-twelve rectangle, shore up the ceiling with boards—another hard-earned carry-in item—create the peephole with the wire or mesh, and then cover everything back up and haul the excess soil away.

Powering down the tablet and Wi-Fi, he stowed them in his pack, mind still going a hundred miles an hour. He had another sixteen klicks to go before he'd gain access to the final clearing he'd marked from the mix of drone footage and satellite imagery. Alace hadn't remarked on the location, but Owen wanted to rule it in or out before he turned back to where his car was parked, now a couple of days south.

Gauging the time left until darkness fell from the sun's arc towards the horizon, he was about to shove to his feet when he heard rattling stones ahead. Listening closely, he caught the muted scrape of leather on rock followed by rustling canvas. *A fellow hiker.* Owen quickly checked himself over, verifying no weapons were visible before he forced his body into a more relaxed position, one knee to the ground as he lifted a water bottle to his lips. When the hiker rounded the hip of the hill in front of him, he intentionally stilled, giving lip service to being startled, then waved in friendly fashion as he took another drink of water.

He automatically marked her physical traits— petite, slim—and focused on what he could see of her face, half obscured by a bandanna pulled up over her nose to keep the dust out. Her blonde hair and blue eyes were bold accents, and he wondered about the rest of her features.

"Hey." Quiet and low from behind the concealing cloth, the woman's greeting held confidence but not even a little excitement.

Interesting.

"Happy hiking." He nodded and stood, making a show of more effort than was needed, playing up the imitated weakness and exhaustion, easily falling back into the habits for which Alace had chastised him. He suppressed a smirk, knowing Alace would be doing the exact same thing in this position. "How's the trail?"

"Clear and in good shape." The woman halted twenty feet away, transferring the grip of her trekking poles to one hand so she could push expertly feathered bangs off her forehead.

That was not a discount cut from a place housed in a strip mall. Her hair was also not sweat-sodden.

The skin on the back of his neck prickled.

Her fingers hesitated over the bandanna, finally tugging it down an inch or two, still keeping her mouth and chin hidden. The wind wasn't right for him to get a whiff of her to evaluate trail sweat, but her appearance had Owen frowning. *Somethin' ain't right.* The maps had indicated no road crossing this trail for another thirty miles, and there were no intersections with other trails either. That meant it was a long distance to where she could have started hiking, yet she didn't look like she'd been traveling more than an hour, not the days it must have been. Even if she'd been one of the other cars parked at the trailhead, it was a long way away. There was something distinctly off about her appearing here, now.

When a hiker had to carry everything on their back, space and weight were at a premium. Clothing was one of the first things experienced hikers left at home, keeping only the most necessary of items and removing unneeded extras from their pack setup. That meant by the end of the first day, pants were wrinkled, and shirts stretched ever so slightly at the hem. Her outfit was pristine, or near enough. Either she hadn't been hiking long, or the brand of starch used in her laundry was industrial strength.

"How far've you come?"

He took another drink before answering, then held the bottle out in a mute offering. She turned him down with a headshake, and he found himself watching how oddly the ends of her hair swung. It moved stiffly, more as a unit than strands of hair. *A wig, maybe?* It was a dark enough blonde to effectively hide any evidence of sweating, no telltale splotches at her nape or the part on her scalp. He named the trailhead where his car was parked, and she nodded. "Trail south is good back to there, if you're going that far."

"That's good news." She took a side-step, edging away from him and towards the drop-off side of the trail. A finger tugged the bandanna over her nose, settling it back into place. With a lifted hand, she muttered, "Be safe." It was an effective dismissal, and Owen didn't move a foot out of place as she passed his position and began making her way down trail, head turned partially so she could keep him in view.

He didn't try to hide his stare, not caring now if he made her nervous.

It wasn't uncommon to meet fellow hikers out on a trail. They could be overtly friendly or less so, gregarious or near silent, whichever suited their nature. Sometimes it would be a traveling encounter, neither party slowing their steps beyond what was required to give way on what was intended to be a single-file path. Sometimes hikers would share a meal, share water, gaining snippets of hiking stories out of those chance companions.

A woman alone would definitely be more wary than most, keeping her distance like this one had. He knew this. So why then did her arrival and subsequent departure bother him? Her appearance hadn't lined up with expectations, unless he was wrong about the up-trail connections this path might have. He glanced around, studying the mountains and trees, gaze skimming the skyline on all sides. Startled by a shape rising from the trees to the west, Owen took a moment to refocus his eyes on the nearby object, then pushed out a hard huff of air, relaxing somewhat when he recognized what he had spotted. *Mystery solved.*

There was a fire tower on the next peak over. It would be only a couple hours' distance easy hiking, and while he didn't remember seeing the structure or any kind of access path to it on the maps he'd pored over, the evidence was right in front of him that he'd missed it. The woman must be a seasonal volunteer. Hired by the DNR, volunteers lived on-site for weeks or months at a time, keeping watch for the first indications of fire. Didn't matter if the blaze was caused by lightning strike during a storm or a careless visitor, the threat of an uncontrolled wildfire was ever present and needed careful attention.

Her pricy pack hadn't been large, not small enough to be a day pack, but far less than his, which was the minimum he'd consider for a multi-day hike. Which made sense if she'd come from the fire tower. Her appearance was consistent with the idea, right down to the neatly trimmed and glossy nails. She must be on the beginning portion of her volunteer assignment, which lined up with the seasons, too. And because she was female, her obfuscation of how far she'd come down-trail made the most sense of all.

Owen settled his pack straps over his shoulders, reaching back to clip the water bottle to the carabiner attached for that purpose. He ran the image of the map through his mind again, verified his position in relation to the clearing, and decided he'd hike at least another five klicks before he started scouting for a campsite. That would leave less than twelve for tomorrow morning, and he could be at the clearing before lunchtime if he got an early start.

He glanced back down the trail, no longer catching any sign of the woman. The route wound through the trees and along the ridges and dips of the side of the mountain, so she was well and truly out of view. Another squint at the fire tower and he sketched a quick salute to her with a silent thanks for watching over the woods.

Gravel ground under his boots as he began walking, taking care to stretch out his legs as he slowly increased his strides and speed. *Places to go*, he thought, jaw clenching as he remembered the body lying contorted in the pit hidden under the half barrel. *And dead people to see*.

Chapter Thirteen

Owen

Eyes on the tiny blue flames, he watched as they began consuming the fuel cube he'd placed in his camp stove, heating the pan of water for his morning oatmeal. His mind was in automatic mode, not a state he worked to attain, just the simple effects of exhaustion and too little food. This was the start of day four on the trail, and he estimated he'd covered more than fifty klicks, not including the distances off-trail to the clearings. His body needed calories to continue at this pace, but by his calculation, even with Alace's extra supplies, he should have already begun rationing food to fuel his impending exit from the forest, having barely enough to make it back to the car parked at the trailhead.

He'd made good time between clearings, that effort part of what contributed to his caloric deficit. When he made it to the third clearing and found what he expected, it had given him a mental boost. Unlike the second clearing, it had looked to be retired, just like the first he and Alace had investigated together. Finding the half barrel tucked in the cache pit for safekeeping had cemented in his mind that the second clearing had to be stil active.

Alace agreed.

She'd come online while Owen was otherwise occupied, and he'd felt a whoosh of relief this morning when he'd booted up the tablet and logged in to see new notes and info waiting for him. Not a word of explanation about the silence, which should have been expected.

Except there's that pesky trust issue between us.

Once they were both online and available, they'd used the shared document to toss ideas back and forth as if they were seated at a table across from each other. Something about having to compose his thoughts to put them into text made it a more productive exercise for Owen, and the half a dozen theories between them by the end of the session felt solid, reliable. Alace would spend the day sorting through what she could, and he would do what he did.

After spending the better part of yesterday afternoon digging through death, Owen had lain in his hammock last night working through ideas to keep an eye on that second field, watching for the killer's eventual return. If he'd had even a single field camera with him, he could have scaled a tree and placed it to catch images triggered by movement. He didn't, though, not having considered they'd be necessary given the information he and Alace had at the time.

Finding that active clearing had been a lot of luck, augmented by his and Alace's observation skills. Luck played a huge part in a lot of what went into investigating killers like this one. Stumbling on a sequence that could be recognized and proved true was the most frequent method of discovery. Long hours of looking at data helped, because that at least cemented the patterns in his mind, but it literally took a chance clue to bring everything together. *Look how Alace and I made the same conclusions based off different data and were both right.*

He blinked, the thought jolting him out of his reverie. The water was boiling fast, bubbles of air rising from the bottom of the pan and bursting when they reached the surface. He changed pans, placing the one holding his rehydrated egg and jerky mix over the flame. Spoon in hand, he added two packets of oatmeal to the water set to the side, stirring slowly until it had cooked and thickened to the right consistency. Using the same spoon to stir the eggs, he judged the moment when they were done enough to continue cooking away from the heat source, placing the pan on a nearby flat rock.

He was almost finished with his breakfast when something cracked and broke nearby, the pop of the splitting stick low, vibrating through the air. Stilling, without turning his head, Owen swept the area with his gaze, not seeing any movement. Then, as if appearing in faded stages, a figure stepped into view across the clearing from between the trees. Owen's heart jolted in his chest. It was the woman from the trail, and Owen saw what had been hidden before, the details his intuition had been complaining about.

Focused as his mind had been on the mystery of where she'd come from, he'd virtually discounted what had been right in front of him, albeit hidden behind a thin layer of fabric. With her distracting hair now covered by the hood on her sweatshirt and without the bandanna, her features were on full display, and the puzzle pieces snapped into place, plain as day.

Holy shit.

One of the Temple twins was standing not fifty yards from his camp.

The common denominator that formed the basis of this investigation was Mackenzie Temple, the woman they were looking for. *It's got to be her. Alace would have told me if the other one had disappeared.* He'd assumed their missing woman been abducted and expected to eventually find her gray-featured face staring up at him from one of the pits—not cast in shadows across a killing field from where he crouched.

She stood still as a wild animal, head turning in jerking increments, following a rhythm of survival he recognized. He had often done the same. Any potentially hostile territory like the clearing would typically be divided into segments in his mind, and as he swept the area, Owen would shift his attention deliberately from one to the next, ensuring nothing was left to chance. If Temple was half as observant as he was, the silhouette of the hammock would stand out to her, as would his own profile.

Sure enough, when the blade of her nose turned his direction, he marked the subtle pause as she momentarily locked on to his position before moving on. Between that, and the unmistakable smell of cooking that hung in the air, fried eggs and jerky having as distinctive an odor as the sweetened oatmeal, he didn't hold out any hope of going undiscovered.

Owen didn't waste any time chasing that thought, instead focusing on why it made him uneasy to be exposed as he kept his gaze fixed on her. He was the hunter, had been behind the scope on so many kills that the black ring constraining his vision would seem to disappear. He was a killer, willing and able to pull off the missions Alace had assigned him so far, the evidence of so many unpaid crimes more than enough to tip the scales of his anger. So why then did this woman make him uneasy?

He controlled the instinctive jerk that accompanied the answer to his question. The unease was the same thing keeping him pinned to the forest floor instead of jumping up to greet the woman by name. She hadn't appeared distressed when he'd seen her yesterday, hadn't shown any indication that her disappearance had been coerced. Which meant she'd gone off grid intentionally. He might believe she'd simply left to do a volunteering gig at the watchtower, if it hadn't been for the lack of closure for the ones she'd left behind. The boyfriend who'd been nearly as vocal as the sister about Mackie's disappearance.

So not only had she vacated civilization intentionally, but now she was hiding her identity. He felt certain the blonde hair yesterday had indeed been a wig and not her own dark hair bleached.

That movement of her head stopped, and he took a breath, waiting for her reaction to him. What he didn't expect was that Temple would simply turn and walk back into the woods, leaving behind only the tiny sounds of brush cracking and fabric rustling to mark her passage. Just before she went out of sight, her hand lifted and swept the hood off her head, revealing not the shoulder-length hair he'd expected but the blurry outline of scalp. *What the hell?* Was this another ruse, a skullcap to throw him off yet again? Why would she even worry about who he was? Except for this appearance at the killing field, he should have been just a random passerby to her.

Brain working overtime on the puzzle that was Temple, Owen quickly broke down his camp, needing only to secure the cooking gear from the meal and his hammock setup. Within minutes, he was ready, shouldering the pack even as he took off, double-timing his steps while moving around the clearing, keeping to the shelter of the woods. Her trail wasn't hard to find. Similar to the one he'd followed to the second killing field, this had originated as a wildlife track, broadened and flattened by multiple passages of human feet.

Given his pace, and the minor length of time he'd been delayed following, Owen expected to catch up to her well within half an hour, maybe even by fifteen minutes. That time period came and went, and still he followed the path through the woods, occasional footprints telling him he was on the right track. In front of him loomed another bramble thicket, and instead of the prints veering off and around, they continued on until he'd run out of room to advance, the brambles reducing the width of the trail, twining together overhead to create a narrowing tunnel. The final footprint was just past where Owen could comfortably go, a solidly placed stride where the only way to advance was on hands and knees.

She duped me.

There was no dew blurring the edges of these prints. Crisp and precise, with the weight balance of the impression mirroring a normal stride, they'd been laid at some point this morning, unbelievably as that seemed. That meant Temple had already known about him before appearing at the clearing, having set this elaborate decoy trail prior to showing her face. He hadn't seen where she'd stepped off the path either, and he'd been watching for it. Well, at least he'd been looking at the footprints, trusting the simplest answer to the question of where she'd gone. He wouldn't have ignored an obvious exit to the forest floor, but there were dozens of places where it would have been simple to step off and onto a rocky outcropping where the only danger of leaving signs of passage would be a brushing of dust from her boot soles.

Owen's skin prickled and he whirled, remaining crouched and balancing easily on the balls of his feet. The narrowing tunnel made the perfect trap, if she was...

It took less than a breath to retrieve the pistol from the side pouch of his backpack, and Owen allowed the familiar weight to settle him, bringing his vision into the narrow focus he'd depended on so many times. Mimicking Temple's systematic movements earlier, he scanned through the bramble thicket and into the trees as far as he could see, searching for anything out of place. No sound or scent reached him, and there were no visual irregularities, no inconsistencies.

Just another day in the deep woods.

He didn't trust it.

She'd spent time laying the false track, invested more time in retracing the path to where he'd barely been out of his sleeping bag, and then made herself vulnerable. Something that Owen would have found difficult to do, even as seasoned a hunter as he was.

She's here, somewhere.

There was a loud metallic crash followed by a high-pitched squeal cut abruptly short. Owen focused on the movements accompanying the sounds. About a hundred yards back up the trail, there was a squirrel writhing in some kind of trap.

I knew it was a setup.

Owen scanned the immediate area around him and identified a faint but distinct round outline of a trap's jaws just to the side of his foot. A footprint lay just to the side, and as he'd done the whole way, Owen had avoided stepping into the outline of the trail he was following, not wanting to mar the marks in any way.

Now that he knew what to look for, he saw another three traps between where he still crouched and where the squirrel had finally stopped twitching. Even more time spent on this endeavor, and he'd give anything to know when she'd begun. Was it last night as he lay in his hammock staring up through the canopy at the stars? Or was it further back, when he'd been sorting through the third clearing's cache pit?

Traps. He'd seen burn marks on one victim that could be attributed to a handheld stun gun. Passive restraints had been used in the form of locked overhead doors and the mesh covering each pit's common opening. *She doesn't lean towards active hunting.* Still, she'd somehow captured and transported dozens of victims to these remote woods. *Resourceful doesn't mean docile.*

Owen caught a faint scent of rancid smoke and frowned at the chemical odor as he studied nearby foliage to map the intermittent breeze. What little wind there was seemed to be coming from the clearing.

He reached out and gripped the ragged end of a deadfall nearby, making enough noise to startle any wildlife within hearing distance, but dragging it close enough to break off a thick branch. He balanced it in his hand, wide end farthest from that grip, and tapped the center of the trap nearest his foot. With a gut-wrenching snap, it closed on the end of the stick, smooth edges indenting the wood with the strength of the steel spring-loaded mechanism. It would have broken his leg, or at minimum have bruised it severely. The trap lifted from the ground easily, an unsecured short chain dangling from the base, swinging in slow circles. The links didn't weigh much, but neither had the squirrel, so he used the trap itself to clear the others nearby, their mouths closing impotently on empty air. He didn't take anything for granted, sweeping the chain across all leaf-covered surfaces nearby.

If she were here, she had to have heard the ruckus, but each time Owen paused to listen, the woods were silent, no breeze present to even rattle limbs together. Standing, he picked the disarmed traps up by their tethering chains and made his slow way back towards the clearing. He located another three traps as he went, at least two of them chillingly close to where his own footprints lay in the dust alongside the trail.

At the edge of the woods, he tossed the traps to the forest floor, staring at the mess now present in the clearing. The cache pit had been opened and dismantled; the only thing left inside was the half barrel, now a charred mess of wood and metal. That wasn't the only thing she'd burned, and he cursed as he stared down into one of the holding pens. Three bodies drug from different pits to this one, tossed in without concern for the dignity of the dead. The scent of diesel was strong, and a thin black smoke rose from where the napalm had been applied to burn the bodies.

He leaned on his stick, having taken no chances as he approached the disturbed areas, sweeping and pressing on suspect sod or grasses. He hadn't found anything, but he was well aware she'd had the time he'd spent tracking a ghost as well as the return trip to leave surprises for him.

Owen faced the direction of the fire tower, wondering if the smoke was enough to gain the attention of whoever was actually posted there. The fire wouldn't spread, the bodies too fresh to burn easily, and surrounded by raw earth as they were, there wasn't enough fuel to give it much life.

Still, he needed to bug out. The situation was compromised in far too many ways.

Gonna make like a tree and leave.

Envisioning the map in his head, he decided to go cross-country back down this side of the ridge, skipping past the second clearing and reconnecting with the southbound trail tomorrow. That would keep him off trail long enough to have a defensible story, since traveling on the official trail itself would take a minimum of three or four days to get to the same location.

He was glad now that he'd taken the time to pack his bag and carry it with him. He winced at the idea of the fallout he would have faced if she'd been able to access the information he had stored on the tablet, or if she'd destroyed his food and water, stranding him out here.

Pulling in a shallow breath, he grimaced as he found it tinged with the nauseating odor of burning human flesh. With a final glance around the clearing, wondering if Temple was watching him, he turned on his heel and strode away, not slowing when he reached the boundary where field met woods, his long legs making good time as he plunged downhill.

Urgency drove him forwards. Alace needed to know what had happened. *Need to report in to the boss lady soon as I can*. That was priority one. Not just as a warning he might have found the woman they were looking for, but to tell her he might have unexpectedly come face-to-face with the killer they'd been hunting.

Faced her and lived to tell about it.

Owen thought back to their discussion about the killer's sex and winced at the memory of his overly confident assessment. *Gonna eat crow for sure*. If he had to stop to sleep tonight, he would put together a report, even if it was necessarily succinct. Just as he had that thought, he decided it might be better to wait until he could fully debrief directly to Alace; listening to her questions would be like seeing into her mind. *I'd learn something, for sure*. Either way, gaining quick distance from the clearing would be preferred, and Owen focused on putting one foot in front of the other.

Chapter Fourteen

Alace

"You're a terrible patient."

Alace flattened her lips, silently curling the corners of her mouth down in a visibly disappointed moue she'd practiced.

"Seriously. Terrible."

Todd Worthson stared at her from the doorway. He was propped on a shoulder and hip, angled into the opening as if he intended to stay there all day, making it into a cozy place to stand and heckle her. The smile he offered didn't quite make it to his green eyes, leaving them cold and distant. He opened a bottle of water and lifted it in a side-to-side sway that indicated the length and breadth of the room.

"Sitting in a chair isn't the same as bed rest. Even if you've got your footies all propped up. Not the same, Alace."

Deliberately clearing her throat, she focused on the laptop screen in front of her, working her way back out of the final layer of folders and network connections one at a time until she was back at the basic log-in screen. She shut down the computer, closed it, then flipped it over and popped a panel on the bottom. Ignoring him for a few seconds longer, she retrieved the battery and re-closed the computer's chassis. Laptop and battery went into a custom-built cabinet within the desk drawer, which she closed and locked with a fingerprint. Only once her work was safely stowed did she look up, reseating her scowl in place as she glared at him.

"Did Eric share why the doctor recommended bed rest?" Todd shook his head at her question, his suddenly trembling fingers clattering lid against bottle lip as he attempted to reseal the container. "No? You're certain?"

"He said you'll be okay." Both shoulders lifted in a shrug she tried to convince herself wasn't as dismissive as it felt. "I told him I'd stop by and check on you today."

Alace scratched along her jaw towards her chin, then rubbed the flat of her palm across the bottom part of her face. It was a physical device used when she needed time to frame a question or statement, and one she'd found herself using with Todd more than once since she'd met him. As anxious as their initial conversation had made her, Alace reminded herself of their connection. *Eric.* "No, you didn't. Or Eric would have messaged me."

"Can't a guy just stop and check on a friend without it being a big deal?" He pursed his lips on a puff of air. "Is it that much of a bother?"

"Not when that 'friend' is me." She'd lifted one hand and composed air quotes around that single word. "Eric would have let me know to ensure *your* safety, Todd. Not because this is an inconvenience to me. You and I aren't friends." *I don't have any friends.* That thought shot through her head like a bullet leaving a rifle's muzzle, ricocheting around the corner of denial she'd kept it tucked behind since Regg. *Owen could be.* That was a thought for a different day. "You forget yourself, Todd." Palms against the front edge of the desk, she lifted her feet from the stool as she shoved the chair back slowly, wheels rolling noisily across the plastic mat. She spun the chair with a quick push of her legs, lining up with Todd's position exactly. "Do yourself a favor. Don't drop in again."

She'd seen him on the security feed long before he'd entered the house using his best-friend-status emergency key and access code. Her on-screen alert had triggered when the proximity cameras picked him up as he turned onto their street.

Todd's movement through the house had been straightforward, not veering off into Eric's study or the kitchen, which meant he'd brought the water in with him. *Interesting.* She couldn't decide if it was intended as busywork for his hands because he was nervous or an unconscious instinct to have something to hide behind.

Her confident stare was unsettling him, evidenced by the tiniest tics at the corners of his eyes. For a man whose profession required him to school his expression, he continued to be far easier to read than expected. "You're leaking."

"What?" He lifted the water bottle, studied the bottom, and swiped across the surface with a finger. "No, I'm not."

"Not the water." She gestured towards him in an echo of the vague movement he'd used earlier. "You. You're leaking. I can tell you want to ask me something." Muscles at the edges of his mouth tensed briefly. "It's got you worried, because you don't want to piss me off. But, you're wondering how much of what you've asked me to do I can do from here." She tipped her chin towards the desk and patted the arms of the chair. "And you're halfway convinced to tell me to pull off, back away, and you'll sort out another way to see about finding this woman you'd like to make a sister-in-law."

Todd's involuntary jerk gave away so much, chin lifting as his back straightened and he settled his weight evenly on both feet, arms swinging ready at his sides, plastic bottle crackling in one fist. Defensive posturing at its finest.

"Todd, Todd, Todd." Keeping him in sight from the corner of her eye, she gave him a view of the top of her head as she tipped her chin down, feigning disappointment. Speaking to her knees, she asked, "Did you really think I wouldn't look at everything to do with the missing woman?"

"No." He sighed, and she saw his shoulders lower, rounding down as he slumped. "I should have told you."

"Yes, you should have." She sat straight and turned the chair, angling it back towards the desk. The folder she'd prepared was waiting in a drawer, and it was the work of moments to retrieve it. She slapped it on the desktop with a loud crack and glared at him, still angry he'd thought to come here and try to do whatever it was he'd hoped to accomplish. "I think the subject has been abducted, but the boyfriend had nothing to do with it. He's got steady employment and a strong family and network of friends, and is financially stable. He doesn't fit any kind of profile. According to those aforementioned family and friends, his grief and anger continue long past the media cameras' withdrawal. There are four witnesses that place her in a different town the afternoon of her disappearance. Absolutely nothing points to a crime of planning or passion, and when questioned using persuasive techniques, the boyfriend gave no indication that his story is anything other than true."

"Persuasive techniques?" Cords stood out in Todd's neck, testimony to how hard he was straining to keep his face expressionless.

"You don't want to know." His imagination would conjure far worse methods than what she'd authorized, the tasteless drug not having any negative side effects other than a tiny bit of amnesia, necessary to protect her operative. "Is that really what you're curious about? I tell you she's been taken, and you're going to get stuck on how I ruled out your main suspect?"

"Who do you believe took her?" His fingers were busy with the bottle lid again, twirling it one way, then the other, repeating the action in slow, steady movements. "Was it someone she knew?"

"Nope. If I'm right about this—" Alace paused, letting the unspoken words settle in that she wouldn't be saying anything at all unless she was more certain that he'd believe. He leaned forward by a fraction of an inch, catching himself and swaying upright. *There it is.* "Then timing and location indicate she's probably the victim of a serial killer hunting in the Rocky Mountains." She gave her next words consideration, deciding that to retain Todd's confidence in her ability to do the job, even through this time of enforced rest, she needed to expose the existence of having a team. "We've patched together reports about bodies found over several hundred miles of remote areas, where there're more than enough similarities to draw parallels between them. Timing fits, too, with the subject one of a small cluster of disappearances correlating to the killer's exposed pattern."

"Mackie." Todd cleared his throat, the rough sound relaying the deteriorating hold he had on his emotions. "Makenzie. Not 'the subject.'"

"I can't personalize things and remain effective, but I can imagine how it would feel hearing it said like that." Alace tipped her head in a shallow nod. "I'm not ready to give you a formal rundown on everything and I won't provide specifics. Not now, because we're continuing to work various angles, and maybe not ever depending on how things shake out. There is an outside chance she's still alive, but you shouldn't hope too much. There have been no rescues to date, only recoveries."

"Is there any good news I can share with her sister?"

"No. In fact, if you've shared at all, I'd be quite displeased." She took a slow, careful breath, leaving him sitting in silence for a moment. "Should I be displeased, Todd?"

His headshake came fast, and was definite, but didn't truly reassure.

"You should make this your last unscheduled visit. Do you understand me? If and when I have information you need to know, I will contact you." Alace stared at him, somewhat mollified as sweat beaded along his upper lip. "Set the alarm on your way out." She turned away, keeping him in view but effectively dismissing Todd in a way he hopefully couldn't miss.

She recovered, reassembled, and booted the computer before he'd cleared the stairs. Focused on the security feeds as he stepped off the bottom step, she watched as he wavered towards the kitchen, then thought better of making himself at home and instead went to the door. He tapped a sequence on the keypad before he made his way through, and closed the door behind him. She could have armed the alarm from here, but making him lock up set a clear impression regarding his unwelcome status. Outside cameras confirmed he left the property, and city tracking picked him up on license plate scans three blocks away, then six, then nine, proving he had kept going.

Good boy.

Alace closed those browsers and slipped her headphones on as she navigated to the video footage she'd been watching before Todd showed, rewound it to the beginning, and pressed the play button again.

"State your name, please." The prosecutor was out of frame, so she couldn't see his expression, but his voice was gentle, encouraging.

"Mackie." The little girl in the center of the video paused, shuffled forwards in the rigid witness chair, and leaned closer to the microphone. The audio system buzzed, and Mackie jerked back until the noise reduced to the annoyance of a mosquito. She licked her lips and continued with her full, legal name. "Makenzie Nicole Temple."

"Can I call you Mackie?" The prosecutor waited for her nod, then reminded her, "We need to hear your words, Mackie."

"I'm sorry." As the young girl cringed, her thin shoulders crowded her ears. "Yes, you can call me Mackie, Mr. K."

"For the record, Mackie's referring to myself as Mr. K. I'm fine with that, as Khosrowshahi is a mouthful for anyone."

Hassnal Khosrowshahi, one-time prosecutor from the Denver DA's office, was about as far from a comforting father figure as Alace could imagine. After more than seven years in that position, two years past the legal proceedings currently under review, he'd taken a swift and messy fall from grace. The allegations of criminal behaviors stretched back not just through his tenure there, but beyond to the time he initially passed the bar. She hated that this vulnerable child had been in his orbit at any point of her life.

Mackie shouldn't have been in this situation at all. She should have been testifying from an isolated room with her support team nearby, or been deposed on tape, with the recording played for the jury without the child being present in the room. Khosrowshahi didn't care about the potential damage being done to the little girl.

He'd had his eyes on a higher appointment and had said repeatedly in closed-door company that this case was the one to bank on. Piggybacking his aspirations on the horrific crimes done to this child. Lowest of the low, but nothing that would have gained him Alace's attention.

Until now.

Alace stopped the playback and made a note, then restarted it to the sound of the gallery tittering at the tiny joke.

"Mackie, can you tell the members of the jury how old you are and where you go to school?"

The warm-up questions continued in this vein for a while, without any apparent relaxing effect on the child. When asked to look at the people seated in the jury area, she squirmed in her seat, casting sideways glances that quickly darted back to the base of the microphone in front of her. Alace made another note regarding the judge, because he could have stopped this at any time and didn't. Two decades wasn't long in the grand scheme of things. It wouldn't hurt to see where his career had taken him. Wouldn't hurt *her*, anyway.

Finally, after many more long and excruciating minutes of testimony from the little girl, the prosecutor got to the meat of why they were here.

"Mackie, is your grandfather in the room?"

If the child had appeared withdrawn and shy before, now she seemed to fold into herself, making her body as small a target as possible. Her whispered "yes" set the audio equipment humming, rising into a painful squeal that made her cringe back in the chair. When asked to point him out, she lifted one tiny forefinger over the balustrade of the witness box, angled to the right and out of frame, gnawed and ragged nail bitten to the quick, quivering in time to the visible heartbeat pounding in the little girl's throat.

What transpired over the next forty-five minutes was unconscionable, the child's agony and terror exposed for everyone to see as the prosecutor asked ever more explicit questions.

Mackie had been systematically molested and eventually raped by her grandfather, beginning at age four and continuing until about eighteen months before the trial, when he'd roughly penetrated the then ten-year-old, brutally injuring her for the final time. She'd been unable to hide the pain and bleeding from her twin sister, and after her humiliated confession about what had happened, it had been

Maddy who'd made things stop by going after their grandfather with a baseball bat.

Why the man had picked one identical twin over the other, Alace would never know.

From Maddy's testimony earlier in the trial, it was clear she hadn't been thinking when she'd run the few blocks between their houses, bat in hand, but simply wanted him to pay for what he'd done to her sister. The protective one of the pair from then to now.

The grandfather had been a serial predator, with victims and witnesses coming forward from various branches of the family to help convict him. Maddy hadn't killed him, had hardly connected with the hickory wood before he'd disarmed her. Fortunately, a sheriff's deputy had witnessed her frantic race—crossing streets without caution—and so had been close enough to hear her shouted accusations.

The encounter formed the beginning of the end for the old man. Alace had checked, her half-formed idea of taking care of him totally unnecessary. He'd been shanked in prison only a few years after being convicted, something she counted as a good death, even if not as protracted a one as he'd deserved.

That had been the first of many life challenges for Mackie. From then until the day she'd gone missing, her life had never been easy. There'd been no coasting, no grace period, no comfortable place to land.

Her school was unforgiving of her fragility, as well as of her more self-destructive coping mechanisms as she grew older. The only stable and supportive influence in her life had been her sister, Maddy. No matter what Mackie did, Maddy stood shoulder to shoulder, supporting and defending her.

From the outside in, the destructive qualities of the relationship were clear to Alace. Maddy couldn't have seen it, not as close as she'd been to Mackie. Alace thought moving to Utah might have been Mackie's last attempt to break from her cycle of codependence.

Up to that point, she'd get into shit and Maddy would rescue her, cleaning up whatever mess was left behind. Maybe if Mackie had been left to sort her own consequences at any point things would have gone differently, but that was a coulda-woulda that didn't matter now. Mackie had met a guy and decided over the course of a weekend that she'd relocate and follow him home. Nothing Maddy could say had deterred her, either, causing the first documented argument between the two.

Police called to a local diner had arrived to find the women facing off in the parking lot. Interestingly, in a picture posted to social media from a bystander, it had been Todd standing on Mackie's side with the potential boyfriend shown only on the fringes of the group.

Alace studied the image closely, noting body posture, facial expressions, and most importantly, the confused look on the two cops' faces. Whatever was being said—Alace would give her eyeteeth for a video with sound but had found nothing so far—didn't match whatever the officers had expected as they'd rolled up.

She leaned back in the chair, recrossing her ankles on the stool set nearby for that purpose.

Something about that single image didn't sit right. Her intuition told her there was more to the story, more than just the more stable one of the pair rampaging about the other sister's wild-hair decision. Todd had known Maddy and Mackie all their lives, and at the time had been Maddy's sometime lover for months. He'd been around Mackie enough to have understood the toll her behavior was taking on Maddy. Yet in this pivotal moment, he hadn't stood by Maddy. *Why?*

Knowing the answer wasn't present in the information currently available, Alace angled towards the laptop and logged into a service feed. She took time to craft the request, being selective both in her keywords and recipients. There were a dozen contacts she'd used for this kind of inquiry before, but only a couple she would trust with something this sensitive. Todd was Eric's best friend. It would not be well received if he knew she was looking into Todd as part of this request.

Her gaze flicked to the image a final time, and it finally hit her. When he'd been standing in the doorway today, his body language had been nearly identical. *Fear*. Whatever Maddy and Mackie had argued about, Todd had been terrified by it somehow. Resolve strengthening, she pushed the button to send the message and backed out of the programs, shutting down the computer and locking it and the removed battery in the drawer before she stood and stretched until her joints popped, slowly making her way to the bed.

She'd checked on Owen earlier and found little additional information uploaded after their chat last night. He'd be on his way back to the car right now and available to collaborate soon enough.

Once arranged on the comforter, Alace texted Eric with a dinner request, knowing he would be pleased she asked. She then took a picture of her socked feet, again crossed at the ankle, this time propped on a pillow, and sent that to him, too. They earned her two messages. One more verbose verifying he'd pick up the meal as requested. The other was a single word, the seven letters on the screen somehow imbued with the same vibrating intensity as when he murmured it against her skin, synesthesia be damned.

Beloved.

CHAPTER FIFTEEN

Alace

A red light blinking along one edge of her computer screen caught Alace's attention. Fingers contorted, she hit a keystroke combination that ran a script to back her out of the darknet node where she'd been chatting with a source. This allowed her to flip to the security system more quickly. The view on the cameras surprised her, and Alace picked up her phone to check the screen and confirm she hadn't missed a text.

Eric was pulling into the garage, the alert tied to movement on the external cameras.

She checked the time, verifying she hadn't been working for longer than the doctor recommended.

Turning the chair to face the doorway, Alace propped her heels on the stool and waited.

With the speed at which he appeared in the hallway, Eric must have taken the stairs two at a time, and she wrinkled her nose in annoyance that he wasn't even the slightest bit out of breath.

"Alace."

Muscles in the back of her neck seized tight at the single fucking, fucking word. The grave tone was so out of character Alace instinctively knew whatever had brought Eric home from work was bad news, and her hand protectively cupped her belly.

"What?" One breath in for four seconds. "What's wrong?" One breath out for four seconds. The expression he wore was anguished and fearful. A glance at her computer showed no alarms for anything to do with her activities. Whatever this was, it had to do with them, the two of them.

"Have you seen Todd?"

So out of left field, the question caught her unawares, and her head nod was jerky instead of smooth. "Yes. I told you last night, he was here yesterday. Came to check up on the sicko." She reminded him of the lie Todd had tried to feed her, more successful because Todd was Eric's best friend. She allowed her fingers a single soft caress against the tiny curve of her body before resting her elbow on the desk. "What's up?"

"He didn't show for court today. Totally unlike him." Eric had fully entered the room while they talked and now paced in short, agitated arcs. "I went to his house. His car's in the garage and the doors were all locked, but there was a smell in the air I didn't like."

"A smell?" Alace retained her relaxed posture, even though her fingers screamed to dance across the keyboard and pull up the cameras she'd put inside Todd's house. Not something she wanted Eric to know, unless the resulting coverage showed something they might need. She'd done it as insurance, to keep an eye on the man who'd been so bold as to approach for her help. "What kind of smell?"

"Medicinal. Faint, but there. I couldn't place it."

Yeap, time to pay the piper on this one. "Don't be pissed." She turned to the computer and woke it with a touch. "I wasn't watching him. I just put them in place when I talked to him about what he needed." A folder on a cloud server held her shortcuts for Todd's house. She opened a log that reflected the alarm usage, then clicked the software for the cameras. "I haven't even looked at anything because there's been no reason. All the movement and info on this gig has been leading us well away from town, no need to check up on Todd."

A review of the alarm log timestamps showed Eric's entry and exit as the most recent activity, but it was a three-peat, because his first entry of the code had alarmed the system, so he'd had to put in the code again to actually enter, and then again to exit. Before that was an entry that corresponded with Todd going home after their interaction the previous day. Nothing in between.

The video had triggered for Eric's visit, and she ignored that piece of footage, opening the previous one instead. It was a seven-second clip from the garage that only showed the overhead door slowly closing.

Alace breathed in and held it for four seconds.

She ignored the next several files from both the garage and interior cameras in the folder, and instead clicked on twenty-seven seconds of video that showed Todd in his kitchen. Due to the camera placement the sound was slightly garbled, something she could clean up later using a different piece of software. Right now she focused on him, because the still image had enough detail to show a surprised expression on his face. The video began at that frame, and his mouth moved in time with more garbled sound as a figure in a hoodie approached him and lifted hands that looked tiny in comparison to Todd's. The figure got close, and Todd's expression changed from surprise to shock, then filled with terror. It was only moments until he collapsed as the figure stepped back, allowing him to fall gracelessly to the floor.

The figure, back still to the camera, shoved something Alace couldn't see into the front pocket on the hoodie. Standing over Todd's body, the figure moved their head oddly, jerking side to side as if to a tune. The sound bar on the recording was flat, telling Alace that nothing was playing in the home, so it was something specific to the person. *To the woman.* Alace could make that determination just from the video based on height and body type.

"What's that?" Heat enveloped her, and Alace sagged backwards slightly, letting her head rest against Eric's chest. He immediately and unknowingly validated her evaluation of the intruder. "What's she doing?"

Alace let the final few seconds of the video play out, then selected the next one. There was a gap between the two of several minutes, the five-second triggered recording delay exacerbated by what she could only imagine was stillness from Todd's attacker. When the video began, the figure had stretched Todd out on the floor and with a strength belied by her size was dragging Todd to the garage door.

Alace's head moved forwards and back, driven by Eric's rapidly increasing breathing. "What?" He was panting, air audibly whooshing in and out of his mouth just over her head. "What's going on?"

"Todd's being kidnapped." Alace didn't consider the terrifying power of the word until Eric made a pained sound, a keening trapped behind his teeth. "Eric, honey. Let me do my job here. Can you get me something to drink?" She glanced to the side and winced when she saw a full bottle of water sitting near her keyboard. "Maybe a snack to help with the nausea?"

"Who's that? Who's in Todd's house?" Eric leaned closer to the screen, taking her head with him until she was crouched over in her chair. "Fuck. Sorry, baby." He shifted to the side and she straightened. "What's going on?"

"Eric." She tilted her head up, staring at her husband's strained expression. "Honey, look at me." His gaze danced sideways, then arrowed back to the screen. "Baby." Another tiny shift, then renewed focus on the screen. "*Eric.*" With more oomph behind his name this time, Alace succeeded in capturing his attention. "I can't do what I need to do with you hovering over me like this. You need to step back, give me some room, and let me focus on what I can find out from the video. The good news is I have footage. That's huge, baby. Let me figure out what's going on."

Eyes drawn into downturned commas, face contorted by the savagery of his suppressed emotions, Eric stared at her a moment then blinked fast as he nodded.

"Okay." She gave him a slower nod in response. "I'm going to figure this out. Just—" She shrugged and tipped her head to the side, jerking it towards the door. "—give me some space."

Eric didn't move for a moment, and she had almost decided to try again when he swooped down and pressed his lips to hers. Chaste and yet more filled with emotion than she expected, he kissed her hard and fast, eyes open and locked on hers. "Okay."

He straightened and she turned back to the screen, hands already moving to the keyboard and mouse. Moments later, she was lost in the video footage, watching the woman wrestle Todd into the back seat of a tiny gray import parked in the garage. The low-slung profile of the vehicle no doubt helped as she lifted his shoulders into the car, the woman climbing out the far side as his feet finally disappeared into the car. In the driver seat and leaving a few moments later, the woman and car vanished as the garage door silently closed.

Fingers flying over the keyboard, Alace navigated to the local public works private website log-in page, gaining entry within minutes, using a brute force method she normally wouldn't employ. She already knew they didn't have the capability of finding her, hidden as she was behind widely spread VPN connections. It didn't take long to sort out the naming convention for the city's cameras, and once she did, it was the work of seconds to locate the closest camera to Todd's house. Backtracking to before the woman showed at Todd's home, Alace found the distinctive vehicle on the screen, with a clear view of the driver, hood not yet drawn up to hide her face.

Short, dark hair matched with petite features Alace was well familiar with helped easily identify the woman as one of two. She had a pretty good idea which Temple sister it was.

Staring at the frozen frame for several slow breaths, Alace considered the options open to her.

Her cameras could be passed off as personal security, albeit with abnormally expensive equipment. Involving the authorities would jeopardize her and Eric. Any interaction with police—and eventually the FBI when this was identified as a kidnapping of a sitting judge—brought significant risk to her door. Her cover was firm and well established, but there was always an element of danger when under scrutiny of any kind. Her hunters would be under threat, too, because her network unavoidably terminated here, in her and Eric's home. Even though she took every precaution, Alace knew from experience that no system was bulletproof.

She could have Eric make the call, worried about his best friend being missing with his car and house untouched, acting out of concern. There was the risk the cops wouldn't see the cameras, and even if she moved the recordings to a server inside Todd's home, pointing all new recordings to the location, they'd be restricted, needing a warrant to seize and examine the computer equipment. It could be days before they realized he'd been taken against his will, and by then the traffic footage would be cycled off and overwritten with new recordings.

Or she could work this like a gig and utilize her resources to find Todd. If he'd been killed, she could do what she had trained to do, and find and penalize his abductor. If worst came to worst, she could even make certain his body would be found and reclaimed by family and friends.

"Alace?" She jerked her gaze away from the screen to see Eric close to her, the trembling tray in his hands threatening to tumble the plate of crackers and vegetables to the floor. He was staring at the screen, frozen on the still frame of the video she'd paused. "Is that Maddy?"

"No, baby." She reached out and took the tray, twisting to set it on the floor to one side of her chair. "That's not Maddy. It's her sister."

"The one who's missing?"

Alace nodded, her movement drawing Eric's gaze to her.

"She's not missing anymore."

CHAPTER SIXTEEN

Alace

"Come on." Her mutter was scarcely audible to her own ears, frustration with the lack of information reflecting Mackie Temple's route through the city. Chewing on her lip, she shoved back from the desk and computer and folded her legs, propping her heels on the edge of the seat. The slight rounding of her belly surprised her, making the position less comfortable than she was accustomed to.

I'm pregnant. The knowledge was no longer new but still took her breath away sometimes. This was a tiny person, growing inside her body, unplanned but definitely wanted. The sense of protectiveness she felt was so strong, her fingers curled around her ankles, holding tight.

The video from the trial of the girls' grandfather flickered through her mind, and she saw Mackie's face again. Charming and innocent, upset by the attention but plainly uncertain why these people cared about what had happened between herself and her grandfather—it wasn't until the trial came to a close that the betrayal she'd felt was clear.

The sweet little girl had never stopped loving her grandfather, even when presented with the reactions of the adults around her.

Alace leaned forwards, pulling up public property tax records, putting in the address from memory.

Somehow she wasn't surprised by what she found. Expecting to find it auctioned off at some point—Alace could have located when the transactions had happened but didn't care, as the end result was enough to know—instead, the house had stayed in the family, still owned by an M. Temple, and the taxes were paid up.

One county and two towns over, and just off a major highway.

"Plenty of cameras between here and there."

She got back to work.

"Alace." Eric's expression was less anguished and more concerned as he appeared in the doorway. "Time to take a break, baby."

Straightening slowly, she rolled her shoulders to work the kinks out of the muscles and glanced at the time in the corner of the screen. "Shit." Six hours had passed since she'd started looking for Todd. "Yeah, okay." Eric stepped close, hand out, and she accepted the help rising from the chair. Hissing through her teeth, she winced as the pins-and-needles woke in her feet. "I need to—" She nodded towards the bathroom door. "I'll be right back." It seemed her gentle dismissal of his assistance went unnoticed because Eric moved closer, wrapping an arm around her shoulders as he turned them and walked alongside her. "I'm okay, Eric."

"And I'm going to make sure you stay that way." The tender touch of his lips against her temple felt like a benediction, and she leaned against him. "Both my babies."

Head pressed to his chest, she sighed. "I'm going to activate one of my guys for this." Eric stilled, muscles stiffening underneath her hands. "You know I can't just call it in." Statement, not a question, but she still waited for his response.

"I know." The sound that came from him was as far from a laugh as it could get. "He bought this when he asked you to find her."

"He did." She reached for the doorframe, pulled away from him, and turned to peer up at his face. "I'll handle with care."

"Go." He gave her shoulder a gentle push, turning her more fully into the door. "I'm going to make you some real food." This time when he laughed, the chuckle was closer to normal, rich and full of self-deprecating humor. "Pretty sure stale crackers and wilted carrot sticks aren't going to cut it." He pulled the door partly closed, then paused to say, "Yell if you need me." The click of the latch was quiet but distinct, shutting her in the small room, separating her from him in a way that hurt somehow.

Business done, she spread her palms flat on the sides of the sink and leaned close to the mirror, studying her face more closely than she had in a long time. *What does Eric see when he looks at me?* Normally, she believed he simply saw the woman he loved. Today, however, with the life of his friend on the line, she didn't believe his view of her was quite the same.

"Come out when you're ready. I've got a mix of things, and if you're a good girl, even dessert." Eric's voice rumbled through the door, and Alace watched her reflection's lips curl up in response.

So damned sweet.

"I'm ready." She opened the door to find him standing right there. "Whatcha got cookin', good lookin'?"

Skin around his eyes tight with concern, he forced a smile for her. "Soup, sandwiches, and juice."

"Went all out, huh?" Alace looped her arm through his, leaning lightly against him. She deliberately lowered her voice to ask, "Where do you want me?"

"In our bed."

Surprised by the jolt of arousal that shot through her from his growled words, Alace glanced up to find him staring at her. The tension in his face had been erased, replaced by the dark look of hunger with which she was well acquainted. As she stared at him, there was an echoing rumble from her stomach, and the expression fled, chased away by a sweet amusement.

"Seems my baby's belly has some different ideas." Eric bent and lifted her, hands on each globe of her ass as he snugged her against his front. Alace curled her legs around his waist and threaded her fingers together behind his neck. Secure in his grip, she arched closer and ran a line of kisses along the edge of his jaw. He captured her mouth with his, holding her tightly before they separated. He placed her on the bed, her feet falling away from his body to the cushioning surface. Gaze focused on her face, he smiled and said, "Let's get you fed, and you can relax for a little bit. You know your brain will keep working at the puzzles you've undoubtedly uncovered. You don't have to be in front of the computer to have it keep going."

"I didn't realize I'd been at the computer that long." She cupped his cheeks in her palms. "I promise. I'm doing everything I can."

"I know you are." With narrowed eyes, he shook his head. "I hate that I'm useless to you with this."

"You're not useless. You realized something had happened and checked on him, and then you came to me." The realization swept over her, a feeling larger than nearly anything she'd ever felt swelling inside her. "You came to me."

Eric blinked at her amazement. The tension that had returned to his features disappeared as they flooded with love. "Of course I came to you, baby. Who else would I trust to figure out what was going on?" She pressed her forehead to his, letting the confidence he had in her roll around and over her. "Alace, baby, there's no one I trust more."

She stayed there, breathing slowly synchronizing with Eric's. "I love you so much." His eyes curved into commas again, this time from a much more pleasant expression. She didn't have to see his mouth to know he was smiling. "More than you'll ever know."

"Oh, I think I know." A broad palm curved over the tiny baby bump low on her belly, and the ease with which he expressed his gratitude without even saying a word of thanks made her laugh. "Get comfy. I've got your food on the dresser."

Alace arranged herself leaning against the headboard, pillow wedged behind her back. Eric placed the folding legs of the tray on either side of her hips, fingers tweaking the end of her nose as she looked down. She grinned, glanced at the neatly divided sandwich wedges, and picked up the bowl of soup, the savory scent making her mouth water. He stretched out beside her, elbow bent, head propped on his hand as he watched her eat. The look of satisfaction on his face was adorable, but she'd never tell him that. Eric had much better kitchen skills than she did, even after months of practice. If the man wanted to be pleased that he'd heated some frozen soup and made a PBJ, she'd give it to him.

Their conversation was necessarily interrupted with silences surrounding her consumption of the meal, and Alace knew Eric was keeping the topics well away from Todd. She didn't know what it cost him to do so, with the fate of his best friend up in the air, but she appreciated the effort. As he'd suggested, it gave her mind time and space to work, picking along the edges of what she knew and suspected, and into areas she hadn't yet touched.

By the time she was done eating, and Eric had felt she'd been resting long enough, Alace had a better idea of what to tackle next. She'd already found Temple's vehicle on footage close enough to the grandfather's home to believe that was her destination, so while looking for definitive proof would make Alace happier about the next steps, it was no longer necessary.

"Hand me my tablet." Eric glanced over his shoulder at the computer and she shook her head. "Not for this. I can stay where I am." Smiling at him, she gave his cheek a poke with a soft finger. "You know that'll make you happier anyway."

He rolled to his back and reached out, grabbing the tablet from the nightstand. He finished on his feet, turned to hand her the device, and then retrieved the tray of empty dishes. Without a word, he pursed his lips and blew her a kiss, then left the room.

Alace wasted no time before booting the tablet, connecting to her secondary Wi-Fi and keying in the pass phrase. Owen's folder appeared a few connections later, and Alace frowned when she saw no activity.

After she'd left him on the trail, he'd checked in a couple of times, answering her inquiries and reporting on the clearing. Alace checked the logs and saw he'd connected a couple of times but hadn't updated. "Asshole." Probably waiting on her to ask for a formal update. He should be out of the woods by now, even if there were more graves or a secondary cache at the clearing he'd been investigating.

Backing out of the system, she stared at the tablet, then shifted her gaze to the computer.

"Do it." Eric's voice was gruff, but when she looked at him where he stood in the doorway, he just shook his head. "Whatever you're trying to do, if you can't do it on the tablet, then get on the computer. Just—" The conflict he felt was plain, mouth twisting to the side before he continued. "Put your feet up or something. Is there anything else I can do, baby?"

Tipping her head to one side as she crawled towards the end of the bed, she grinned and joked. "Rub my toes?" As she settled into the rolling chair, Eric pulled her footstool out from under the desk, set it just to the side, and plunked himself on top of it. He motioned towards her feet with curled fingers, and she laughed aloud as she lifted her feet and placed them in his hands. "I was joking."

"I know." He smiled back at her. "I'm just going to stay close anyway. Might as well make myself useful." A stiffened thumb dug into the ball of her foot, and Alace lifted her chin at the soothing sensation. "If I'm a distraction, I can stop."

"No, no." She woke the computer, going through the usual routine to get logged into the system she needed. "I got this."

The satellite images she found were recent, timestamped the previous day. She accessed the ones she wanted, zooming in close and shuffling the picture around until she located the first clearing. From overhead, it looked the same as the day she'd walked down the trail back to the parking lot.

Opening another window, she navigated to Owen's folder again and opened his report. Making a note of the location, she returned to the overhead images and searched for one that covered the area. She zoomed in quicker this time, easing the image around until she saw a break in the tree cover. Scanning the screen, she saw nothing out of place, a flat field in the middle of a stretch of woods. She flipped over to the folder with Owen's write-up and saw what she remembered. He'd left the half barrel in place as she'd instructed. Now, however, the clearing held nothing foreign like that. Nothing at all. She could see the outline of the holding pits, and what was probably the cache pit, but other than that there wasn't anything exceptional about the clearing at all.

Owen had been right. It had been an active field, and the killer had returned at some point in the past three days, putting it to bed.

Now Owen wasn't checking in.

Fuck. She should have tagged his bag or something inside so she could find him now. Maybe this was how Regg had felt, what had led to him bugging her clothing and supplies? She shook her head. It didn't matter. The fact was she couldn't find Owen because she hadn't. Had even gone so far as to tell him she wouldn't do it.

Something about the folder bothered her, and she navigated back to it, looking at the contents again. Nothing had changed. Since she'd left Owen in the forest, he'd logged in twice, once updating the document they used to share information, and once just to look around, maybe just as she was doing now.

He'd logged in.

Because I left him the satellite Wi-Fi.

Which she *could* track, even if it wasn't actively transmitting.

In seconds, she'd accessed the system she needed, and it took only a few additional keystrokes to bring up a map. There was a blinking green dot on the map, hundreds of feet away from where she knew the established trail was. She turned on the topographic overlay and saw the dot was at the bottom of a ravine. It could be just the pack, but she didn't truly believe that.

Back to the satellite imagery, she found the correlating place and zoomed in as far as she could. *Dammit.* The tree canopy was too thick to see anything on ground level at the bottom of the ravine.

Angling back in the chair, she tore her gaze from the screen and tipped her head back, staring at the textured ceiling overhead. Alace allowed her gaze to follow lines and whorls in the texturing, finding random patterns that required no effort to trace, tracking back and forth across a small section of the ceiling. The same basic patterns appeared in different segments, and she found her gaze drawn to one repeating pattern, an imperfection in the finishing tool perhaps, a particular twist of muscle in the movements required by the laborer. Similar to how she solved puzzles, finding the replicating complaint and zeroing in on the causative agent until it could be removed from the equation.

She needed Owen out of the woods to go after Temple and save Todd from whatever the woman had planned for him.

Planned wasn't a mistaken conclusion. Mackie Temple had arrived at his home and entered using a code similar to the one Eric had used, her car parked in the garage protected from spying eyes but exposed to Todd when he'd driven in. He hadn't been upset to see Mackie in his kitchen. Surprised, yes. Mad? Not at all. From that, Alace concluded she'd been a frequent enough visitor to have worn away the shock of Todd seeing her. She was currently listed as missing, and he was dating her sister with intent to take the relationship further. She was missing, and the subject of great distress for that sister/girlfriend, and he didn't immediately go for his phone to call Maddy and relieve her distress.

Was she really missing after all? Alace hadn't mapped her trail to Utah, not closely. She'd followed up with the boyfriend and witnesses, but nothing leading up to the change in location. *Maybe it was Maddy, not Mackie? What possible reason would Maddy have to drug and abduct Todd?* That line of questioning led nowhere, because there was absolutely zero explanation Alace knew.

Alace closed her eyes and sighed. The heat from Eric's hands registered, curled around her calves, holding her legs steady in his lap.

"How well do you know Todd?" Eric started to answer immediately, and she held up a hand to halt him. "Hear me out." He made a sound and she pulled in a breath, hoping to get through the next few minutes without seeing the hard edge of his anger. "You've been friends forever, but do you know him behind closed doors? He's dating Maddy, we both know that, you from meeting her and me from my investigation. Dating Maddy and hoping for more. But I found evidence he might be seeing Mackie, too. And I think Maddy found out. Just before Mackie moved away, there's an argument and I surfaced a photo that showed him backing Mackie, not Maddy. The footage I looked at today, Eric, he was surprised when Mackie showed up at his house. Shocked, even. But, what he *wasn't* was ecstatic that the missing sister of his girlfriend was standing in his kitchen. So I'll ask you again—how well do you know Todd?"

"Not as well as I thought, clearly." The ache in Eric's voice caused her stomach to clench, and Alace lifted her head to look at him. He was staring at her legs, gaze following the gentle up and down movement of his hands. "I thought Maddy was the one for him. That's what he's been saying, anyway. He's known them forever. You knew their parents were friends?" Alace nodded, mentally marking it as yet another area she hadn't investigated deeply enough. "So he's known the twins since they were all kids. He and Maddy, though, they have been super close for the past few years. Timing was never quite right for them until now, but he's carried a torch. Why would he risk that to have...what? A fling with Mackie? That doesn't make sense." Eric's eyes drifted up, and their gazes locked together. "I can't imagine him doing that, love. I really can't. There's got to be a different explanation for the picture you saw."

"And his reaction to her being in his home?"

"Fuck, Alace. I don't know. Maddy's convinced Mackie's boyfriend had something to do with her disappearance. If she's not missing, then where has she been?"

"I don't know. I can see if I can find out. I've got to get my guy out of the woods first, so he can go after Todd. Whatever is going on, the way she attacked him doesn't give me a lot of confidence that she's firing on all cylinders." Alace glanced at the clock on the computer, brows scrunching together at how late it had become. "I've got a couple of other things to follow up on. If I can't get my guy, or I think it's getting too late, I'll activate someone else. First I have to be sure where she took him."

Eric continued holding her feet and legs as she rolled back towards the desk and computer. She was sitting sideways, twisting to reach the keys, but there was no way Alace would complain about the position. If Eric needed to touch her to remain in control, she'd give him every opportunity he wanted. Alace was about to minimize the tracking software when she realized the dot had moved. As if she'd done it with her mind, wishing and hoping Owen was still mobile, and poof—the tracking showed he'd traveled about a hundred feet. He was angling down the ravine, and studying the map closely, she saw the notch in the ridge he was headed towards. If he could get over that rise and stay on track towards the lot, he could cut two days off the trek out.

Still. There was no guarantee he would be in any shape to go after Temple, and even if he made it to the car in record time, he was still hours away from where she needed him.

A hunter named August Brooks would be her next choice to activate, and she knew he was one who'd do exactly as asked without question. Which was part of the issue she had with cueing him up for something this sensitive. If he truly trusted and believed material presented in a brief, August wouldn't be swayed, moving forwards with conviction towards the goal. He was like an ICBM in that fashion, with no recall button and no reset.

A minimized window flashed at the bottom of the screen, showing activity.

Alace somehow wasn't surprised to see it was Owen's assignment folder.

***

Wilderness area

The ground shook underneath their feet as the very air around them began pummeling against all exposed skin in rapid pulses. The replacement wig, their prized sacrificial covering, threatened to fly away in the face of the driving winds but was held in place with one hand.

Chin lifted, their eyes stared overhead, wide and unblinking as a dark object plummeted towards them from the sky. Ominous, large enough to block out the sun, it slowed in descent, finally coming to rest only yards away.

Their shirt and pants were plastered to the front of their body, fabrics stretched taut by the force of the downdrafts caused by the machine.

The side yawned open, and they didn't need any more invitation than that.

With a quick step, they strode towards the noisy monster and climbed into the darkness inside.

CHAPTER SEVENTEEN

Owen

When he opened his eyes lying at the bottom of a gully folded into the surface of a mountainside, Owen took a few seconds to realize what had happened. The dried blood and tender-to-the-touch goose egg on the back of his head told part of the story, but his landing position more than a football field length downhill from the game trail he'd been following was another part of the answer. The what and how of his fall determined, he spent a few moments trying to sort out the why, finally deciding it mattered less. No matter if the edge of the trail had given way or his ankle rolled on an unfortunate stride—he was far more concerned with the condition of his body and pack to give it more effort than that.

He sucked in a sharp breath and held it as he ran his hands along his ribs, finding an entire section where pressure against the skin made sweat bead along the back of his neck. Not broken, he made certain of that by palpating them enough to diagnose only bruising, but their current state didn't make it easy to do anything like remove his pack or twist around to look for a water source. It was a struggle, but with the pack finally retrieved, he hunched over it as he waited for his breath to settle down; each reckless drawing in of air poked sharpened swords between his ribs.

Delving into the depths of the pack, he found his food and water were undamaged, but of all the damned things to be broken, the tablet hadn't survived. Not intact. The surface was shot through with cracks, and he grunted in disappointment at the loss. He didn't even try to turn it on, digging back into the pack to find the satellite Wi-Fi Alace had left with him. That seemed unscathed, not even a scratch on the sides, and when he turned it on, the lights cycled in the normal fashion, finally landing on a steady amber that told him there were no available connections. Whatever network the device worked from was either blocked by the trees or the satellite wasn't in orbital sync. Not entirely unexpected, given the remoteness of his location, but a definite damper on his mood on top of the unrelenting pain from his torso.

Fortunately, the ribs were the bulk of his damage from the fall. He had a multitude of scrapes and bruises, but nothing else of note. Owen repacked the backpack and strapped it in place with effort. Then, using a nearby tree as a leaning post, he worked his way upright only to nearly collapse again, the rib pain now extending farther around his torso. Hands on his knees, he fought the overbalancing weight of the pack until he could stand a little straighter, avoiding landing on his face through sheer determination. Inch by inch, he adjusted until he hit the point where he could no longer ignore the throbbing, holding there while he caught his breath. Then, with gritted teeth, he pushed past the pain to fully upright, fingers gripping the bark of the tree tightly.

It took him three hours to travel half a mile, the deadfalls and rock piles seeming to join forces to block his way. *At least the movement loosened me up.* He smirked, knowing better than to attempt a laugh, his shoulder pressed hard to a tree in exhaustion. He gave himself only a moment of respite. It was less than five minutes before he was moving again, getting closer to the parking lot with every wavering stride.

"Time to camp." The idea of relaxing into his hammock was overshadowed by the pain he knew would face him in the morning when it came time to exit the cocooning fabric, but right now he didn't care. Food, water, painkillers, and sleep—that was the recipe to a more productive day tomorrow. He'd lost hours today unconscious at the bottom of the ravine, and as much as he'd tried to ignore the frequent bouts of dizziness that attacked as he bent and twisted, stepping under and over the deadfalls in his path, he'd field-treated enough concussions to recognize the signs in himself.

Two hours later, he had a full belly, was well hydrated, and had cleaned the blood from his head wound, giving him a chance to finally settle down into the hammock. Owen had nearly drifted off to sleep when he remembered he needed to check the Wi-Fi again for a signal. Eying the backpack leaning close but clearly out of reach against a nearby tree, he evaluated the effort needed to get there from the hammock and extrapolated the amount of time it would take to regain this level of loose relaxation, and very clearly and distinctly said, "Fuck it," just before he went to sleep.

The next morning showed the wisdom and foresight he'd had in taking both a bottle of water and the painkillers to bed with him, because it took the maximum dose and nearly thirty minutes before he felt like attempting to get out of the hammock. *It woulda been the same if I was in a tent. I'd just be layin' on the sticks and rocks I wouldn't have been assed to clear out before I set up.* Once he had a fuel cube lit and a pan of water beginning to boil for coffee and hot cereal, he rose from his crouch and was pleased he didn't stagger at all. That lasted only moments before tripping on air as he took the three strides to the backpack. "Dammit."

He retrieved the broken tablet and Wi-Fi device, placing them nearby as he reclaimed his position next to his cooking spot. Edge of a tarp under his ass, he settled with his back against a tree and sipped the hot coffee as he booted up the Wi-Fi, keeping one eye on the cycle of lights along the front edge while he poured a careful amount of water over the oatmeal mixture he'd measured into the second enamel mug. Setting his breakfast aside to steep, he huffed in surprise when he saw the signal had settled on green, indicating a strong connection to a satellite overhead.

Finger to the button on the tablet, he held his breath as he pushed it gently, shocked when the screen lit up, the words on the welcome screen disjointed and fractured by the cracks spiderwebbing through the surface. The lock-screen of the tablet waited for his credentials, and Owen just as gently laid his thumb on the fingerprint scanner, grinning fiercely when it was accepted and the screen brightened. He watched as the device found the connection and a folder opened on the screen, a document automatically opening.

He leaned closer, tilting his head to the side as he read what Alace had written to him. Only brief updates since he'd told her about the second field, followed by a series of demands of increasing intensity that he check in, unsurprising since he had basically fallen off the radar. *Heh. Fallen.*

Owen rotated the tablet, the on-screen keyboard flipping around with the movement until he had the keys over the less cracked section of the screen. His first touch resulted in the screen darkening ominously, and he wondered how long he had before the touch recognition gave up the ghost. With that in mind, he sipped the rest of his coffee and ate while he sorted out in his head the report he needed to give, trimming it down to the most succinct debriefing he could.

Dishes set to one side, Owen gripped the tip of his tongue between his front teeth and with one finger tentatively tapped out his report, then rotated the device so he could see the icon to save the document, touching it with a final motion.

Third field found, retired like first. Means second is her active location. Yes, you were right, killer is female. It's Mackie Temple. She showed on-trail, then at field. Not dressed for long hike, so base probably nearby ranger fire tower. She knew I was there, tracked me. HUNTED me. I evaded, was headed to trailhead bushwhack-style but descended ravine in unorthodox manner. I'm fineish, tablet much less so. Will continue to car. Full debrief soon.

The folder indicated Alace had just been active, so she'd see his report right away unless she was in the process of moving on with her day. Owen looked at the battery meter with a frown. The tablet was draining much faster than normal, and he cursed his fall again.

The document changed color, glowing briefly, and Owen saw a familiar light green cursor blinking at the end of Alace's last update. His cursor lay after his closing punctuation and was blue. She was online and was reading what he'd written.

The green cursor moved down line by line until a new paragraph opened.

And Alace brought him up to speed on the fuckery that had been going on, with all the pieces that didn't make any sense laid out in her direct way.

Rotating the tablet so the on-screen keyboard was at the least-shattered end again, he mentally composed his response.

Hours from location.

He felt his face twist with distaste at what he had to say next. Few things bothered Owen more than not living up to his commitments, and telling Alace the truth would put him on the sidelines—given where he was and the condition of his ribs. His failure burned like an ember in his belly.

Secondary assistance may be needed.

The surface of the tablet flickered, dimming until the text on the screen was nearly unreadable. "Dammit."

Moving now. Tablet dying. Will keep Wi-Fi on. Not tracking me, my ass. Thanks, boss lady.

Save icon tapped, he verified the changes had uploaded, then watched the screen. Alace's cursor moved down and opened a new paragraph just as the surface went black.

Dishes cleaned and pack reorganized, Owen pushed to his feet, not bothering to restrain the groan that slipped from his lips. He lifted the pack, briefly considered abandoning it, then yanked it up and shoved his arms through the straps with a series of painful movements. Head and side throbbing, he leaned back against a tree as he took a few experimental breaths.

Yeah, telling Alace to activate another asset was the right way to go, given he couldn't even put on a half-filled backpack without breaking a sweat. Didn't mean that ember wasn't still ablaze in his stomach.

With a final rib-expanding inrush of air, he pushed away from the tree and started the slow process of climbing out of the ravine, heading up the opposite side, angling to where the trailhead and parking lot awaited.

CHAPTER EIGHTEEN

Alace

Following Owen's progress on the satellite feed was worse than watching paint dry.

Alace hung her head over the back of the chair, letting her neck roll slightly side to side with a tendon-popping stretch. Noises downstairs told her Eric was back in the kitchen, his go-to place since he'd declared he was home for the duration. Cases reassigned or postponed, it had only taken him half a day to sort out his schedule, but the intensity with which he listened to her brief updates told her how serious he was about this.

Todd was still missing.

Cameras near the suspect's house had captured Mackie going and coming several times over the past day, none of the trips eliciting the same amount of suspicion as the original footage. If Alace didn't know better, she'd believe the young woman was headed out to work or meet and greets with friends. When Mackie left and headed downtown, the deeper she moved, the harder it was to follow her, any necessary video path jumping from traffic cameras to security ones with bad angles, and eventually to those at ATMs and other sidewalk vendor positions. Poor lighting, sidelong images, and blurred backgrounds made it hard to even verify it was the right woman sometimes. Alace had other databases, of course. Those listing credit cards used for parking meters, plate recognition systems to identify the vehicle, loyalty cards for the coffee shops and diners Mackie frequented—but Alace liked to have the visuals, too.

August had taken his time answering his messages, long enough that Alace finally tracked him down to find he was out of the country with his daughter for several weeks. Once she found that out, she'd erased all the details of the gig from his folder and wished him a good vacation. He deserved to be able to take time with family, and the longer Alace thought about the way Temple had taken Todd, the less likely she thought it was that he would be greatly injured.

Still, they were coming to the end of day two, and without understanding the motive behind the kidnapping, it was impossible to have complete faith in her assessment.

All the information they had said Temple only took and killed women, and each death involved a ritualistic torture not easily available in a home setting, especially not positioned as the house was in the middle of a family-filled subdivision. Owen would be out today, and Alace had arranged for a package to be placed in his car containing a new tablet to replace the one he'd reported damaged. Her network held assets for far more than the services her hunters specialized in, and as she'd organized the delivery, Alace had briefly toyed with the idea of setting up true surveillance on Temple's house. The idea held merit, but the chances of a shadow being noticed were a consideration, and she eventually decided against it.

A glance at the tracking screen measured her exasperation in millimeters of progress. Alace blew a steady stream of air through her nose and forced her mind away from the situation. Being tied to the bed or chair, figuratively if not literally, was compounding the frustration, and she was fighting against resenting the pregnancy.

Something about the Temple girls had been bugging her, and Alace drew in and released another deep breath, then rolled her shoulders and logged into the darknet node where she'd planted a request yesterday, pleased to see a handful of responses.

There'd been no reason other than her twisted desire to know exactly how the patriarch of the family had died. After reading what he'd done to Mackie and repeatedly watching the girl's harrowing testimony in court, Alace had hoped he'd earned a grisly death. Curiosity often unraveled mysteries, and she'd followed a hunch, posting the request as a low-risk ask for her normal resources. Easy money for them, and a way to scratch her unsettled mind for her.

Temple had been last in a short line of connected prisoners when an inmate traveling the other direction in a narrow corridor had shanked him, using a shiv made from hardened plastic. The official information available in the secured prison system had been skimpy, lacking detail. More a "this happened, ho hum, on to dinner" kind of report than an inquiry.

What she had now was very different. Alace read through the conversation transcripts and skimmed the coroner's report quickly. The hair rising on the back of her neck had her retracing her steps, and she pulled up one of the transcripts again. Comparing it to the report, she didn't take long to pinpoint the discrepancy.

The official record had his body cremated, the coroner's report had him surrendered to family, and the transcript of the off-the-record conversation with a guard who'd been working that night had the body transferred to a nondescript van the same night he'd died, which wouldn't have allowed time for even an autopsy.

There was a folder labeled with a date, and inside she found three images. She'd seen Temple's inmate photo before, hair still wet from the delousing shower he'd been subjected to slicked back and away from his face. Another was a picture of the man on the floor, bent double, with arms wrapped around his middle. There were hands reaching into the frame with keys, supposedly to release the chains connecting him to the line of men. The final image captured her attention, and Alace enlarged the photo repeatedly. It was of a white van backed up to a loading dock, doors wide open. Temple lay inside the van, neck twisted so his face was captured by the camera. Alace's attention wasn't on the body as she refocused the image on the screen, instead centering on the pale face of the person standing near the open doors, glancing over their shoulder. Female with dark hair, and while the image quality wasn't good enough to have an unblurred look at the features captured in the photograph, Alace had an idea who it might be.

She touched the screen, tapping gently with the tip of a nail, staring.

Mackie or Maddy, she didn't know, but one of the girls had been present when their grandfather's body was retrieved from the prison the night he'd been killed.

The body on the floor of the van caught her attention again and Alace stared, then flipped back to the image of the man curled on his side post-stabbing.

The blood staining the man's shirt was clearly visible on the image taken from what looked like a corridor security camera. As was his inmate number tag, affixed to his loose shirt high on the right front shoulder. The photograph of the body in the van showed a shirt without staining, and when she zoomed in on the identification tag, it showed a different number.

Fingers clacking the keys, it was the work of moments to match that number to a different inmate. One who had conveniently also died of pneumonia while incarcerated, just a day before Temple had.

Either the medical staff had redressed Temple in the wrong shirt, something that didn't make sense at all, even given the unorthodox release of the body, or the right shirt wound up on the wrong body, one destined for the crematory furnace at the funeral home servicing the prison.

"He's not dead." She flicked the screen with her fingernail again, tapping the woman's face. "The question is, who are you? And how do you factor into what's going on today?"

Quick math gave her the timeframe, and another glance at her notes had her shaking her head. The old man would be nearing eighty if he were still alive. *Unlikely.* There had been no reports of him out in public since his reported death. Not even a whisper of a rumor about him.

"Beloved." She turned at Eric's call from the doorway, taking in the adorable way his ruffled hair gave him a look of just-woken little boy. "I've made you some food."

She tipped her head at the stool and patted the edge of the desk. "Come here. I need to run something past you."

Tray deposited on the desk as she'd silently requested, he sat on the stool and stretched out his legs, hands reaching for her ankles. Captured limbs arranged in his lap to his satisfaction, he smiled at her crookedly. "Hit me."

She did, retracing her steps, skimming over the reasons why she'd looked deeper into the old man's death, staying succinctly focused on what she'd found. Eric's brows had shifted from low and drawn together to reaching towards his hairline by the time she finished.

He shook his head. "So you think one of the girls arranged a complicated breakout for him? At what, fifteen? Sixteen? You're saying one of the twins masterminded a jailbreak at that age? Alace, that just doesn't compute." His thumbs dug into the ball of her foot, and she winced at the sensations of pain and pleasure. "I'm not buying it."

"She's right there." Fingernail flicking the screen, she brought his gaze back to the image. "I'd bet money that's one of the girls."

"Look at the height." His hands fell away from her feet, and she frowned as he leaned closer. "Maddy's not tall, and you said they're identical, so Mackie's petite, too. That woman"—he gestured to the screen—"is closer to taller-than-average than she is petite. See where her head measures against the hinges of the doors? Maddy wouldn't come up to the bottom of those windows, and this woman could see inside if she wanted. I don't know who it is, but that's not one of the girls, honey."

Gaze fixed on his face, she let her mind drift back through the information surrounding the trial. The old man had been outed as a serial predator, not restricting his molestation to family but also taking advantage of neighborhood girls if the opportunity existed. Maddy and Mackie's father had died several years before the trial, and the girls and their mother had lived only a few blocks away, evidenced by Maddy's ability to run to his home when she found out the news. Their mother, married to the old man's only son, hadn't appeared in any photos so far, nothing in the coverage around the trial, and Alace now found that highly suspect.

She pulled the keyboard closer, fingers once again tapping out a request to the county servers.

The reason the woman wasn't at the trial was she'd been ordered to stay away. She'd threatened to kill the old man, and rightfully so, given what he'd done to her daughter, but the courts had taken her threats seriously, barring her attendance. Alace exited that server and navigated to one in the state's system, accessing the DMV database.

An image from the woman's driver license appeared on the screen, and Alace stared as Eric shifted around so he could see. Alace noted the license was expired, nearly a decade old. There were no newer records.

"Damn, Maddy looks just like her mother." He inched closer. "Woman's the right height, too."

"Yep. After what he did to Mackie, if their Mom broke him out of jail—incapacitated or not—he probably didn't last long."

Eric's finger teased her bottom lip from between her teeth, and Alace shot him a small smile.

"Sorry." He didn't like it when she chewed her lip, saving it from her unconscious torture frequently. "She's a mom. I can get behind what I imagine she did to the old man after she got her hands on him, but how could she not have known what was going on?"

"What?" The tilt of Eric's head told her more than his frown did. He was entering what she called his scolding lawyer mode. "If the old man was good at threatening his victims, then how would she have known? Didn't the prosecution make a big deal during the trail regarding the level of coercion and threats he'd taken with the girl? As someone who's prosecuted these bastards, I know the fear they can instill in those they've victimized. Threatening to kill loved ones is a too frequent tactic, and as young as the girl was, it would be terribly effective. Especially since her father was already dead. The idea of losing her mother would silence her."

"But shouldn't she have known?" Alace closed her eyes at the raw pain in her voice. There was no hope Eric would ignore it, and it wouldn't be long until he figured out why it mattered.

"You would have. You would have seen something, and started digging, and figured it out before anything happened at all. You—" He leaned closer and lifted to press his mouth to hers, the intensity of the kiss more potent for the setting. "—you can't know what went on in that house to have the mother be blind to the pain her daughter suffered, and you can't know she was. Maybe he was abusing her, too. Don't judge yourself by the measuring stick of someone else." His hand caressed her stomach, and breathing was suddenly hard, her throat tightening with the emotion that gentle touch evoked. "You are going to be the best little momma. My babies."

She drew him to her, fingers wrapped around the back of his neck as she lined their lips up for another kiss. "I love you." He gave her that same shuddering breath in response that she'd become addicted to, and she smiled against his mouth as they kissed again. "Love you so much."

When Eric moved away, the skin around her mouth and lips burned, abraded by his unshaven whiskers. Alace loved the feeling, a way of accepting she was his, a claiming mark that she didn't mind at all.

"*Beloved.*" The vibrating word filled her ears and lifted her heart to fluttering heights.

Then an idea hit her, and brain reengaged, she shoved back in her chair, creating distance between herself and Eric's startled expression. She repeated his words. "Maybe he was abusing the mother, too." The tiny furrow between his eyebrows was adorable, and she kissed a fingertip before touching him and smoothing it away. "I need to look into the father's death."

Eric wordlessly bopped the end of her nose and scooted back, pulling her feet back into his lap. "Eat first, baby. Humor me."

Baby.

Alace held her hands out to be helped from the chair.

Fucking, fucking Eric.

CHAPTER NINETEEN

Owen

Muscles in his thighs burning, Owen pushed himself the final strides up and over the bank of the roadside ditch, crossing the narrow gravel road to reach the parking lot. His car was the only one occupying the lot, and he didn't try to hold back the groan that escaped as he swung the backpack from his shoulder, carrying it in front of himself as he dug into a side pocket for the keys.

With a twist of the wrist, he unlocked the driver door and slung the backpack across the console and into the passenger seat. Then he saw the package on the floor: a cellophane-wrapped box proclaiming itself the latest and greatest tablet.

"Bingo."

This was why Alace was the boss. She had sources everywhere, and the woman could manufacture or source nearly anything.

The new tablet wasn't keyed for the normal network or his folder, so after connecting to the Wi-Fi, he logged into the email he used infrequently. Another soft "Bingo" fell from his lips when he saw a new message from an A. Divine. *Divine*. He laughed through his nose. *So sweet*. Inside looked to be a short missive from a dyslexic aunt, with starts and stops to the story being told, odd paragraph breaks and punctuation as if it had been done via voice-to-text translation. The message closed with a "family" recipe, and that's where the real info was.

He input the digits for the imaginary ingredients as an IPv6 number, isolating the eight groups of hexadecimal digits with colons, and ran it through a secure converter to identify where Alace expected him to log in to communicate.

Once into the new network, he studied the folder selections. Alace was the queen of traps, paranoid to a level he completely respected. If he selected incorrectly, there were any number of consequences he could envision. Her bricking the tablet was the least of them, and he had been out of contact for too long as it was, given the volatility of the situation.

Available folders were named tr*glody7e, c*nfl4gration, and perf0r4ti*n. He sighed. "I'm neither a caveman, nor have I razed any cities lately. I'm going to go with door number three and hope this is a reference to our knife play." *Games, Alace? Really?* He tapped the folder icon and watched the other two turn red and disappear, the selected destination pulsing green twice before the display changed.

The new view had a copy of the shared document they'd been using, with new text at the end from Alace. It also had an application installer labeled simply: Click me.

Owen propped the tablet against the steering wheel, head in hands as he roughly massaged his scalp with the fingertips of both hands. Running through the past few days in his head, he isolated what felt like the critical moments and reviewed them in detail. Finding the first cache, identifying the torture implements, debriefing with Alace about the intelligence each aspect showed in their subject. The adrenaline rush when he identified the active field. Remembering the moment when he saw the planter standing in the middle of the second clearing sent a flush of pleasure through him, an acknowledgement of his body that he'd enjoyed outsmarting the enemy. Always had, always would. Identifying Temple, the unfamiliar sense of being stalked, and the legitimate thrill of winning against her made his teeth clench to hold back a victory yell. Regardless of the fall and resulting injury, he'd made it out of the woods still well under the time it would have taken on-trail, and that was another win.

The battery light on the tablet changed from green to yellow, indicating it needed to be charged. Typical for a device out of the box, and he pulled the cabling from the package. Shoving one end into the USB plug in the console, he connected the other end to the device. The battery indicator stayed yellow, not showing a charge. *Duh*.

Chin to his chest, he reached for the car keys, hand hesitating just above where he'd shoved them into the ignition switch. Alace had sent the tablet, he believed that to be fact. She'd known his car was here, something he'd volunteered the first hour they'd talked on the trail. Alace had taken that info and provided it to someone so they could break in and leave the box.

Alace had no reason to hurt him. He knew it deep inside. Her actions had been helpful, not malicious.

Still. Someone had been in his car. In and gone without leaving any trace, other than a factory-sealed box of electronics.

Unable to shake the sudden sense of unease, Owen climbed out of the car and dropped to the ground alongside, gaze sweeping the undercarriage for any evidence of tampering. *Nothing*.

Why the feeling of unease, then? He stood and stared out at the woods just yards away. The trees were thick here, a lower elevation plateau scraped flat and modified for the forestry service's use. All around him the trunks were broad and tall, rising dozens of feet into the air, blocking out even the view of the surrounding mountains.

I have no reason not to trust her.

Back in the car he rolled down the window, took a deep breath and held it, then twisted the key. The car engine started immediately, running smoothly. He let the breath out with a small hum.

Why am I so spooked?

His gaze flicked to the mirror and he saw exactly nothing in the rest of the parking lot, precisely as it had been when he arrived. Reversing from the parking spot, he maneuvered to the middle of the lot, creating a fifty-yard buffer of open space on all sides of the vehicle.

Better, but not enough.

The body of the car created blind spots he couldn't stand right now. He killed the engine but left it on auxiliary power and grabbed the tablet and Wi-Fi, getting out and leaving the door open behind him, the charge cord trailing behind like a tether.

Owen used the frame as a step, then the window, and swung his ass on the roof, lifting his legs to fold them crisscross. From here he had the advantage of being able to both listen to the surrounding forest and still sweep the tree line with a twist and a glance.

Better.

The tablet had gone into hibernation mode, and as he woke it his brain unhelpfully supplied, *Unless there's a sniper here, in which case I've just made myself a clear target.* "Shut up."

Fingertip to the installer icon, he let the app guide him through the two steps needed, leaving him staring at the log-in screen of a video chat software. The document held few clues, just two words: Install me—something he'd already done.

Owen racked his brain for ideas, knowing Alace had provided him all the clues he'd need. He just had to see them. After reviewing the information so far, he settled on using the recipe title as the name, and the complicated folder name as the password. He breathed a heavy sigh as the software began to load, then laughed when he saw a single contact in the address book within the software. A. Divine had made a second appearance, it seemed. He tapped the name, grimacing when the message appeared: Sufferin' Succotash is calling A. Divine. "I hate you."

The tablet buzzed in his hands and the video slowly resolved, one strip of the image drawing in at a time until he was looking at an empty chair. Shadows moved across the far wall, the corner of a table and lamp in view. There was the low murmur of quiet talking, nothing urgent, just the rise and fall of normal conversation. He muted the sound from his end, increasing the volume for the speaker to more clearly hear what was going on at Alace's end.

"No, I've tabled everything else for now. Todd's kidnapping takes precedence over anything else I had going. With August out of the country, Owen is the only one I trust with the gig. I'll evaluate his condition when he finishes hiking out and we'll go from there."

"Beloved." While the previous speaker had been Alace's distinctive voice, her tone even and calm, almost reasonable, the new entrant into the conversation uttered a single word so resonant with emotion it sounded intimate. It also sounded deeply concerned. Whoever the guy was—and Owen had an idea just from the one word—he was heavily invested in getting Todd Worthson back safely. "You can't go. Not you. Not with things as they are. The doctor said it was a warning, but one we should take care and heed. You can't go. If Owen can't do it, then we call in the police."

"Not a good option, and you know why, Eric."

Identity of the second speaker confirmed, Owen decided this would be an opportune time to interrupt and decide for himself if the idea of rescuing a judge was one he wanted to take on. Tablet unmuted, he held the microphone opening near his mouth and cleared his throat. Loudly.

An instant later, Alace appeared, hair rumpled amusingly. It almost looked like she'd just risen from bed to answer the call, and he searched the background for any clues. The table he saw could be a nightstand, he supposed, which would indeed put her computer in her bedroom. Interesting, especially when paired with her husband's comment about the doctor and Owen's suspicions based on Alace's behavior while on the trail with him. Now to decide if he wanted to show his hand this early in the mission. Owen gave himself a mental shake. Alace wasn't the mission, she was the boss lady, and he couldn't think in terms of restricting her access to anything. He'd never know what might be the bit of info that she could later turn to his benefit, including his knowledge about her condition.

"There you are." He gave her a minute to catalogue the injuries she could see. Bruising on his face underneath the unwashed layer of dirt and grime from the days of hiking, the tear in his shirt along the shoulder, that being on the side where the ribs still made their presence known with a bone-deep aching. At least the worst of the pain had passed, but he wouldn't turn down a hot shower to help soak out what remained. "Show me." Owen rolled his eyes at her demand, then adjusted the angle of the tablet as he pulled up his shirt. The tiny image in the corner of the screen gave him a glimpse of the bruising he hadn't been able to visualize, not without twisting painfully. Dark purple spread in an oblong pattern along his ribs, telling him that his guess of bouncing off a tree as the cause was probably correct. "Damn, boy. That looks like it hurts."

"You done, Momma?" The screen froze and he stared until he realized the shadows were still moving behind her. It was Alace that had locked into place, not even a breath disturbing the statue-like stillness at his response. "I'm okay." He shrugged, and when he didn't bother to hide the wince, saw her take in a slow, careful breath. "Ish. Good enough for what we gotta do. Bring me up to speed. Let's chat."

A man's hand circled her shoulder, fingers wrapping around her upper arm and pulling her sideways. Alace's head dipped forwards, breaking their technologically enhanced stare-down, and she lifted a hand to scratch at the crown of her head, fingers threading through her hair repeatedly. Partly out of frame at first, the man inched his way onto the screen until he was glaring at the camera and Owen. His words weren't for Owen but carried more than a hint of anger as Eric asked, "You told *him*?"

"Dammit, Eric. You're not supposed to engage." Alace's words lacked the sting of true rebuke.

"Oh, hey there." Owen shook his head, keeping a grin off his face with effort. "No, sir, she did not. I just picked up on the clues. I'm right though, right?" He nodded at the camera. "I'm Owen. Your woman and I work together." That last was just to dig at Alace a little; reducing her to an object owned by the man as well as an equal of Owen's would make her respond, and hopefully move the conversation along. Owen still felt profoundly vulnerable and exposed here in the clearing that composed the parking lot and wanted back inside the car and away from the woods. That feeling of unease was as annoying as an itch that couldn't be scratched.

"Owen, stop it." Alace hadn't lifted her head, and he saw an unfamiliar expression on what he could see of her face. Resignation, and anger, but with a hefty mix of embarrassment. *What the hell?*

Eric didn't move, even when Alace shrugged her shoulder. "Eric."

"I'm just trying to get a sense of the guy who spent two days with you but didn't pay enough attention to see what you were doing to yourself."

Owen had only a few cues from the guy: the possessive but not restraining hold, the masculine posturing, the distress on his face and in his voice. Something had happened after Alace returned home. Something that threatened this relationship he'd built with Alace. It must have something to do with the pregnancy.

"Is everything okay?" A medical emergency of some kind fit what he knew and filled in certain gaps of what he didn't. Alace's unaccustomed silence for those couple of days, the computer in her bedroom, and

Eric's presence at home in the middle of what should be a workday. "You good, Alace?"

"I am." She leaned her cheek against Eric's chest, and her shoulders sagged the slightest amount. "Everything's fine."

"Then tell me what's goin' on, boss lady." It was a better idea to reestablish his and Alace's working relationship than earn points with her hubby, and he flashed the man a grin that hopefully shared his admiration for the woman who connected them in this tenuous way. "What do you need?"

Her fingertips made another pass through the hair on the crown of her head, and Owen watched as Eric brought his lips to the thin skin at Alace's temple, pressing a kiss there. "Beloved." The murmured word was scarcely loud enough to be picked up by the video software, and the intimacy caught at something inside Owen, a quiet longing he hadn't paid attention to in a long, long time.

Not something I have time for. He squashed the thought, instead focusing on Alace's face.

"From what I overheard, should I take it the subject remains unaccounted for?" *Gimme something. Anything.* "Do we still believe the perpetrator is the one sister, the one I saw in the clearing? I don't know how she could have gotten there in the timeframe you've established for the abduction. Help me out here, Alace. Tell me what's going on."

"No changes. Worthson is still missing. There's been zero activity on the system I have at his house. I've got street-level footage of the two approaches to the suspect location and have seen only the one actor heading in and out." She looked at the camera, and he saw a microscopic frown tightening the skin around her eyes.

"You don't believe that. Not totally." Her gaze sharpened and he grinned, wide and goofy, the one that had disarmed so many targets in his careers. The tension left Eric's arm, although it remained in place around Alace's shoulders. "They're twins, right? Are you sure it's the same one each time?"

"No." The admission freed something in Alace, her brows lifting a fraction, showing surprise. "But I haven't observed two departures without an arrival in between, so if it's both of them they're taking turns, which is a serious amount of caution given the fact no one officially even knows Worthson has been abducted."

"You said you had video?"

She quirked her lips. "I do."

"Can you screenshare it? Two eyes, and all that."

Alace leaned forward, Eric's arm slipping away even though he didn't move out of frame, standing as a solid bulwark behind her. Owen chanced a guess the positioning was more than symbolic, given everything the couple had been through.

"I can share." Her hand disappeared from view, closer to the computer than the camera could capture, and it was only a moment before the screen split, half still showing Alace and Eric, half showing the contents of a document folder. The cursor entered the screen and touched an icon, then that half of the screen went black. Alace cursed under her breath, her arm shifting, and the dark portion of the screen came back to life, showing an elevated view of a kitchen.

The icon in the corner of the video surprised him, and Owen involuntarily asked, "Nostago?" Alace nodded and he whistled. "Pricey system." Muscles around the corners of her mouth tightened and he grinned at her suppressed smile. Then the figure came into view on the footage, and he was glued to the interplay between the woman and the man he assumed was Worthson.

"I've spliced things." Alace was still, not shifting in her chair as the viewpoint changed to the garage. "Patched in the street-view stuff, too."

He nodded, stunned by what he saw captured by the cameras he assumed Alace had planted. Whoever the tiny woman was on the screen, she exhibited significant strength, something he hadn't expected. And something else was off. When the woman lifted a hand and shoved hair back from her face, he realized what he'd seen and barked out, "Freeze it."

"What?" Even through the camera he felt the intensity of Alace's stare.

"Zoom in on her hand."

Alace did, the high resolution of the camera holding true enough to see the woman's fingers, hidden behind a hank of hair.

"Advance slowly, just until we can see her nails."

"What are you looking for?" Alace didn't wait for a response, manipulating the view a couple of frames at a time until her fingers, including nails, were in view.

"Woman I met on the trail had carefully tended nails." He didn't have to explain anything. The raggedly bitten nails and cuticles on the woman who'd kidnapped Worthson said it all. "That's not her."

"No, it is not." Alace rolled her top lip between her teeth and bit down, flesh turning bloodless and white from the pressure. "Lemme see if I can get a shot of hands from the street vids. It'll take me a little while to go through it all."

"I can be driving." He straightened his spine, the roof of the car underneath him creaking and bending as he shifted. "My first stop is gonna be food."

"You didn't find the cache left for you?" Alace wasn't looking at the camera any longer. Owen was amused to find Eric had moved away while they were engrossed in the video, and he hadn't noticed until the man appeared back in view with a stool he plunked beside Alace. When seated on it, he came up shorter than Alace, his head slightly lower. Owen was surprised by the positioning, given the man's masculine posturing earlier.

"What cache?" Owen started the process of climbing down from the roof, the tablet tossed into the driver seat for a moment, no doubt showing a stellar view of the ceiling. "The tablet was the only thing I saw."

"Your passenger seat has a swing case now." She still wasn't looking at the camera, something Owen noticed when he thrust his head into the car to stare down at the tablet. "Lifts from the back. Code is the IPv6 number minus the zeros and letters."

Eric was smirking, gaze fixed straight at Owen.

He leaned across to shove the bag out of the way, suppressing a grunt of pain as his ribs caught at the movement, then lifted the bottom cushion of the passenger seat from the rear. It had been hinged along the front edge, and the space underneath filled with the smooth surface of a custom-built safe.

"How long has this been here?" The ten-key lock blinked once when he input the digits, and the lid lifted an inch. It hinged opposite the cushion, creating easy access to the contents. He saw two bottles of water, another bottle of his favorite diet soda, packets of tuna and corned beef, and half a dozen portions of his favorite jerky. "Doesn't matter. You're the bossest boss lady I've ever had, Alace. This is golden."

"I'm the only boss lady you've ever had. Still, I take care of my boys." When he glanced down at the tablet, Alace was looking back at him with a tiny smile, while Eric was once again glowering in the background. "Eat up, then you need to roll. There's a burner in there, too. I've texted it from a new one here, so let's keep contact clean, hmm?"

"I'm not a boy." *Really, Owen?* He held up a hand, palm towards the camera. "Don't respond. I'm gettin' hangry."

Alace made as if to say something, then caught herself, bottom lip curling in on one side, trapped between her teeth. An expression of resolve developed on her face, jaw firming and chin lifting. "There's a tracker in the burner. Passive, only runs when the battery's engaged."

"I like insurance." He shrugged and picked up the tablet, folding into the driver seat as he reached into the cache of food. "Thanks for helpin' keep me safe, boss lady."

Her tight nod expressed her gratitude for his easy acceptance, and he gave her one in response before the secure call disconnected.

A glance around at the trees crowding the lot decided him, and Owen turned the key in the ignition, the engine rumbling steadily. He ripped open a package of jerky with his teeth, tore off a big chunk and leaned his head back, chewing happily. Once that first swallow hit his stomach, he picked up the soda and used the edge of his hand on the twist-top, letting it drop discarded into the open cache as he upended the bottle and drained it.

Something vibrated in the safe, and he leaned over to see the phone's screen had lit up from an incoming text. An address. Owen grunted and chomped off another big bite of jerky. The phone lit up again, and he laughed aloud at the incoming message.

As he tapped in a brief response, Owen muttered, "Patience is a virtue, boss lady."

CHAPTER TWENTY

Owen

"Body camera." Owen waited a beat for Alace's response, that freeze-frame effect the only indication he'd surprised her. "And an earwig."

"You want me in your head while you go in?" Alace's ear tipped towards her shoulder, and she shook her head slightly. "Why?"

He'd made better-than-average time on the drive, cleaning out the food cached in the car along the way. Two and a half hours ago, he'd pulled into a no-tell motel, paid cash for a room, showered, changed clothes, swapped out weapons to the favorites he'd stashed under the false well of the trunk, and crashed for two hours. The nap had taken the edge off his exhaustion, and the hot shower had worked wonders for the remaining soreness in his shoulders and ribs. So had the pain pill he'd swallowed. He'd also woken with the beginnings of a plan, and after studying the blueprints Alace had gotten of the house they suspected Todd was being held in, those beginnings had moved to more solid.

"Because you're smarter than I am, and you look at things differently. I go in, I see what I see. *We* go in," —the emphasis was intentional— "we see so much more." He scanned the room out of habit, then looked back at the tablet propped in front of the TV. "If I get in there and need anything, you're only a subvocalization away, not a wait-until-I-extract-my-own-ass length of time. I'm—" He stared at her image and decided to lay it all out there, knowing it would be an abrupt change to an uncharacteristic amount of transparency. *She'll get it. If anyone could, it's her.* "I've been on my own during a lot of missions. Many of them, even if I'd had a handler in my ear, I woulda done the same damn thing anyway, regardless of the orders barked. There're too damn many though where I'm still second-guessing myself, and that shit eats at me. I didn't hate getting to know you. I think we work well together, and back there in the woods, I know for a fact we saw things the other missed or misread. I think I'm pretty damn good at my job now." Her stare seemed less emotionless and more focused, but still lifted the hair on the back of his neck. "I think I'll be better with you in my ear."

Owen clamped his lips shut and waited, a parade-rest form of forced stillness that he'd used on so many missions. This wasn't unlike lying in a high hide, waiting on the target to turn a corner or take a single step into the clear. He was ready to jump into action in a nanosecond but could hold this position for hours if Alace needed that long to process.

She didn't.

"I've decided I won't do any more gigs, personally. I'm retiring from that side of the business, officially. As of now."

From offscreen, there was a relieved-sounding sigh, then a rustling, and Eric's hand came into view, the backs of his fingers trailing down Alace's cheek in a slow caress before disappearing back offscreen.

"What you're offering me feels like a good fit for this partnership, but you need to be sure." She'd leaned into Eric's touch, and now straightened her head, stare never wavering from the camera. "This work, this 'mission' as you'd call it. It's been part of me for a long time. At one point, I truly didn't have anything other than the work. Giving it up won't be easy." Her lips lifted for a second in an expression more grimace than smile. "The gigs were my life until I met this guy." A head jerk indicated the side of the room where Eric waited. "And now I've got so much more to protect." The muscles in her throat worked, but her voice was steady as she continued. "If you put me in your ear, give me a voice during the gigs, I don't know if I'll be able to give it up if you decide it won't work."

Owen let his shoulders droop, a forced relaxation he didn't truly feel. What Alace was doing was unheard of. Adrenaline junkies like them didn't give up the fix voluntarily. There was no way in hell he could ever do that, no matter who might ask him to. If she was being honest about her motivation, though, Alace might be the only person he knew who could actually do it. The idea she'd get a vicarious thrill riding along on his missions was amusing, but as he studied her face, he realized she was deadly serious. She recognized she'd be trading one addiction for another and setting the tone for the rest of their partnership together.

"What's your middle name?" Owen's question clearly surprised her, the dilation of her pupils giving that much away.

"What? Why?"

"What's your middle name?" Owen leaned forwards an inch and added a strident tone to his repeat of the question, keeping their gazes locked through the electronic device.

"I don't have one. Why?" Alace shifted slightly, the movement abruptly terminated, but her discomfort had already been telegraphed.

"If we're gonna be besties, I think I should be able to use your middle name if I need to get your attention or call your ass out on bullshit." Rough, masculine laughter rumbled through the speaker. It seemed the off-screen Eric did not disapprove of his tactic. *Noted.* "Me and Alace Sweets, besties."

Eric remained engaged, shooting back with, "You know she took my last name, right?" Muscles around Alace's mouth tightened at the statement.

"All the more reason to know her middle one." Suspecting Eric could see him, even if the camera's field of view didn't extend that far, Owen adjusted his position to look towards where the man probably sat on the stool, a positioning that still didn't entirely make sense. At her side but not equals didn't strike him as acceptable for someone like Eric. "Help a brother out, man."

"She doesn't have one." A shadow on the wall lifted a shoulder, head angled to one side in a casual stance. Eric was comfortable with this exchange. *Good.* "No lie."

"Then I reserve the right to give her one. Alace Ward will work for now." Owen reached out and picked up the tablet, bringing it closer to his face, returning his gaze to Alace. He liked the easiness he saw there, an acceptance of the careful joking he'd introduced. "I'm gonna roll. Tell me where to pick up the camera and earpiece. Goin' with my gut, boss lady. I'm feeling a sense of urgency on this one."

"I'll message you." That was all Alace gave him before the video call disconnected.

Owen grinned at the image of himself reflected on the tablet screen. Adopting the most Southern accent he could muster, he told his reflection, "She's gonna be my best frand."

Laughing, he finished packing and exited the room, and once in the car cranked the engine, giving it only a moment to warm up before he was back on the road. The burner phone was plugged in and charging when it gave a soft, discreet ping indicating an incoming message. Gaze flicking ahead and back, Owen looked for the gleam of metal in places where it shouldn't be. The last thing he needed was to get stopped by a local cop for using the phone while driving.

Tapping the screen, he navigated to the text message and glanced down. Selecting the map link that had been sent, he enabled the directions and settled back into his seat, listening to the monotone voice telling him it was nearly an hour to his destination. That put it within thirty miles of the house, which was a good position to launch their op from.

"I like her." Owen rolled his shoulders, the pull from his ribs less than only a few hours ago. "She'll do."

Working with Alace was a unique kind of thrill. She could manifest items seemingly from thin air, like the stash of goodies she'd had left in his car. "Or a pair of electronics that should be hard to come by yet turn out to be available within ten minutes of the request." He shimmied in place, hands tapping out a rhythm on the steering wheel. "Intoxicating."

The drop location for the devices was low-key scuzzy, the back room of a bar where all he had to do was walk in through the kitchen entrance. Without a word spoken, the man occupying that room looked him up and down with a quick nod, then tossed Owen a zipped plastic pouch before turning back to the wide griddle. Owen took the hint, swiveling to sidle out through the door, one eye on the cook while he surveyed the parking lot. Still empty.

Returning to his car, he drove a couple of blocks away, pulled into a shopping center, and parked.

Only then did he open the pouch, finding a tiny earwig in a protective case, a camera that looked shockingly familiar, a set of individually wrapped flesh-colored bandages, and a pair of clear glasses. In lieu of a helmet to secure the camera, it had come with a harness that would hold it stable against the side of his head; the connecting cable would snake down his back to a pack he would put on his belt. *Easy peasy*. His phone pinged, and he glanced down to see a message saying only, **Call me**.

With the ringing on speaker, he was free to continue to fiddle with the camera, grinning at the tiny weight as he held it in his hand.

"Which will you use?"

No preamble, no lead-in, just straight to the chase with Alace. Owen shook his head. "Which?" He glanced at the glasses, seeing the tiny opening in the center of the nose piece. "Oh hell, glasses. All day long, the glasses." He ignored her laughter as he lifted them from their case and found a lanyard underneath, intended to secure the glasses. "Why'd you do two options?"

"Look at the backside of the larger device. It's intended to clip to clothing in addition to being head-mounted. If you get into a position where the glasses break or get knocked off, it's a good backup option."

The luxury of having what was needed on a mission was thrilling, and Owen laughed under his breath as he asked, "If I wanted an ORSIS T-5000 Tochnost, could you get me one?"

"A Russian sniper rifle?"

Owen blinked. "My estimation for you just went up by like a million points." He scoffed lightly. "You just pull that from your giant brain, or what?"

"Or what." She didn't laugh, but humor vibrated through her words. "I've got a voice search running on this call, and it pulled up the result while you were still talking."

"Holy crow. Okay, make that a billion points." He shook his head. "You coulda played it off like you just happened to know the most elite sniper rifle in production today, but you gave up one of your secrets." He leaned back in the car seat and smiled out the windshield. "Million billion."

"Is this you being relaxed around me? This humor and shit?"

"If I say yes, will you admit we're besties now?" Owen closed his eyes and shifted, finding a more comfortable position. "Because we totally are."

"Either camera will work. Both together is a better idea. The glasses connect to the throat mic and stream live, as long as there's at least an LTE data connection. I've already checked the coverage maps; the house shouldn't pose a problem. The more traditional camera stores to the box but also streams. It's higher quality, so needs a better connection, which also won't be a problem at the location." Alace had swung right back into work mode, and Owen matched her change in trajectory.

"I'll use both. Do you have a heat detection overlay on the floorplan?"

"Yeah. I can port that to the tablet now and we can go over it. There's something wonky about what I'm seeing."

"Well, if Alace Ward says it's wonky, I know that shit's completely fucked up."

He caught her muttered "Jesus" and grinned.

"Send away, boss lady." The tablet dinged, and he looked over to see an image on the screen. "Let's walk through this."

"I expected two signatures, at the most three. I see four." When the image moved unexpectedly, Owen realized she'd not just sent the file but had tapped into the device and was currently controlling it. *She's all kinds of badass.* "See the large dark spot in the center, that's the stairwell. There's an oddly placed wall at the bottom, but that's the only structural anomaly I can find." A floorplan flicked into existence, then became opaque, showing the yellow and orange blobs through. The darkness did line up with the stairs, but he frowned at the difference in hue. "There's two anonymous signatures showing on the first floor." She huffed in what sounded like annoyance. "I've got another pass scheduled in about ten minutes with much higher resolution. Should be able to tell male or female from that one. It wasn't in sync, so I had to wait for the satellite to complete a rotation before I could retask it."

He blinked. She spoke so casually about redirecting a multimillion-dollar piece of equipment to look at a house, it took him aback. "And I thought I had contacts."

"Yeah, well." There was a rustling on the phone, and he wondered if she had retreated from the chair to the bed. Considering what he thought the medical issue might be, he hoped she was taking it as easy as she could. Alace let out a growl of frustration. "When you've helped as many people as I have, you make some unique friends."

"No friend like me, though. Am I right?"

She ignored his comment, saying, "I got access to some earlier footage." The view changed on the tablet's screen, and he watched as Alace flipped through a series of images. Two of the shapes moved around the building, appearing in various rooms throughout the period the footage covered. There was a third shape, slightly less concentrated, that stayed pretty much in place. There was slight shifting side to side, but he couldn't discern any great amount of movement. Owen kept his mouth shut, waiting for Alace to show him what she'd found. Then three became four, and that fourth shape appeared in several images, just inside the main door, then into a bedroom, and then still in the bedroom but much less concentrated, becoming more like the third shape. "That ties to the time Todd was taken."

"You think that fourth figure is Worthson." Not a question, Alace's own statement said as much, but Owen wanted to verify.

"I do."

"Then who is that third one?" He studied the image. "Can you roll backwards to the pictures where that third shifts a few inches to the side?" On demand, the images moved, finally pausing at the one he'd indicated. "Is that solar loading, maybe? Sunlight coming in through a window? Why would it be so dim, though. Doesn't make any sense if it's on the first floor of the house." He reached out and touched the screen, grinning when it reacted. Quickly changing the page view of the floorplan overlay, he grunted when lines and colors matched again, but differently. "They've got a basement."

"Makes total sense if they moved Worthson to the basement. Still not sure what that other thing is, though. Don't forget that we have two unaccounted for subjects with the mother and the grandfather, but since neither has been seen for years, it's a slim chance it could be either of them."

Easily mapping distances given known standards for things like doors and stairs, he committed the layout to memory. "It's vague enough in outline, it might be an overheating appliance, or even a furnace. Given the nighttime temps, it could be something like that. No sightings means deep graves somewhere, probably back in the woods." He rearranged things to show the first floor, and memorized that, too. "Do you have outside imagery of the structure itself, and the surrounding buildings and approach?"

"Yeah." The view disappeared, then reappeared. "You done with this?" He grunted and it disappeared again, replaced a moment later by an overhead view. "I bought time on a drone earlier. My guy just sent this like ten minutes ago."

"A million million billion," he muttered, watching the changing background in the video. It zoomed up a street that he saw turned into a cul-de-sac, not his favorite residential area layout because it only allowed for a single direct approach and egress. A car was backing from a driveway, and the drone gained altitude, dropping back down at a stomach-wrenching pace once past the vehicle. Whoever the pilot was, he knew his shit. It paused in front of the next house, and the image zoomed in on the street address, verifying the location, then the video methodically mapped the outside of the house. One story plus the basement, unlike most of its neighbors, the house appeared older than the surrounding residences. They'd had their roofs raised, added attached garages, eaten up available yard with expansions. This house was tiny in comparison. From the floorplans, he knew it held several rooms at ground level, two bedrooms with a Jack-and-Jill bathroom between, master bedroom with its own bathroom, a den overlooking the backyard, and an open-plan kitchen, dining, and casual living room that were lined up across the front of the house. "No windows into the basement, but lookie there." He touched the screen and the video froze. "That was a window well once." Right at ground level, there was an indentation in the foundation. "See? And another one nearer the corner." Touching the video again caused it to continue, and he wasn't surprised when it rounded that corner and he saw two more. "They've been closed off. From the weathering on the material, it was done a while ago."

"Whatever they did, the windows are no longer present, which means there's no solar loading in the basement." Alace sighed in his ear, and he analyzed the sound for tones of exhaustion, finding them. "What else do you need, Owen? Do you want to wait for dark to attempt entry?"

"I've got a thirty-minute drive, which means I'll get there just before sunset. I'll scope what I can—" He touched the video screen and exposed the player controls, using the rewind button and running the footage backwards until he was at the approach again. "What do you know about the houses around theirs? That one where the car just left, who is that?"

Rustling, then tapping of keys meant she must be on a computer separate from the one connected to this tablet. He ran the footage forwards and backwards a few times, taking stock of the woman driving the car.

"Single owner, she works an evening shift at a local hotel as hostess in their restaurant." More tapping. "No kids, and her history doesn't show an active boyfriend." A pause, then lowly, "No vet bills since her dog died last year."

"That's my hidey hole, then. I'll gain entry to her house and use the proximity to the subject's residence to figure out my next move. I'll have you in my head, and you'll see everything I see. We got this in the bag, Alace."

"I'll monitor what I can until you get in place. I do see a low-level security system at your launch point, so you'll have that to deal with."

"Got a make on the garage door opener? That'll help cut down the time I spend idling in the driveway." He laughed. "I have my tools, too." She rattled off the name of a popular national brand and he grinned broadly. "Roger that, boss lady. I'll let you know when I'm in place."

CHAPTER TWENTY-ONE

Alace

She hated this.

Not the takedown portion of a gig, which was the culmination of hours of research and investigation. That was satisfying to the extreme.

She hated being sidelined. Relegated to observer status.

It was a necessary demotion, not just for the pregnancy, but because of her promise to Eric. *I won't knowingly lie to him, ever.* Still, being downgraded to watcher status sucked ass.

"Base, do you read me?"

Owen's question came through her headset loud and clear, so she flipped the microphone down, engaging it, and responded, "Roger that."

"Roger." His response was quiet and clipped, but enunciated in his own voice so she knew he wasn't subvocalizing yet. The glasses setup she'd procured provided bone-conducted audio via the temples, and when he applied the adhesive microphone to the underside of his jaw, allowed him to communicate without speaking aloud. The engineer she'd tapped for the device was anxious to hear how it worked in what would amount to a combat environment, because he had a defense grant for development. That meant he sent prototypes to his contact, which were tested in controlled situations, and only limited feedback was provided. The DOD was notorious for keeping the true specifics of any test confidential, no matter the security clearance of the individual actually doing the development. The engineer was also a professor at a highly respected university, so he had tenure riding on the successful culmination of his development. She had a feeling that she and Owen would deliver exactly what the developer needed.

"Entry achieved."

Alace blew out a soft stream of air at that transmission. The video from the clipped-on camera changed from the blank surface of the door at the house beside their target to an interior view. She clicked on a window displaying on a just-added-today third monitor and activated the thermal imaging from a hovering drone. It took a couple of seconds for the display to change, showing a bright orange blob for Owen's position. She keyed in a change and sent the instructions, watching the details grow smaller as the device gained altitude and shifted slightly north, positioning between the two houses. The second house, the target location, showed the two minimized heat signatures from the basement—Todd and the one that was so small and motionless she still assumed was probably a furnace—and one more distinct signature in a room on the far side of the structure from where Owen stood in the other house.

"Subject one at location K1. Repeat kilo one."

"Roger." There was a pause while the view on the camera changed, but she couldn't hear anything. No background noises at all. *Hmmm. Maybe the subvocal was a mistake.* Without a more standard microphone pickup, all she would receive in terms of sounds were things spoken or subvocalized by Owen, no ambient or environmental noises. "Do you have the assets in place to watch for subject number two's return?"

"Roger." She flicked a glance at the screen of video feeds, twelve in total, the first positioned nearly three miles away from the house, at the first location where many paths became one. "I'll have a minimum five-minute warning for you."

"No time like the present, right?"

The view changed as Owen retraced his steps partway through the house, diverting from the side entrance to the rear for his exit. Once Owen got outside, the drone's heat signature for him changed, becoming a bright yellow against the darker orange of the surrounding grass and ground. She could see more detail too, and noted the darker outlines against his body, knowing they were his weapons.

"Still at K1." The figure in the other house hadn't moved. Alace leaned forwards and brought up another window, taking a moment to scan the pending command already typed in before she hit the Enter key. Numbers flashed over the screen, the twelve-digit number rapidly decrementing as integers locked into place. When the display had stabilized, all twelve figures were filled in, and she copied the result, pasting it into yet another window and submitting with another keystroke. "Alarm is neutralized."

"Roger." Owen would still have to use his lockpick skills to gain entry, but she'd done everything she could to ensure things went smoothly.

The view from his bodycam was disorienting, depending on his body position for a picture of anything that made sense. While he was bent over to take care of the lock, the picture was of his crotch, and she groaned when Eric's hand coasted up her arm, warning her before he bent across and set a bottle of water down, whisking the empty away.

"Nice view."

She clicked to the image from Owen's glasses, showing the face of the deadbolt just as he withdrew the lockpicks. Eric moved away without being asked, seating himself on the bed behind her so he could see the monitors. They'd talked about the need for focus, and he'd made it clear he wouldn't interfere.

"What?" That was from Owen, and showed her microphone was plenty sensitive if he'd heard Eric's muttered comment.

"Nothing. Keep going. Kilo one for subject one." She verified no alarms were showing on the street-level footage. She'd tied a rudimentary identification program to the feeds, knowing the make and model of vehicle they were watching for. "No sign of subject two."

Given the two women were identical twins, they had no way of knowing which had left and which remained in the house. Owen would depend on the indicators they'd noted as differentiating the two to identify which one he was confronting. At this point, with Maddy kidnapping Todd, and Mackie looking like the serial killer—coming face-to-face with either was potentially deadly.

"I am in." The words appeared on the screen as she heard them, marking the change to subvocal communication. The voice had changed, too, losing so much of the intonation unique to Owen. "Crazy is in the house tonight. Oh, fuck. Did you hear that?"

"Roger." Alace kept her tone even.

"Shit, boss lady. This will take getting used to." The video shook side to side slightly, and she read that as Owen shaking his head, literally trying to put behind him the disconcerting knowledge that distinct thoughts would be translated as intentional speech. "Okay. I am ready. What the hell. Jesus. Stop it." Another shake, and this time she wasn't able to keep her snort of laughter quiet. "Stop laughing at me. Stop giving her something to laugh at, fool. Jesus."

"Settle, Owen." The view from the bodycam shifted, and she recognized it as his chest expanding and contracting with a deep breath in response to her command. *What if I had biometric details?* She leaned over and wrote a note to look into a full military system for the next gig. "You got this. Just focus, and don't distract yourself."

"Easier said than done. What the hell?" Another deep breath, then the glasses camera shifted down and back up. *He'd nodded.* Okay, she was getting the hang of this. *Wish we could have built in time for a test run.* She shook her head, knowing there hadn't been a chance to do more than the limited testing they'd performed. Battle ready meant exactly that, and she knew Owen would get past this rocky start and dial in on what was needed. He proved it with his next transmission. "Roger that, boss lady. Status update?"

"Kilo one and no activity."

"Roger." He moved up the hallway, the video stream showing blurred images of framed pictures on either wall, a carpeted runner to muffle his footfalls, and when he glanced back, an umbrella stand next to the door. All the comforts of home, but the twins also had individual residential addresses where they ostensibly lived. "If I buy it in the combat zone. Shut up, head."

"You're not going to die." His advance up the hallway paused and the video angle subtly changed. He was standing straight. "I won't allow it."

"But now I have to finish it, boss lady." *Oh hell*. Well, she certainly understood how that worked. Compulsions didn't go away because they were inconvenient. "Might as well get it over with now."

"She's still in the kitchen. Kilo one." Which was only two corners away from his present position, but he knew that as well as she did.

The replication of his voice adopted a singsong cadence, and in her mind, she imagined a younger Owen jogging in lockstep with his brothers as they chanted, "If I buy it in the combat zone, box me up and ship me home. Pin my medals on my left breast, tell my people I've done my best." He sighed heavily, at least based on her interpretation of the body camera's movement. "There. Now I am ready."

"Roger." Even if he could see the words on the screen, she was glad Eric couldn't hear the tension in Owen's voice. "No status change."

"Red leader, I am going in." Silence for a moment. "Boss lady?"

"Yes?"

"You can ignore most of this, you know?"

"I know."

"Good." The video feeds showed him advancing, the heat signature moving at the same pace. He paused before rounding the first corner, and the glasses angled towards a picture on the wall. She realized he was using the reflection to check the room ahead and noted it. Same thing she would have done, had she been entering blind. He wasn't, but they didn't truly trust each other. *Not yet. We'll get there.* That was something she had an ever-increasing confidence in, and hoped to have a chance to express to him soon. "Lima one clear confirmed."

"Roger. Kilo one still in play." One figure on the screen stayed stationary, while Owen's figure moved, making his way through the house.

"Any chance of listening on her phone?"

Alace cursed the lack of environmental noise again. If Temple was focused on a phone conversation, that could explain why she'd been standing in one place so long. The fact Owen could hear at least one end of the conversation but Alace couldn't was frustrating.

She leaned forwards and changed windows on her main monitor, leaving the thermal and Owen's videos visible. She brought up a program she'd used before and logged into the carrier's business website, then stripped down the URL to the base before adding in a colon and what would seem to anyone else to be a random string of letters and numbers. The screen went black when she entered the code; then a message displayed on the monitor and she smiled. "Hello, Alace, indeed."

"What?" A glance at the video showed Owen hadn't moved.

"Gimme a second and if she's on a registered phone, I'll have it." Her investigation had uncovered only two mobile numbers on the account, one for each sister, and if the house had a landline, Alace hadn't been able to locate it. She'd bet money it was one of the mobile numbers. Audio flooded out the computer's speakers, and she grinned. "Bingo. Can you copy like this?" It would be easier if he could listen in with her, rather than taking the time to route to their communication channel. He'd already proved he could hear background sounds from her mic, so this should be a cakewalk.

"Roger."

They were silent as they listened.

"—sure there's no progress in the case? I'm so afraid for my sister." That had to be Maddy, then. But if Mackie had left the house not an hour ago, why would she be so worried? "Have you questioned her boyfriend again? I left a message last week about something he'd posted on social media."

"Ma'am." The deep drawl held a massive amount of strained patience, in just a single word. "There has been no progress in locating your sister. If she's even missing. She's a grown woman, and there are no laws against taking off in the middle of the night and leaving everything behind. As long as she didn't default on any debts, there are no civil issues, either. You already confirmed her accounts are set up on automatic payments with ample funds, which means she may have been planning this for a while."

"She's missing." Maddy's voice was shrill and gave the impression her emotions were out of control, but the lack of movement on the thermal imagery highlighted the lie. She should have been moving and throwing her hands around, especially given the parking lot image Alace had seen of the argument between the sisters. "Why can't you understand that? She's in danger. I feel it in my gut."

And my gut says you're a lying piece of shit.

"Ma'am. If there's nothing else, I have critical matters requiring my immediate attention." The speaker was not saying her sister's supposed disappearance wasn't important, just that other things were more pressing. It should have elicited an angry response and didn't, which was the biggest crack in Maddy's façade Alace had noted so far.

When that call terminated, Alace watched closely to see if the woman would move, but instead another call initiated. The number showed it was Worthson's work. *What the hell?*

"Judge Worthson's chambers."

"Christine, is Todd available?" Maddy was on a first name basis with Todd's assistant. *Interesting*. But, given he'd had to recuse himself from her recent case, maybe it wasn't unexpected.

"Hi, Maddy. No, he's been out for a couple of days. Probably holed up at home with the flu. He texted me that he was sick." *Shit*. Alace should have checked Todd's phone records for activity. The device must have been on him when he was taken, because she hadn't seen him set it down that day. Not on camera, anyway. "Want me to give him a message when he calls in?"

"No, no need for a message. Thank you."

The call disconnected and there was no further activity, so Alace minimized the phone company's website to expose the street cameras. Still no alerts there, which was good.

"Owen, what are you thinking?"

"I am thinking I need to go in soft, see what she knows. I can pretend to be a PI looking for Worthson, maybe tracked his phone to here." He was improvising, adjusting on the fly, just like Alace would have had she been there. "Take her temperature."

"Sounds like the right call." Even as she spoke, he was retreating, going back down the hallway towards the back door. From this angle, she saw something she'd missed before.

"Stop. Back up two steps." He complied, with a quick glance over his shoulder. "She hasn't moved yet. What's that on the right?" The view swung, and Alace saw a depression beside a picture frame. "What's that—" Before she could finish the question, Owen touched the indent, smoothing his fingertip down the surface until he paused, then pressed firmly. A section of the wall shifted, now inset by a couple of inches. He placed both hands on the surface, turning to face it fully, and pushed to no effect. Then he slid his hands to one side, and the section moved with him, revealing darkness behind. "That is a basement access that is not the stairwell. Also not on any floorplans I've seen."

Her immediate internal dilemma was between asking him to explore and pushing him to head outside to approach from the front door using the PI ruse.

Owen took it out of her hands by stepping into the darkness and turning in a half circle. The shift to infrared video was seamless, and she saw the outline of the tiny staircase clearly.

"Holy shit." Owen's reaction told her the glasses had worked correctly, imposing an opaque overlay on the streaming video visible on the inside of the nonprescription lenses. In normal light, the streamed imagery was imperceptible, because it matched exactly what the wearer expected to see. In low or no light, however, they could be a crucial advantage over non-wearers. "Ah yeah, my boss lady has the best toys. Billion billion. Racking up the points, lady." He scanned left to right, then turned and closed the sliding door behind him, leaning on it until it settled into place. "Going to check it out."

"Let me look for electronics at that level." She'd scanned and ruled out any internal video surveillance system for the main floor but given the time constraints hadn't moved forward with the basement. The plan had been for Owen to confront and subdue before exploring, but with him going off script, she wanted to be certain to provide the best chance of success. "Going forwards, we won't enter until I've locked everything down. Hear me?"

"Oh, I hear you, boss lady. I hear you."

The drone was set up for signal recognition, so she enabled that filter, using the basement layout as an overlay. Three signatures appeared, two near the furnace, and one— "Back up. There's a camera over your head." He did as ordered, the glasses video view changing as he looked up and she saw the camera housing. "It's aimed towards the base of the stairs, not where you are. I don't think you'd show on it yet. Let me find the monitoring station. Hold tight, Owen."

"Holding." His confirmation wasn't necessary, as she'd see any movement from the videos, but it was nice to hear regardless.

Alace looked at the drone view, changing the layout overlay to the main floor. There was a significant source of interference in a small room behind the kitchen, and she suspected that was the computer with the security system software. *Now to get into it.* Her first two attempt trajectories were met with a brick wall, but the ISP-supplied firewall was weaker, and she slipped in through an unblocked port. There was a central storage device filled with images she didn't take time to review and an IP assignment that led her to a switch. From there she utilized a common bot-placed backdoor, shaking her head at the idea of thanking the Russian hackers for distributing their keylogger so widely. And then, she was in the computer. Careful to not disturb the hibernation mode currently in play, she opened a remote session to launch the surveillance software. Settings confirmed alerts would be sent to the two women's cell phones, which wasn't unheard of for normal alarm systems. This one was completely focused on the basement, however, and that level of scrutiny for an internally accessed area raised her hackles even more.

"Okay, I've got things shut down for now." She'd rerouted the alerts to a burner she used for things such as this. "You're clear to move forward." She minimized that window, opening the surface video again. One of the portals was outlined in red, and she watched as the next one in line pulsed red, the car passing in and out of view within a second. "But there's a problem incoming."

"Just got to keep it interesting, huh?"

"Ya know, keepin' you on your toes. You still want to go down now, or back out and neutralize the known subject?"

"Going to keep going. These are nice toys. You keep things locked down on the security front and we will be fine. Why does it keep doing that? I said we will, not we will. Huh." The bodycam captured a wide angle of the stairs as he descended. "The throat mic cannot do contractions."

"So that's not just you gettin' über formal during stressful situations?" Alace laughed dryly. "Noted."

He rounded the landing on the way down and must have stutter-stepped, because the timing with his "Holy shit" matched Alace's own "Jesus Christ" reaction.

The basement floor was divided into a grid housing what looked like four low, metal containers. They appeared to be squat structures independent of the house itself, but each of them was outfitted with internal viewing portals, like a child's view of an aquarium. Whatever was being kept in those was intended as entertainment on demand, unable to hide in a corner.

"Check the thermal." Owen's diction was crisp, all business, the casual play from before cast aside like an old set of shoes. "Look at me, and then look at those ghosts."

"That's why they're so dimmed. The metal surrounding them diffuses the signature. You show up just as clearly as you did in the hallway above." Alace glanced at the center monitor, seeing another three views had gone red, indicating Temple had passed their positions. "Closing in on three minutes. I'm going to reactivate the perimeter alarm so they have to disarm to come in through the garage door. That traps you inside the house, Owen."

"Roger." He'd reached the bottom of the stairs and stepped off onto the main basement floor. "The dimensions are wrong. This space is about half as big as it should be. There is a wall that crosses the full width. See?" His glasses cam swept from side to side. "Internal stairs must end up in that smaller side. This entire setup is hidden from casual view." His bodycam moved up and down with a deep breath. "If Worthson is in the left-hand enclosure...fuck, Alace, it is a holding pen. Remember the clearing?" For the second time, Alace noted the audio software didn't pick up nuance of inflection. *Another reason to see what improvements can be made to it.* Her connection would be thrilled with this kind of feedback, and she made a note to debrief Owen about the wearer's experience with the software specifically. "These dimensions are the same. I would bet money on it."

"Check the one to your right. It's fully dark on the thermal. It'll give you an idea of what you can see inside the others." Alace's fingers trembled as she minimized the street view videos, easing her way into the residential alarm system to silently reset it. Then she worked her way back to the computer off the kitchen, looking for the possibility of a secondary video monitoring system. *Bingo.* "I think there's probably video inside the pens. Verifying now." The first two she pulled up were blank, the wireless devices' batteries dead, cameras inactive. The third showed a man from behind, angled over his head as he reclined on a mat on the floor. There was movement near his groin, and she realized he was jerking off, but something was odd about the image. Alace manipulated the camera and zoomed in to see he wasn't using his own hand to touch his cock. He had a dismembered doll's arm and was using that to flop his semi-hard penis from side to side. It looked disturbingly like a child's hand touching him, and Alace jerked backwards in her chair, fingers flying to change the camera's focus again. The device must have made a sound as the shutter shifted, because he craned his neck around, looking up at the camera. He was old and grizzled, beard trailing down to the middle of his bare chest. He was completely naked, she realized, and when he grinned at the camera, she saw rotted teeth, broken and splintered from untreated trauma.

"Who is that?" Eric's voice came from right behind her as Alace sucked in a breath. "What's he doing?"

"What did you find, boss lady?" Owen's video had moved as she worked with the surveillance camera. He was close to the holding pen she'd requested he approach first, and she watched as he leaned over to look inside via the center portal. "Empty." His words matched the image displayed, and she suddenly knew which was the holding pen for the video she'd seen. "Got anything for me?"

"Worthson is to your left. Cattycorner to that one, there's an elderly subject being held. Leave him there for now, he appears...perhaps unstable." Rapidly clicking controllers, she cycled through the camera from over the stairs until she found Todd's image. He was seated against a wall, shoulder and head propped up by the metal surface. He, thankfully, was not nude, and when he turned to look at the camera, she saw only rage in his expression. Whatever was going on, not only wasn't he part of it, he was seriously angry at being kidnapped and restrained in this fashion. "Worthson's awake and alert. He's probably not in a frame of mind to be patient, so stay away from his pen." She changed windows to see the car pulling into an open garage door. "Subject two is back. What's the plan?"

"You're leaving Todd behind?" Eric's disbelief echoed through the words. "Alace, what are you doing?"

She shook her head and listened for Owen's response.

"Tell the fretter I have this. I can rely on my poise and good looks." He backed up, turning when he reached the stairs. "I am still locked in the house, right?"

"Alace."

"Eric." She turned and fixed him with a glare. "Please." He subsided back onto the edge of the bed, elbows propped on his thighs as he leaned forwards. "Owen, you're correct. Once subject two is inside, I can kill the system again."

"Roger that." At the top of the stairs, he pushed against the section of wall for the hidden door, shifting it to the side when it opened at his touch. He muttered, "Hidden doorways and secret basement hideouts look like fun and games in action movies. So much less so in real life."

"Thermal shows they're both in the kitchen. Subject one and two are in kilo one." Alace cut the alarm.

"Security disabled." Movement on the thermal had her barking, "Wait." One figure moved out of the kitchen and into the living room. "You've got one coming your way. Unknown which." The two women had blended together at one point, and she no longer knew which was which. Not that they'd really known before, just identifying them as the one who'd left and the one who remained. "She'll be on you in seconds."

The video from Owen's bodycam moved, sprinting up the hallway, and she wished again for a standard mic to round out the experience from her end. He must have heard something, because he slowed to time his arrival at the corner with the woman. She came into view, mouth opening as Owen's hands reached for her. The view from the bodycam went dark, and from the position of the glasses video she saw the top of the woman's head. He'd gotten her into a lock position and was dragging her back down the hallway.

"The vid from the holding pens, you got that shit locked down?" Owen's grip shifted, and he slung the woman over one shoulder, arm around the backs of her legs. She was unconscious. "Alace?"

"Yes." She'd disabled local controls, so even if the other sister logged into the computer, all she'd receive were error messages prompting her to uninstall and reinstall the software, which would take half an hour, minimum. "Locked down. What are you doing?"

"Dishing out some of her own medicine. Figure both sisters are in on this. You found surveillance on their joint computer at the home where neither live but both are hanging out while they have abducted folks stashed in their basement. Tit for tat, man."

"I don't disagree. How long will she be incapacitated?"

"Not long enough." Something the software interpreted as a grunt came through the speakers. He was near the bottom of the narrow stairs when she saw the other woman start to move.

"Bad news."

"It's faint, but I hear her footsteps." Good, at least he wouldn't be taken by surprise. "Door is closed, maybe she will think this one went outside." He stood over one of the empty pens. "Simple latch here; at least they make it easy to get inside." The entire top of the pen lifted, hinged along one side. "Would not have taken much to put one of these together. Little metal, little welding, little soundproofing, and you have yourself a place to secure a kidnapping victim. Inside it is a lot like what we saw in the clearing, too. The viewing bubble doubles as a hatch for food or water, waste removal. Locks from the outside." He laid the woman in the pen, having to adjust her position so she stretched corner to corner at an angle. "These are smaller than they look, Alace. Would be a tight fit for a man like Worthson."

"She didn't go outside."

"Figured as much." The lid swung shut, closing off Alace's view of the unconscious woman. "Nowhere to hide, really. I can hunker down next to Worthson. That is about it."

"Do that. I'll ring her cell, see if I can distract her." Alace went back to the phone company's software and initiated a call.

"Stop." Owen's voice came through loud. "Disconnect. Wrong phone."

"Shit." She'd been so certain of the idea. Shifting to the other number, she dialed and waited, watching. The thermal imagery showed the woman hesitating outside the basement door, then moving away. "She's going back to the kitchen." Alace let the call connect before terminating the contact, hearing a faint "Hello" from the computer speakers. "Owen, you've got to get back up there."

He was already moving and didn't bother responding. At the top of the stairs, he opened the door and stepped through, turning to the back door. Alace watched as he opened and closed it with a slam, then ran up the hall to wait just at the corner.

"Genius," she breathed out, and saw the woman's image begin to move. "She's on her way back."

"I got this." As he had only moments before, he stepped into the woman's path as she rounded the corner into the hallway, using her own momentum against her to pull her back to his front in a choke hold. Alace saw the individual movements this time, paying attention to how he pulled and swiveled. "Shhhh." That was directed to the woman who was struggling against his hold, her movements rapidly becoming less coordinated. "Give it up." She sagged and Alace took in a breath, the first since Owen had slammed that door.

In another repeat of things that had just transpired, he lifted the woman's limp body to his shoulder and carried her downstairs. This time, when he lifted the hatch on the holding pen, there was a surprise. Not empty as Alace had thought, it held a woman's body. Nude, her desiccated skin was on display, bones visualized underneath that thin covering.

"Uh." Owen paused. "What now, boss lady?" He raised his head, glasses video focused on the pen where the sister was stashed. "Subject one is awake and angry. I am going to not open that up right now."

"Open Worthson's pen. He's awake." She checked the video feed for his enclosure. "And he's aware something's going on. Be ready for him to be combative."

"I got this." Owen shifted to the side, standing over the latch to Worthson's hatch. A lock was threaded through the hasp but not snapped in place, which would make it simple to retrieve him. His voice sounded, so very different from the system voice she'd almost gotten used to. "Dude. I'm going to open your cell. I have a chick you might know in my arms. She's a bad guy, and I need to secure her. Can you climb out when I open things?"

"One way to go about it." Alace shook her head. "Still, be ready."

"I got this, boss lady." Owen's boot flashed into view as it tapped on the side of the metal box. "I'm with Alace. You get me, man? I'm a good guy here. This chick is a bad guy. Me, good guy." Whatever he heard must have convinced him, because Owen stooped and removed the lock, flipping the hasp back as he lifted the hatch. Todd stared up at him, blinking, and Alace remembered it was dark in the basement.

"He can't see you." Todd shifted towards the edge, sidling towards where the opening was. "It's too dark in there."

"Oh, my dude. Trust, okay. Climb right on out. There you go." From the cadence, Owen had adopted his hiker/beach bum persona. The "dude" was a clear giveaway. She liked to hear that, his easy flow of words, would like to have heard Todd's response. This proved just another reason for a more typical mic as part of the setup. With Owen encouraging him, Todd carefully completed the process of evacuating the pen and tumbled into the open walkway. "That's right, my dude. Now, in she goes." He followed the same process as before, aligning this Temple sister with the corners so he could stretch out her limbs. "And let me find a light switch." Hatch closed, he pushed the lock through the hasp and snapped it tight. Subvocally, he told Alace, "She is taken care of for now."

"Tell him to shield his eyes." Alace kept her gaze on Todd's face for a moment. "There's a switch on the wall at the top of the stairs but probably one at the bottom, too. Try just behind you."

"Lights on in fifteen seconds, Worthson." Owen unerringly went to where she now saw a light switch against the wall. "Probably be bright."

When Owen turned back to Todd, the grays of infrared were gone, replaced by the grays of cement and painted metal. Todd was on his feet, one hand shielding his eyes. His mouth moved, and while she made out a few words by lip reading, she had to wait for Owen to respond to understand his question.

"Yes, Alace's aware you are okay. She's in my ear but cannot hear." The bodycam shook and she realized he was laughing. "I rhymed, boss lady."

"Dial me in, Owen. The op is finished. Well done."

"Beloved." Eric's hands landed on her shoulders, and she leaned her head back against his solid frame. "You did it."

"Tell your man that *we* did it. We make a good team, Alace." Owen had the glasses in his hands and lifted them, pointed at his face. "We done good, boss lady." His wide grin filled the screen.

"Yes, we did."

***

Todd

Fingers running lightly over the upper half of the steering wheel, Todd Worthson stared at the old house sitting only a few blocks away at the end of a well-known cul-de-sac. He'd just come from the third floor of the small county hospital where Maddy and Mackie were being held, the antiseptic smell of the mental ward clinging to his clothes. He still experienced tiny bursts of bitterness on each indrawn breath.

I just don't understand.

Oh, of course he had the mechanics of what had happened. Well remembered the surprise of seeing who he'd thought was Maddy in his house, how he'd imagined for a moment her having let herself in was a sign they were moving forwards. The shock when he'd realized it wasn't her.

Waking in darkness, inside an enclosure not tall enough to stand up in, mapping it on his knees to find four corners and no doors—he wasn't ashamed to say he'd panicked and pounded against the walls. He cleared his throat, the burn of overused vocal cords a painful reminder of the hours he'd spent screaming and shouting.

That house. That damn house.

He hadn't known.

How did I not know?

He'd been eleven when Maddy and Mackie disappeared for a time.

He remembered the day they'd disappeared with crystal clarity, because it was also the day *it* had stopped for him. The last time old man Temple had teased Todd into *that* house with promises of candy and cartoons.

When they'd showed back up in class at school, he hadn't cared when they wouldn't answer questions about where they'd been. Todd had just been ecstatic his best friends in the world were back.

And the monsters had retreated to the darkness where they belonged.

Until they'd shown back up in his kitchen, clad inside the skin of his girlfriend.

His phone buzzed against the hard plastic of the console, and he scooped it up. Gaze fixed on the house, he answered without looking at the screen. "Judge Worthson."

"What are you doing back there, Todd?"

The spit in his mouth dried to dust.

If he'd ever thought old man Temple was frightening, he'd been wrong.

Terror was a diminutive woman named Alace Sweets.

Dread prickled under his arms as he cleared his throat, the pain less of a factor now he couldn't spare any thought to it. "I grew up around the corner."

"I know that." Of course she did. He was finding that Alace knew everything. "Why are you back there now?"

"I knew them all my life. My whole life. I can't…I don't understand what happened."

"I suspect we'll find their mother wasn't very stable. Some things are genetic, Todd." He shook his head, the idea that simple ancestry was to blame for everything. "Don't shake your head at me." Todd froze. *She's watching me.* "Yes, I know. Deal with it. Remember when I told you that taking the first step was proving intent to plunge fully down the rabbit hole with me? This is part of what I meant."

"How long?" He wasn't even sure exactly what he was asking, but Alace seemed to understand immediately.

"The evil things that happened to them would have played a part. But their mother orchestrated a prison break for their abuser and then made them responsible for not just his life but keeping a huge secret in order to keep their mother safe. Their entire lives were organized around ensuring Grandpa was fed and watered, kept breathing. Imagine it. Vacations coordinated, nights out, college plans set aside for local schools because once Mom was gone, it was all on them." Alace sighed as if the very thought was exhausting. "Mom died and Mackie, she was done. But Maddy started taking off unexpectedly, disappearing for months at a time. Do you remember that?"

"Yeah. We hadn't started dating yet. I was building my career, starting my run towards election. I'd have dinner with Mackie once a month or so. She was always complaining about how unreliable Maddy was. Then after Maddy and I got together, she seemed to settle down for a while."

"Then Mackie decided to move to Utah." Alace's voice was quiet, musing in tone. "That announcement set Maddy back on her heels, didn't it?"

"Oh, God. The arguments those two had. I didn't understand why Maddy was so angry. It felt disloyal, but to me it seemed like it was just Mackie's turn, you know?"

The front door of the house opened, and the distance was far enough he couldn't recognize the male figure that walked out. Then, he watched in disbelief as whoever it was turned to wave at him from the porch steps. While he sat there, stunned, the man took the final step down to the sidewalk and turned away from him, heading around the far side of the house.

"What is going—"

"I do know, Todd. I know the draw of that feeling of not having any responsibilities beyond what I choose to take on. This is me helping you put things behind you. You aren't responsible for what happened to those women. You also aren't responsible for the crazy things they did. You were Maddy's last anchor to reality. So Mackie took you away." Alace's breathing changed; then he heard the light tapping of keys in the background. "You should turn the car around now and drive away."

"What? I don't understand—"

Flames licked into view behind the windows a moment before the front of the building blew out in a gigantic ball of fire. The resulting concussion rocked the car, and when he lifted from where he'd ducked behind the dash, he saw a few windows of houses closer to the blast had shattered.

"Drive away now, Todd." The sound on the call changed, as if Alace were inside an enclosed space like a barrel. *Or a cage.* Sweat trickled from his hairline down his temple. "You can't be there."

He pushed the button to start the car's engine, put it into gear, and drove away from the curb, putting the call on the Bluetooth speakers. He turned at the next street and drove steadily, even as his hands shook.

"Alace?"

"Yeah?"

"That house…" Trailing off, he wasn't sure what he'd meant to say. *That the house had exploded?* "It housed more than one set of nightmares."

"I know." The pain in her voice had his teeth grinding together. "You didn't deserve anything he did, Todd. None of you did." Silence fell between them, and he blinked back tears.

His voice cracked when he whispered, "Thank you." Her simple acknowledgement of something he'd never voiced made his spirit lighter somehow.

"Now, Todd, I have one final instruction for you." With an upbeat tone, she asked, "Ready?"

"Yes. Anything."

"Lose this number."

The speakers spat static and hummed; then the dash screen indicated the call had been terminated.

Fuck, she's scary.

CHAPTER TWENTY-TWO

Alace

In the end, it was Todd who had decided how to handle his abduction and subsequent release. Of course, all he knew at the time was that the two sisters had a secret concentration camp in the basement of their grandparents' old home. A location where his sometime girlfriend's sister had imprisoned him inside one holding pen while the body of the women's mother was in another and their completely insane grandfather in yet another.

And that's all he needed to know.

The official story was Mackie had drugged and abducted him—there would be security footage from inside his house to back that up—before taking him to the family stronghold. There, he'd been held against his will until he saw an opportunity to overpower Mackie as she passed him food. Then he'd managed to also incapacitate Maddy and secure her before immediately calling the authorities.

Now that the house was gone—such an unfortunate explosion from a leaky furnace—the only evidence was what the police had been able to extract in the first few hours. Alace had expedited an order to lock the house for a federal investigative team in order to get the scene shut down, and then Owen had taken care of the rest. All footage from inside the holding pens was gone as if the cameras had never been networked into their system. Any irregularities with the alarm logs would be written off due to the mental state of the sisters.

The older Temple had been returned to the state's custody, heading first to the local hospital, after which he undoubtedly would be placed in a different facility from the one he had supposedly died within. That was definitely going to stir a corruption investigation, but since the ownership of the prison had changed hands in the meantime, it would be difficult—if not impossible—to track down the guilty parties.

Alace had already decided Temple wouldn't have long to enjoy the state's hospitality. Insane or not, he didn't deserve to keep breathing. The image of the tiny doll's hand kept intruding into her thoughts.

There had been quite a bit of confusion about Mackie's presence, since she had officially been a missing person, but Eric said he expected it to die down fast. No matter the stink her own sister had made about Mackie being the victim of an abduction, her simply being there played even more into the growing theory that both sisters were as nutter as their grandfather.

Alace had her own ideas about all of that. The timeline of construction would tell the authorities a lot, but she'd bet money the dungeon and original holding pen had been constructed especially for the grandfather's imprisonment after he'd been freed from official custody. Owen had reported from his very brief review of the mother's body that she likely had died from natural causes, no obvious trauma inflicted on her person.

Imagine being so small and abused by someone you trusted, then your whole family is torn apart until suddenly Grandpa's home again but Mommy's mad. The Temple girls' mother had certainly exacted her revenge, and Alace was itching to get into their heads. She had an idea how to secure an interview with them, something she and Owen would have to discuss. *Being a writer has some perks.*

Alace leaned against the kitchen counter on a stiffened arm, slowly stirring the spaghetti sauce. Eric had done the actual cooking, which was their norm, since she still struggled with all but the simplest of meals. He was upstairs showering, and her job was to not allow the sauce to burn. As low as the heat under the pot was, she thought the assignment of stirring was more busywork than actual saving the meal—but if Eric asked it, she'd move heaven and earth to make it happen.

Owen was coming over for dinner.

Hence the need for busywork, because she was absolutely antsy with nerves.

It was what she wanted, no doubts about that at all. She liked how they'd worked together yesterday, at the end of the Temple gig, which had turned into more of a collective effort and less of the handler and hunter relationship they'd had up to that point.

She straightened and cradled the tiny bump low on her stomach. The pregnancy had made her promise to Eric of leaving behind her active roles in the retaliation aspect of her gigs far more real. Just saying the words hadn't been enough. Nearly losing the child had worked better than any rational discussion could ever have. Alace knew that without the promise of the baby, she would have found a hundred different and valid reasons to reenter the field with every gig—just as she had on this one. Being the boots-on-the-ground agent was what she knew and was most familiar. Being the person behind the keyboard wasn't going to be easy to adapt to, but it would help to have a partner like Owen. *Partner. Handler. Ground control.* She snorted at that last one, his latest contribution to their ongoing text discussion. She owed it to him to be the best possible whatever-they-were-going-to-call-it that she could be. No matter how uncomfortable it was right now.

The sauce bubbled and spat hot droplets of red on her arm, and she realized she'd stopped stirring at some point. *Shit.* Grabbing potholders lying nearby, she moved the pot to an empty burner on the stovetop, then stirred vigorously, thankfully not encountering any resistance that would indicate burning on the bottom. Stovetop off, lid askew on the pot, she set aside the spoon for now and checked the clock. Again.

Definitely nervous.

Her phone pinged and she dug it out of her pocket, scowling when she saw the incoming message. She unlocked it and navigated to her text exchange with Todd.

He'd written, **Why do I feel like there's more I don't know?**

Alace sighed. Because he didn't need to know about the murders, at least not yet. Not until she and Owen had decided how best to handle things.

Lose this number, Todd.

Nothing in response, but she didn't expect anything. Not for a couple of hours. If he stuck with his current schedule, he'd wait for a time and then send a different version of the same question. And he'd get the same response. They hadn't been texting buddies before his problem became hers to solve, and they wouldn't be now.

But she wouldn't block his number, just on the off chance she might need him.

It didn't hurt to know a judge who owed favors.

Her phone buzzed again as the doorbell rang, and as she stalked to the door, she unlocked the device to see a news alert about the Temple sisters. She scanned it quickly, then flipped to a different utility to see Owen's face as he stood in front of the door.

Identification verified via the security app, she opened the door and motioned Owen in. He had his phone out and was studying it in much the same way she was, and Alace laughed. She asked, "Did you see what they're calling you now?"

"No, what?" She let him keep reading as she closed the door behind him. He'd stopped walking two steps into the room and now was distractedly running a hand over the top of his head, apparently in search of the beanie he held in his hand. "Motherfucker. Seriously?"

"Yeap." She passed him and motioned him to follow her into the kitchen. "You're now a delusion caused by a psychotic break from reality. Both women, same time. Same delusion, same psychoses. The twinsie freaks are going to go nuts about this." It was Owen who had showed her the forums online where people venerated the more notorious identical twin pairings. "Would you like something to drink, Mr. Delusion?"

"Water, with a little whiskey. Maybe a tad more whiskey than water. Tell ya what, save the environment and hold the water." He pulled up the neck of his shirt and hid his mouth behind it as he continued reading. Alace wondered what the tell would expose, if she were to dig. It was a youthful pose, which meant the mannerism was a holdover from his childhood. "I can't believe the crazy chicks haven't said anything about the bodies. Neither of them, which makes me wonder if I got it wrong. For which sister did what, I mean."

"For what it's worth, I believe we got it right."

He glanced up at her and seemed to realize what he was doing, straightening his collar with one hand while he gripped his phone tightly in the other. He opened his mouth, then closed it before looking towards the stairs. She turned and saw Eric walking down them, a towel draped around his shoulders. His entirely *bare* shoulders. Alace grinned. She'd told him a hundred times that the partnership with Owen was never, ever going to go beyond friends, but here he was, making a very male gesture of staking his claim.

"You're ridiculous." Alace tipped her chin up as he got close, lashes dipping to her cheeks when he dropped his mouth to touch against hers. She cupped his smooth cheek in her hand, thumb sweeping over the freshly shaved skin. "Absurdly handsome, but ridiculous."

He wrapped an arm around her shoulders as he turned them to face Owen. Who was standing there with his trademark broad grin, eyes sparkling at the domestic scene he no doubt imagined this becoming.

"Eric Ward, this is Owen Marcus." She gestured between the two men. "Owen, meet my husbutt, Eric." Two heads swiveled to look at her, and she laughed. Leaning close, she pressed a kiss to Eric's bicep and felt the touch of his lips against her temple. "Put on a shirt."

Thirty minutes later, polite conversation had withered on the vine, leaving them sitting in awkward silence only broken by the scraping of tines across plates as final bites of food were chased down.

"Jesus." Alace threw her fork at her plate. "This is weird."

"So weird." Owen's head bob agreed with her. "You weren't this quiet walking through the woods."

"Take that back." Alace stared at him. "I have skills." She laughed through her nose. "Unlike you, focused as you were on becoming the spider whisperer."

"That first web you walked into—" He broke off, laughing aloud. "Inventive cussing at its best."

"You're a jerk." The feeling that coiled through her chest wasn't the same as what she held for Eric. Not love, but she recognized it as a deep fondness. "But at this point, you're my jerk, because I'm keeping you. We work well together."

"Hell yeah." He offered up a fist pump, looking chagrined in the middle when he realized what he was doing. "I mean, yes, we do. I—" He shook his head. "I don't say this lightly, and you've gotta know it. I trust you, Alace. I *trust* you."

"What a tangled gig this one has been, yeah?" She pushed her plate and cutlery aside, absently thanking Eric when he stacked it on his. "From the time Worthson approached me for help finding his girlfriend's sister, to leaving him behind to make the call for the cops, it was filled with twists."

"Which one do you really think was the active killer?"

"Depends on which one we believe took Worthson." Alace lifted a finger. "The nails were a giveaway to tell one from the other, but they're identical, so unless I care enough to get into the local cop shop's database to get their fingerprints or see if there are CODIS matches, we only have their word for who they are. Historical images show Mackie'd been a nail biter way back when, so I think it was her who took him, but I have a theory that Maddy wasn't as stable as she'd portrayed herself through the years."

"Do tell?" Owen leaned back, arm slung across the top rail of his chair. "Let's share theories, shall we?"

"You remember the debrief on their childhood trauma?" Owen nodded. "There was something that bugged me about the police report from the day Maddy found out what their grandfather was doing to Mackie. She grabbed a baseball bat, sprinted the blocks to his house, and attacked him. Not very effectively, because he disarmed her before she could do any damage, but the cop who followed her reported she had shouted 'something that sounded like *I'm your girl*,' end quote. I think she was less upset about the ordeal her sister had been through and more concerned with losing her standing with their grandfather."

"So you think he was molesting both girls?" Alace nodded. "Makes sense. I mean, what little girl tries to kill a man like that? A crazy one, that's what. If she was supposed to be Grandpa's special girl, it'd piss her off to find out he was doing Mackie on the side." Lifting his beer, he swirled the last two inches of liquid round and round as he considered her theory. "Why was Grandpa in the house?"

"Mom. Eric called it when we were looking through photos, because the girls were too young at the time. They didn't organize shit at that age, certainly not something as complex as a prison payoff to extricate a prisoner in a way that officially killed him." Alace picked up her glass, glaring at the plain water for a moment. "Second theory is he didn't necessarily start with the girls. Maybe he waited until his son was dead, maybe he didn't. I'm planning on looking into that death, but we'll have to take it at face value for now. Mom had to be impacted by what happened to her daughter, even if she only knew about Mackie's abuse and not Maddy's. I don't think that's enough to fuel the kind of rage necessary to create a dungeon, break the old man out of jail, and keep him for more than twenty-five years. He never had a moment of freedom, going from prison to dungeon. Personally, I think he started his extracurriculars with Mom, then branched out later."

"But wasn't Mom kept in one of the cells?" Eric's question had both Alace and Owen shaking their heads. She gestured to Owen to go ahead and he grinned, offering her a tiny genuflection in response that made her smile back.

"Mom didn't die in the holding pen. She was laid out in state, the circulation fan turned off so it was as airless as it could be without sealing the structure. But with the viewing ports, the girls could still see Mommy." He lifted the bottle to his lips, draining the final swallows. "She became a relic, holy. Mom might have been batshit crazy, but the girls revered her. You couldn't hear what they were shouting after they both woke up." Alace shook her head. *Damn mics.* "They were most concerned with which pen each of them was in, neither wanting to be the one who woke up Mommy. Crazy talk, and it unsettled Worthson pretty good."

"Then who killed all the women in the woods?" Eric leaned forwards, elbows to the table, clasped hands in front of his mouth. "And what will you do about telling authorities where the fields are?"

"We may never know for sure—" Owen stopped and looked at Alace. "What do you know that I don't? Because from that face?" He made a stirring motion aimed her way. "You know something."

"The forestry service keeps good records." His ah-ha expression was amusing, and she laughed at the round "O" created by the surprise. "Seems Maddy had been volunteering for years. First during a sorority push for diversity. Not sure what working in the woods has to do with that, but maybe they were looking to bolster their ranks with girls who had activities other than cheerleading?" Alace shrugged. "Doesn't matter, except the first trip Maddy took, one of the girls didn't make it back. Her body was never found, and it was assumed she'd run off with an unsavory boyfriend who disappeared at the same time."

"You think that was her first kill? A male/female couple? That's a dicey setup even for someone with lots of experience. A twofer isn't something to just dive into." Owen shook his head. "I could buy tragic accident for one and opportunity for Maddy with the other one."

"Maybe. Until you or I want to voluntarily head into lockup and pick her brain, it's not likely we'll know. But I do think that weekend's missing couple had everything to do with Maddy." Alace looked at Eric. His brows were drawn into a deep frown, tiny lines appearing between. "She would have been eighteen." She left it at that, hoping he would draw the correlating lines without her having to speak them. *Just about the same age as me when I started.* "We won't know if there were any kills between that and the bodies in the pens up north, but I suspect there would have been if something fell into her lap in terms of opportunity. The first abductions, however, line up with Mom's probable death. One abduction, then two in quick succession, and we know she kept them alive for a time."

"Alive and tortured." Owen tapped a fingertip against the table in a slow cadence. "Who knows what she used with the early victims, but she'd refined her activities by the time we found her caches. Napalm for food or water denial, and the staging for whatever her fantasy was."

"That one I can't figure. Overalls over layers of girly clothing, and a trophy wig. I can't wrap my head around it." She snorted. "Wonder if we'll ever really know?"

"She dressed up as Mom. Not sure about the blonde aspect of the wig, but while Worthson got ready to call the cops, I did a quick sweep of the house. Mom's room was a shrine, and her closet was filled with shape-obscuring clothing like overalls. Muumuus, shapeless sweatshirts, and pants. My guess is Mom not being all there in the head showed in her wardrobe selections. Hiding her femininity, but underneath was where she allowed herself to be vulnerable." The tapping increased in speed, evolving into a pattern of sounds Alace thought sounded familiar. "The holding pens were a makeshift replica cell from the dungeon. The first ones were without a viewport, but she eventually figured out how to build an access window she could cut off in an instant by shifting the barrel over the top. Can you imagine being the person inside, watching as this crazy lady shut down your access to light and air?" He flattened his palm against the table, staring down. "I'm leaving tonight to go back to that active clearing. I just have to make sure no one's left behind. The fact she visited it between when I saw it and when you did a sat sweep is concerning."

"Good call." Alace shoved her chair back from the table. "And good timing. I've got a new com we can test."

"Yeah? Already? Cool." From the sound of things behind her, Owen had left the table too, and was following her. "New tech acquisitions are fun times. Whatdja get?"

"ESA has a new development, and I got my hands on one of the newest prototypes. It uses a MEO base, which means there's a longer coverage, and it can skip to a different bird when one hits the horizon. Lightweight, too." She paused on the stairs and looked back to see Eric's smile beaming her way. "We're gonna talk shop, but you're invited."

"Nice of you to invite me up to my own bedroom." The sideways quirk of his lips told her he wasn't truly annoyed, and she rolled her eyes in response. "I'll be up in a minute, but what's ESA and MEO?"

Owen offered up the meaning behind the acronyms, his knowledge impressing her as he no doubt intended. "ESA is European Space Agency, and MEO means a satellite in medium earth orbit, which offers more coverage than one closer to earth but still keeps transmission time fast." Owen hooked a thumb over his shoulder to where Alace waited on the stairs. "The fact your woman has connections to acquire this level of technology like that"—he snapped his fingers—"is impressive, and just adds to her point tally." He laughed, and Eric joined him. "She's got the best damn toys."

"There can only be one resident geek." She turned and continued up the rest of the stairs. A couple of steps later she realized she'd given him her back without question or thought, and the understanding of how much she instinctively trusted him only drew the tiniest shiver from her. "I've fully occupied that position. All new applications will be declined."

"Oh, man. I missed out." Owen's soft chuckle mapped his distance behind her, which despite his longer legs wasn't decreasing. Whether he was keeping away out of fear or respect, she didn't care. She'd take it.

"Yes, you did. But, if you're a good boy, I might be convinced to continue to share my toys." Their teasing wasn't sexual in nature, not at all, and she knew Eric understood when he joined in.

"Do good boys get dessert?" She glanced over her shoulder to see him uncovering the container of cookies he'd baked earlier while she worked. His own way of keeping busy.

Eric had stories about sitting on a stool next to his mother and stealing bites of dough as they mixed the batter. Alace found her palm was again cradling the baby bump she never quite lost awareness of, and she wondered if his mother would take their child to her heart. *A grandmother.* Something to discuss with Eric and find out when he'd be comfortable telling the people important in his life. She didn't have anyone. That knowledge didn't dig as deeply as it would have even a couple of months ago, the raw emotion of losing Regg slowly covering with new friendships. Her gaze landed on Owen, and she saw his attention on the placement of her hand. While they hadn't completely clarified things on the call yesterday, he'd made his knowledge clear. If anything had been left to question, her actions now had confirmed it.

"Yes, good boys get dessert. Bring a couple up with you when you come." Eric lifted his gaze, and she felt the weight and heat of his focus. It affected her the way it always did, and she shivered. "Don't take too long. I'm snackish."

"Feed my babies." That calm assertion did things to her insides, and she blinked back a sudden onslaught of tears. "Be there in a minute, beloved."

"Don't make the pregnant lady cry." With that firm order thrown into the air between them, she turned and made her way into their bedroom.

"Everything okay with the pregnancy?" Owen's low question cut the silence as she settled into her chair. Alace glanced over her shoulder and nodded. "But you're on restrictions, right?" Slowly, she nodded again. "And that kills you a little." He paused, studying her. "No, that kills you a lot. I get it. I had to sit out a couple of missions because of injuries, and the worst of it wasn't doing the research, studying the data and providing analysis, because then I was at least pulling my weight." He huffed out a laugh that didn't seem to hold any humor at all. "Worst was sitting in a chair and watching the screens as my team stepped into hell without me at their backs. Listening to the calls on the com. Listening to the silence between transmissions."

His mouth twisted and he shrugged, one shoulder lifting and falling with a sigh. "What I mean is I get it. I understand. This is a change, and an unwelcome one, I'm sure. By the time you get used to it, you'll be ready to jump back into the field, no doubt."

She stared at him and his smile faltered and fell away.

"You're not going back into the field." Not a question, but the tentative statement wasn't too far removed from disbelief. "Ever." She shook her head and he looked away, a low curse falling from his lips. "So many layers to all that is Alace Sweets Ward."

"You and me." Her words brought his attention back to her, and she sat quietly, letting him look his fill, leaving her expression open for easy interpretation, knowing he'd understand how much that meant. "I want to partner with you. Going forwards. We can find the tech that suits us both, and figure out what that means, what it looks like. Right now I've got two other hunters, but I'm going to put them to pasture for a while. I want to get comfortable with you and give you the opportunity to build the same level of confidence. What we do, Owen." She shook her head. "It doesn't make us models of conformity, that's for sure. But to be the support you need, I've got to be in sync with you. We'll be a team."

"This mission was extreme." Feet apart, hands clasped behind his back, Owen stood at parade rest in the middle of her bedroom, and Alace took a breath and allowed herself to appreciate the surrealness of the moment. "Things moved so fast, but having you in my ear, knowing you were just a whisper away, it meant more than you probably understood. Most of my targets haven't been as up close." Lips a thin slash across his face, he shook his head. "Not to say I can't or won't do wet work. God knows I've done enough in my day. But it's not my specialty."

"Are you turning me down, Marcus?" Alace tried to create distance by using his surname, but his quick grin, so at odds with his last statement, gave her hope that she'd read him wrong.

"Oh, hell no, Sweets." She stuffed down her humor at his attempt to turn the tables on her and paid attention, not just to his words, but his posture, expression, the vibe rolling off him—all of which told her he wasn't lying, that he hadn't been closing the door on this fledgling partnership. "You can't get rid of me that easily." He unlocked his knees and brought a hand around to scrub across his jaw, the aw-shucks aspect of his putting-a-mark-at-ease persona in full effect. *Asshole*. "What I'm saying is it meant a lot to me, you being willing to be with me the way you were during my time in that monster house. It was creepy as shit listening to the crazy lady talking to herself. Knowing you'd move heaven and hell to get me out if things went south, and that you'd know immediately, not waiting for the next satellite overview pass—it gave me confidence. Not in my abilities, because hell yeah, I always had that shit on lock, trust. But in the survivability of the mission. Not always a given in the past, and when I worked off grid—" He shook his head, gaze dropping to the floor between them. The tension in his shoulders spoke volumes about the scenes he must have running through his head. "Let's just say I appreciated you more than you'll know."

"What do you know about my former handler. Partner?" Time to fess up to what had gone sideways, even if she'd never be ready to talk about Regg's death.

Owen glanced around and grimaced at the stool near her chair, shaking his head. He took a knee where he'd stood and settled back, crouching comfortably over his heel. Once relaxed, he drilled her with a solid gaze. "Not much. Just what you've shared about them spying on you without vetting the idea first."

"When I started my path, I didn't know a lot. I'd had some advice from a friend of my mother's, who put me on the idea of an alternate identity. Regg was my paper guy to start." Just talking about the beginning brought back so many different emotions, not many of them good. "Then, on like my third gig, I ran into trouble. I sorted it out but realized I might need more than an identity going forwards. I'd developed what felt like a long-distance friendship with Regg, so I walked my idea past him and he took it and ran with it. Before long, it seemed like he could produce anything I needed. We set up drop locations, and things progressed."

Eric appeared in the door to the bedroom and paused just long enough to note where Owen was crouched. He shook his head and approached her, snagging the stool with one foot to move it to the side before sitting down. One long arm reached out and hooked her ankles with his fingers, lifting her feet to his lap.

"I don't know exactly when things changed for him, but he started hiding things. Mostly motives for pushing a certain gig my way, which all turned out to be financial in the end. On *his* end. He used his association with me to further a money laundering career, blackmailing his way into the bed of a powerful man's daughter. And me?" She scoffed slowly. "It's not so simple to explain what he was to me. I thought we were friends. Thought he had my back, no matter what. I was young and naïve, and so very lost in what had happened to me, and what I was doing. I'm still that, honestly. I spent so long under his thumb, believing his statements like they were gospel so I didn't have to create connections. Even in a long-running gig, I'd only carve out whatever part of me was needed to produce the person needed for the gig, and no more. None of it was real. I'm stunted."

Eric's hold on her feet tightened, and he leaned closer, whispering, "Beloved."

"I am, and you know it. I'm learning." She cupped his jaw with her hand, thumb ghosting across his bottom lip, tugging it one way then the other. "I never had friends, never had anything until you latched on to me and wouldn't let go." She glanced at Owen. He was watching them, a complex array of emotions racing across his expression. "That's a story for another day. I'm telling you about my only other partnership for these gigs." He nodded while Eric's head moved in her hand. Alace bent forward at the waist, surprised at the extra pressure from the—*that's the baby*. Blinking back tears for the second time in a short while, she touched her forehead to Eric's.

"Regg used me. Long and short of it, he used me to fund his lifestyle, which was lavish. I'd be holed up in a no-tell motel for months on end and he had a three-story McMansion to roam around in. Not that I knew about any of that. Part of the using was the lies. The most he'd brought me into his life was when he claimed to have met his soul mate." Eric's fingers were firm bands surrounding her ankles, holding her steady. She straightened in her chair, fingers falling from his face back to her lap, where they twisted with her other hand. "It was about that point he started protecting his investment, bugging all the items he'd provide me for any given gig. Gave him a way to keep tabs on me. Even when I thought I was in private, I wasn't. My chosen gigs have always been a lot like yours in terms of motivation. I want to even the scales for people who've been fucked over by the legal system, or by someone who believes themselves untouchable. What we just did isn't my typical. You know that already by the couple of gigs I fed you before this one." Owen nodded, but she appreciated his silence. Letting her get this all out in one go would make things easier for everyone. "I found out Regg had manipulated information, doctoring data so he could steer me towards gigs that had dollar signs attached to them. I've never been about the money. Half of anything I earn still goes to charities and foundations to help girls like I used to be. That single thing, finding out how he'd used me, felt like such a violation."

She swallowed hard, blinking back another infuriating round of tears. "Dammit, I'm not a weeper normally. That shit's gonna piss me off for sure. It needs to knock it off." That earned her a pair of masculine chuckles, one she loved and the other she was becoming fond of.

"I gave him every chance to back away. But he'd groomed other hunters, groomed and discarded when they didn't produce like I did. And by discarded, I mean ditched, as in rolled them into one. His last living hunter got sicced on me. I didn't know it. Didn't know that's what he was." It felt like she was trying to justify her actions, and maybe she was, but dammit, in the moment, it had been her or him. *I walked away breathing and came home to Eric.* "Regg had set him up, linking him to a killer I was hunting until we were pitted against each other. When that gig was done, I went to Regg. His reaction didn't earn him forgiveness." *There, I'll leave it at that.*

A glance at Owen showed her his thoughtful nod, and Alace blew out a silent breath of air.

"I don't trust easily." Eric's thumbs had started digging into the balls of her feet, and his touch faltered at her words, then continued. He knew it was true; she wasn't revealing any great secrets here. Not to Eric, anyway. "I have Eric, and that's pretty much it. I might give the benefit of the doubt to those he trusts, but even that's only to a point." She shrugged, happy to be nearing the end of this monologue that felt far too close to a confession. "And now, I find myself trusting you." Elbows propped on the arms of the chair, she pinned Owen with the flat stare she used to unnerve people. "I don't like it. I've never been that person. But I trust you, anyway. I like that you aren't perfect, and you don't hide it. I like that you aren't afraid to call me on my shit. I think we could be good partners, but only if that trust, that faith and belief, goes both ways."

Their locked stares held for fifteen seconds that stretched to thirty, then sixty—and finally Owen's face split in a broad grin that had Alace rocking back in the chair in reaction.

"Called it. We're besties."

Alace's internal response was immediate. *Jesus Christ. I'm going to have to kill him.* Externally, she held his gaze without providing any feedback to his brash statement. He wasn't intimidated, the grin never wavering.

"Dibs on changing your nickname, though."

"No." At Alace's one-word denial Eric's touch changed, stuttering, and she broke the stare-down with Owen to glance at him, not really surprised to see his shoulders shaking. "Really, Eric?"

"Hey, Alace." Owen's call tore her attention away from her manically cackling husband, and when she saw the unexpectedly somber expression on Owen's face, she readied herself for whatever was coming.

"Yeah?"

"That girl you were? Don't hate on her anymore. I mean, sure, you already know it's okay to mourn the things she didn't get. To be pissed about the way life fucked her over. She got caught up at seventeen and might have stayed there for longer than others. But you aren't stunted, not like you think. You might have hit pause for a while, but you're fully engaged in life now. That girl is your past, and that shit might be sordid and painful, but it's in the past. A brutal fucking lesson, not a life sentence. That past is so damn messy, and I can only marvel at how well you came out of the fire that forged you. But it's not you. Not now." He settled to the floor, legs sprawled and knees cocked out to the side as he leaned back on his stiffened arms. "Dealt a shit hand and then had insult to injury added by that shit stain Regg. He set you up to be alone so he could control you. Years, you suffered. Alone and lonely." Owen's eyes blazed as he stared at her. "You aren't lonely now. You might not recognize yourself yet, but the woman I see in front of me is strong and powerful, able to tackle any challenge directed her way." He gave her a tiny smile, the barest glint of teeth showing through his parted lips. "You are going to be one fierce momma, and I'm honored that I'll get to see it. The trust you demand, it's there between us, and will only become stronger. I didn't expect it. Hell, I bet neither of us did, but it's where we are and I'm not too upset about it at all." His laugh was low and soft, a transition sound to let her know he was done with the hard topics. Moving on to his more normal humor. "A partnership with the renowned Alace Sweets would be cool and all, but getting to work closely with my good friend Alace Ward?" The grin grew, the corners of his eyes crinkling as his cheeks lifted. "In the words of that damn TV ad, it's priceless."

Eyes burning with unshed tears, Alace didn't bother trying to mask the depth of the emotions he'd stirred up. She sniffed and blinked, swallowing hard as she fought her chin for control, not wanting to lose her composure entirely. Breathing deeply through her nose, she eventually won the battle without a single drop escaping.

When she thought she could depend on her voice not to break or waver, she cleared her throat and nodded. "Thank you." Eric's fingers threaded through hers, and when his mouth opened, she shook her head at him. "Nope. Nuh-uh. Don't do it. I've got all of this under control right now, but it's not far away. I'm a woman on the brink, my husband, and I don't know what to do with all of these feelings." Another huffed sigh had him cracking a smile at her, and she was reduced to the routine of sniffing, blinking, and swallowing again. "Stop it. I want to show Owen the tech I got for his nighttime hike. If you make me cry, I won't get to it for a long time. There's a chance that the Temple woman had an opportunity to take a final victim. She was in the woods for a reason when she met up with Owen." The longer she talked, the more in control she felt, and Alace felt herself settling. Neither man would be upset if she had dissolved into tears, but there was work to do and it wasn't her way. Had never been, and wouldn't be, if she had anything to do with it. "Owen, there's a chair in the hallway. Grab that and come sit so we can share the screen. I've got toys."

"Yes, ma'am, boss lady, ma'am." He unfolded from his position on the floor, flowing upward to standing without any apparent effort. Flashing her that damn grin she was coming to depend on as a barometer for his mood, he angled towards the door.

She couldn't let his repeated ma'aming go without mention, though. Following his direction, she offered him a little Alace-style humor. *Dominant, but still playful. Sure, we'll go with that.*

"Are you looking to be killed? Because that's how you get killed around me."

CHAPTER TWENTY-THREE

Owen

Pausing at the top of a ridge for a quick breather and much-needed drink of water, Owen pivoted in a slow circle as he took in the surrounding peaks with forested shoulders and valleys. Just over the top of a pass to the west, he could see the ranger fire watch tower he'd noticed when he was here before. A shiver worked down his spine as he remembered the feeling of being stalked, tables turned in a way he never wanted to experience again.

"What's wrong?"

Owen blinked, and he lifted the water valve to his lips and bit down again, taking a long, slow drink. "Just takin' a minute, boss lady."

"Your heartrate spiked for a moment."

"I knew letting you do the biometric harness would be a mistake." He shook his head and tapped the microphone attached behind the hinge of his jaw. The adhesive was strong, and it couldn't be sweated off, or so Alace's source had promised her. Didn't mean it didn't pull and tug at his whiskers. "I shoulda shaved before I let you tape me up."

"Noted."

He didn't doubt she had a running list of things they could do to fine-tune the rig. That was just her style. And his, if he wanted to admit to it. They'd worked on the setup until after midnight; then he'd climbed in his car and set off for the trailhead. She'd dialed in mid-morning, and he didn't know if that was because she'd slept in—something that didn't seem her kind of thing—or if that was simply the first time the satellite they depended on for communication had swung into place. His pace had been quick, a determined trail-running stride he could keep up for hours, only slowing for extreme climbs like the ridge he'd just topped.

He used the bite-valve for the bag stored in the light pack suspended between his shoulders to take another deep drink, propping a hip against the column of a tree. "Anything I need to know?"

"No new missing reports in surrounding towns, and no buzz about anything the local authorities might have stumbled onto. I don't think she had time to pick up anyone new."

"From your mouth to God's ears. Wish we'd had time to figure out her transport process. Woulda given us a better idea if this is a rescue or the beginnings of a recovery. I know she manhandled Todd's body easily, but we're talking dozens of women. Takin' that risk over and over doesn't match with the intelligence of the twins." Breathing deeply, Owen pushed off the tree and set his feet on the downward-angled trail. Launching into a jog and then picking up the pace, he asked, "Audio and visual okay?"

"Yeap, we're golden so far. I do like this better. I can hear your footsteps."

He grunted, grabbing a tree trunk to swing himself around a switchback corner of the trail without bleeding off too much momentum. It was a sheer drop from where he was, at least a football field to the bottom of the ravine, the slope of the mountain covered in squared-off boulders and forest.

"Uh." Alace's alarmed vocalization cut off, and he grinned. She'd been doing that since she synced up with him. Never quite telling him to be careful, and not even reminding him it hadn't been that long since he had fallen down a mountainside. But her reactions were nervous tells: each time the stream from his bodycam changed direction abruptly or he jumped down a steep slope, leaping multiple feet at a time, it was obviously killing her to be quiet.

"In a hurry, remember?" Each syllable was its own tiny effort, and he decided to keep quiet unless speech was needed. Not that he expected to find anything except empty holes and bones. But on the off chance there could be someone to save, he'd do so much more than just bust his ass in a quick march.

"You're averaging twelve-minute miles, you're going fast enough as it is. Don't—" Alace sighed, the sound echoing through his head as if she were running right next to him. "Just be safe, okay?"

She must have taken his grunt for a response, because she let the subject die away. One thing about Alace, she wasn't afraid of silence, and neither was he, but he wanted to know one detail. *Worth the effort*, he decided, and took a quick drink to wet his mouth.

"When are you due?"

There was silence for so long he'd started to believe the com link had broken, which wasn't a disaster but would put him out here entirely on his own. *Nothing I haven't handled before*, he reminded himself. Then Alace answered him.

"They count things in weeks, did you know that? The doctor who read the ultrasound said I was about sixteen weeks. That was a week ago, so I guess in five months? He wrote a date down, but Eric took control of the paperwork and I didn't pay attention to that." Her voice cracked, and he shortened his strides, listening closely. "I could have lost the baby. What you're doing right now, I could have done that three months ago. Today it would cost me…" He heard a gulp and understood she'd swallowed back a sob. "…everything."

"Life changes." Owen slowed, settling into a fast walking stride that would leave him enough air to carry on a conversation. "And we roll with it. That's what you're doing right now with me. You're still right here figuring out how to roll with the changes. Not doing too shit a job, either. I'd say you're a keeper."

"Flattery will get you new toys." The fractured quality had fled from Alace's voice, and he grinned to hear her sass back in full force. "You're only a couple of miles from the first field. Why'd you slow down?"

"Boss lady, we measure things in klicks, not miles. So that means I've got about three klicks to go before I enter the first target." He took another drink and picked up the pace again. "For your information, I was going slower so I didn't make you motion sick."

"Should I call it a landing zone instead of clearing, too? Klicks sounds stupid. Like training a dog. Klick, klick, what a good boy."

"Boss lady—" He huffed out a laugh and picked things up another notch. "—you can call it what you want, but my mind measures distance in klicks. You wanna see me as a dog, that's cool, but make sure it's a chill breed like mastiff. All guardy and stuff."

"Definitely not a mastiff. You're all bark and no bite, so Chihuahua is out, too." She was laughing now, and he liked hearing this less stressed version of her. "What are those military attack dogs? Malinois? Yeah, I can see you as a Malinois."

"Knock, knock." He didn't know if she'd play along, but he hoped she'd take the bait.

"Who's there?" *Boom*. He liked knowing she was someone who could be silly sometimes. It would make it easier to work with her during the tense encounters.

"Patsy."

She laughed through her nose but kept the game going by asking, "Patsy who?"

"Pat zee dog on zee head, zee likes it." She groaned, and he grinned. "I got a million of 'em."

"Well, keep 'em to yourself. That was terrible."

He'd covered half the distance to the clearing before she spoke again.

"Owen?"

"Yeah?"

"Are we friends?" Static filled his ears and she muttered something unintelligible, then came through loud and clear again, leading him to believe she'd covered the mic on her end. "Never mind. Focus on the gig."

"Oh, I'm on point where the mission's concerned. Do not worry your twisted little mind about that." He shook his head, knowing she'd see the movement for what it was, a way of discrediting her attempt to derail his reaction to her question. "Where you're concerned, things are a little muddier. Are we friends? I'd say yes, we are, but kinda fledgling friends. Like I enjoy working with you, but we're both still holding back."

"I thought we were besties?"

He scoffed at her attempt to defuse the intensity of his words. "You need to stop being so prickly, Alace." He slowed when he saw the fallen tree he'd fixed as a marker in his mind. "I'm at the place where I need to turn off the trail. Bushwhacking coming up."

"I'm not prickly."

"Just saying that makes my point for me. You're so prickly you could be a hedgehog." He stepped over the deadfall and off the trail, paying close attention to the footing. Within a few strides he'd found the faint track he and Alace had followed that first day in the woods. "Maybe I'll make that your new nickname."

"I don't have nicknames."

"Oh, sure you do." He settled back into the running pace. "Skyline Sweets is one. I picked that up when I looked into you before working our first gig. Your work in Chicago is legendary." Ducking under a branch, he ran into a cobweb stretching the width of the trail. "Son of a bitch. Goddamn it." He flailed around to clear the clinging web from his face and hair. "I hate that shit."

"Hey."

He grunted, still wiping at his face. "What?"

"You didn't hit any webs on the main trail, did you?"

Owen straightened, his head coming up as he locked attention on what she was saying.

"No, I did not. My car was the only one in the lot when I parked. I didn't see any sign of anyone, and I've been cooking with gas on the main stretches of trail. You think I've been following someone? Someone with as much motivation as I have to get to the clearing fast?"

"Maybe. It'd be more suspect if you were completely alone, I think. Still, something to watch out for. You're—" She paused and he heard the clicking of keys in the background. "—about half a klick from the clearing now."

"I'll keep my eyes peeled." He bent over and found a stick, holding the wood balanced in a loose grip. "Did it hurt just now?"

"Did what hurt?" Her tone was more relaxed than a moment ago, and he suspected she knew he was joking with her again.

"You said klick instead of mile."

"Whatever. Shut it." Quiet for a breath, then a soft, "Be careful, Owen."

"Totally besties." His mutter made her laugh, as did the next cobweb he saw and twirled expertly with the end of the stick.

"He can be taught." Her chortle had him grinning. "Clearing in thirty seconds."

"See it through the trees." He paused where he was and dropped to put a knee in the soft dirt of the track he'd been following. "It looks like it did when we left here. Nothing changed. No disruption to the pits we know hold bodies, and the cache looks to be undisturbed, too."

"Copy that. Do you want to look closer or move to the next field?"

"I think heading to the next one is best. That's the one that was active and is the most likely location for any new captives. The third field was as dead as this one, so while I'll be covering that one, I don't expect anything there. Plus there's the fact the bitch burned shit." He took another hard pull of water from the reservoir in his backpack. "I'm gonna run short on water. Can you look at the topo and see where the best place to filter some replacement agua would be?"

"On it." The keys clicking told him she was doing as advertised, and when the answer came just a moment later, he suspected she'd already been anticipating the request. "Due north, there's an all-weather stream. I think the track you're on will cross it. The main trail doesn't. The water flow runs parallel until the stream dips under the rocks. So good news, this side trek wasn't useless after all. You'd need to be where you are to make the best path to the stream."

"Yay." He stood and oriented himself, then followed the track north, web stick poised and ready.

A trek that had taken him hours when he did it previously passed much quicker, but the sun was still heading down behind the peaks to the west before he found himself on the approach to the second field. The haunting memory of traps snapping closed had him wary of staying on the track, so as he had before, he shifted several feet to the side and remained parallel to keep his bearings. Alace's conversation had been brief and staccato in nature, one long period of silence broken by an extended chat she'd had with her husband. Faceless Eric no more. Owen had listened to their back and forth with a grin on his face.

Just when he'd been about to remind Alace to let Eric know Owen could hear him, the man's voice had come from close to the microphone. "Be well, Owen. We're both rooting for you."

Be well. Not good luck, not anything offhand or throwaway. Owen grinned at the memory as he mentally approved of Alace's selection in a partner.

Not that my validation matters. Rustling leaves to the other side of the trail had him crouching, scanning the area.

"What?" Alace clearly hadn't heard it, and he made a note to tell her about the sound so they could determine if the level of environmental sounds was adequate.

Then he saw what had caused the noise, a shape moving through the woods. Bipedal and tall, the figure flitted from tree to tree, heading from the clearing back towards the main path.

"Oh my God." He breathed out slowly. "Please be Bigfoot. Please. I could totally get behind discovering Bigfoot today."

"I see what you're seeing." Alace didn't miss a beat, and her basic business tone made him grin even as he shook his head. "That's no Sasquatch, Owen. That's our killer."

"Bigfoot would be awesomer." He shifted to keep track of the figure as it moved through the woods. "Just sayin'."

"What do you think? Continue on to the clearing, or follow the killer?"

"How can you ignore the fact that this could indeed be Bigfoot?" He pushed to his feet as the woods grew lively around him once again, birds and small animals beginning their scurrying and calls. He hadn't even realized how silent it must have been for him to hear the passage of the killer. "Clearing. I'm too close not to check it out first. It kills a little, though. He's right there, and if Temple one or Temple two isn't the killer, then we're back to the fundamentals here with no knowledge about the target. We've got patterns and seasonality, but other than an apparent height that defies the female persuasion, nada else. Still, creepin' up on the dude without knowing anything about him or what he might be packing seems a quick ticket to badsville, too."

"Okay. There's not much I can do here other than watch." The sigh he heard was filled with frustration, and Owen found himself commiserating with her.

"You're doing a lot, Alace." He grabbed the branch and moved forwards warily, tapping the ground ahead every few steps. "Last time I was right here, not having someone at my back left me feelin' vulnerable. I didn't like it. With you now?" He saw the open field ahead, trees thinning as he got closer. "The barrel is moved. It's not gone like you saw on the satcom imagery, which means it disappeared, reappeared, and now it's definitely moved. Shit."

Resuming his crouched position, he scanned the area.

Alace chuckled. "Infra for the win. Stand and do a slow circle, let me ensure you don't have a visitor trying to access the clearing."

"I didn't know the new cam had infrared. That's boss, boss." He did as she asked, making his way round the tree he'd had at his back, giving the bodycam a clear view of the forest surrounding the clearing.

"The barrel is hot. It's clear on the infra that the base is significantly hotter than the ground around it."

Owen was moving before she finished talking, jogging across the field in a zigzag pattern to avoid depressions indicating underground holding pens.

"Owen, remember the traps. We've only really mapped dead fields. Neither of us has seen what might be in place for an active victim."

He pulled to a stop a couple of feet away and stared at the ground around the barrel. Damaged grass stems surrounded the iron-bound bottom, and he could see a deep groove leading away to a spot where a circle of grasses and ground were depressed slightly, as if the barrel had been placed there and then rolled away. Moved from that position so recently the flora hadn't yet recovered.

"If there's someone in the pit, any prepared countermeasures might be expected to silence the prisoner as well as take out whoever discovered them. Be careful, Owen."

"My instinct says the killer would not risk the captive doing injury to themselves. They like to watch too much, building their own version of the viewports used at the Temple house." He'd shifted to subvocalization, once again appreciating the tech Alace had brought to the endeavor. Her acquisitions that were so casually mentioned...he wasn't sure she knew how fantastic the things were. "I do not see anything of note surrounding the barrel blocking the wire you and I both know is underneath. I found no indication the killer boobytrapped the other pits I excavated. No pockets in the dirt. No left behind pieces of wire. I do not think our guy is so sophisticated." One knee to the dirt and grass, he leaned forward and placed his hands on the edges of the half barrel. "Just another walk in the park."

It was heavier than he expected, too much so to lift directly off, so he reversed what he thought the killer must have done, yanking it up on one edge and rolling it to the side.

"Jesus." The stench from the pit was overwhelming, and Owen breathed through his mouth to escape it. "Be glad you do not have Smell-O-Vision." The running narration substituted "translation not available." That made him laugh aloud, because they'd run into this before and it made Alace crazy to not know the specific word. He activated the audible mic and repeated the word aloud, "Smell-O-Vision."

At the sound of his voice, something shifted in the pit, pale fingers coming into view as they clutched at the wire covering the opening. Then a tiny, triangle-shaped face appeared. Dirt covered the woman's skin, and he saw her mouth moving, no sound coming out at first. The distinctive jaw movement and lip shape told him everything he needed. The word "help" repeated again and again.

"Boss lady, you seeing this?" He stood and maneuvered the barrel well away, kicking it onto its side for good measure, rendering it more difficult to return to the previous position entrapping this woman.

"Making the call now." That would be the not-quite-anonymous call to the authorities they'd discussed. Alace would call using an alias, and give his alias, saying he'd contacted her but been unable to get a call through to emergency services. "Get her out of there."

"On it." He offered a small grimace to the woman in the pit. "I'm going to open the pit, but it's certain to be locked."

"Yes, I have a confirmed person requiring assistance in Antanga National Forest. Air rescue will be required. My authorization code is tango-alpha-lima-alpha." *TALA* was the acronym Alace had mentioned when they were talking about the gear yesterday. He made a note to ask her about it later. "I've been in touch with a person on the ground and am calling a scramble response ASAP to these coordinates."

He blocked out the rest of her call as he walked around the holding pen. When he arrived where he expected to find either a latch or hinges, he explained to the woman in the pen what he was doing. "I'm not leaving. Won't do that. I'll be here until we can get you some help. But we've got to get you out of there."

"Be careful, he's going to be back." Alace's words were overlapped by the first broken utterance from the woman.

"Help me."

"I've got this," he promised both of them. Pulling a gun from the holster strapped to his thigh, he told the woman in the pit, "Go to the other end, protect yourself as best you can." Her eyes bored into him, brown pools of disbelieving despair that nearly broke his heart. "I'm getting you out, okay? I promise."

"He'll hear the gunshot."

That made Owen hesitate for a breath; then he was shaking his head and repeating his instructions. "Go to the other end. I'm getting you out. Boss lady, unless the killer's packing, I doubt he'll return to investigate someone who is clearly well armed. Gut call, and I'm makin' it."

"Got you." He was glad she didn't argue and liked the fact she trusted he could handle not only the situation, but also any repercussions that came about from it.

"On three." He locked gazes with the woman trapped in the pit in the ground and nodded. "One, two" —she lifted her hands and cupped them over her ears, head turning at the last second—"three." The lock split cleanly, with none of the shrapnel he'd feared from a poorly forged device. "Okay. I got this." The top of the pit levered open like a bin, and the woman scrambled towards him on all fours, too anxious to get out of the confining space to attempt to stand. "Come on out. Come here."

"Shift left. Let me scan the woods again. Shoulda launched the drone." He adjusted his body position as Alace had asked, and twisted his torso in a short arc as he released the latch, the woman having made it to the grass beside him. "Okay, you're clear. Take care of her."

"No time to deal with the tech." Owen dropped to his knees next to the woman, who was stretched out flat on the grass.

She looked like she was trying to claw herself away from the pit behind her, muttered phrases interspersed with piercing cries. He managed to isolate a couple of words, and winced as she sobbed, "I'm out. I'm okay. Not dead. I'm out."

"Shhhh. What's your name?" The woman flipped to her back, heels digging into the dirt and grass as she attempted to shove away from him. The stark fear on her face tore at his chest, leaving behind a burning hatred for the bastard who had done this to another human. "I'm not going to hurt you. Are you hungry? Thirsty? I've got water and food." He pointed to the backpack he'd dropped at the other end of the pit, not having even registered when he discarded it, so focused had he been on moving the barrel to see what lay underneath. "A friend has already called the authorities. I expect we'll hear a helicopter within an hour, but I can help you until they get here. What's your name?" It took him a split second, but he remembered the alias Alace had set up for him before he made an irrecoverable mistake. "I'm Mathew, Mathew Smith. You want some water?"

She nodded, short bursts of silent movement, her introverted muttering gone as if she'd never spoken.

"Water, got it. I'm just going to go over and get my pack." Her gaze flicked down and back up to his face, and he realized he was still holding the pistol. "I'm not putting this up just yet. The man, the one who did this to you, if he comes back, I want to be able to keep you safe. I'm going to keep you safe, okay? I'm not going to hurt you. Promise." Owen eased to his feet and took a step away from the woman, seeing how even that small distance gave her more comfort. "I'm just getting my pack."

It continued like that for the next hour. At one point he'd heard a helicopter, but Alace had quickly confirmed it wasn't the one dispatched to his location.

He talked the woman into accepting food and water, and the flimsy-feeling space blanket from his pack. Each thing was yanked from his hand as if he would pull back the offering at the last minute. He watched her eating and couldn't take the way she kept her gaze on him the whole time, glancing away but quickly moving it back to him, ensuring he didn't do anything alarming.

Keeping his communication with Alace on the subvocal level, he asked for updates. While handling the controls of the tiny drone he'd finally launched at her insistence, she was also tracking the information relayed from the police to the forest service, and finally the nearby fire tower. That would likely be the first person they saw, because the helicopter he expected was farther away but on track to arrive within the next thirty minutes.

He asked, not sure he wanted to know what Alace thought but needing to put it out to the universe, "Do you think she was here somewhere when I was here the other day?"

"No way of knowing until she'll give you a name." Keys clacking in the background told him Alace was already trying to solve the mystery. "I've got the names and descriptions of the most recent disappearances you and I thought were suspect. Maybe we can start with those?"

Owen studied the woman currently curled into a tight ball, arms wrapped around the blanket covering her legs, taking up as little space in this wide-open field as possible. He lined up her apparent age with the missing women he'd spent so much time studying and fought a grimace when he realized her likely identity.

"Nyla Davison?" The way her head snapped up gave everything away, and he gave her a small smile even as he heard Alace laughing in his ear. "That's you, right? Nyla?" She nodded slowly. "You went to work but didn't get there. They found your car parked in a car wash."

"There was a man and a little girl standing next to a broken-down car." These first coherent words from her were a revelation, and the first crack in her eerie composure. Tears tracked down her face as she said, "She tried to tell me. I didn't understand, but she told me the boogie man would get me. 'Don't talk to strangers,' she said. 'The boogie man will kill you.' But I didn't listen. I'd stopped, because there was a little girl. I didn't see the van. Didn't see what he did to knock me out. I came to inside the van, and the little girl was tied to me." She sucked in a breath that caught a half a dozen times, gaze fixed on the ground in front of her bare feet. "Locked together. He kept us in the van for days. Then he parked it and was gone for so long I thought we'd die there. Chained to the seats like we were, we couldn't get away. No, we couldn't, could we? No. The earth shook. It shook and was loud, and when he opened the door, it was like thunder; then I woke up here. I woke up in the dirt. In the earth, with dirt over my head. Surrounded by dirt. I'm not dead, am I? I was buried."

"The little girl." Owen knelt, one knee in the dirt, every muscle strung tight. "Where is she?"

"She's dead." Stated so baldly, the woman's matter-of-fact recitation tore the ground out from under Owen. "He said he left her in the van. She was too young, but she was the daughter of a woman he knew. He said he knew me, too. But he didn't. I don't know him." Her voice had gained in volume and pitch as she talked, eyes widening until the white sclera created brilliant slashes across her face. Owen watched as she lost the bit of composure she'd had, tangled hair flopping forward over her bony knees. "I didn't know him. I didn't know what he'd do. I stopped because he had the girl."

"Nyla, you couldn't have known what kind of monster he was. You were doing good, being the responsible citizen and trying to make sure your fellow humans were safe. You did good. You couldn't have known." More than anything, he ached to wrap her in a hug and convince her she was safe now. There was no way she'd accept the touch as comforting, though, so he shoved down the impulse and kept talking to her instead. "You survived, and that's pretty amazing." She settled as he spoke, eyes hidden by the fall of hair, but the tension flowed out of her muscles. "You're here, and alive, and you can tell the authorities about what he's done. You couldn't have known how twisted he was."

"I didn't know." Nyla rocked forward, cheek to the tops of her knees as she stared at the woods. "I'm alive."

"Get her to tell you about him. See what you can get before the rangers show up. They're bringing sheriff's deputies with them, just FYI. I guess the helo they wanted isn't where it needed to be, so they picked a bigger bird." Alace sighed. "Which means because they've got the room, they're bringing more bodies."

He stood and turned his back on the woman, facing the woods as he took several steps away. "Same story we settled on?" He kept his voice low but used the audible version of the mic, not wanting the unsettling sensation he felt when he used the subvocal unit too much. "Did you send the info about the other fields? I want all the women to get home, Alace."

"They will, Owen." Her tone was soothing, and he realized he'd fisted his hands, clenching and releasing over and over. *She's reacting to my tension.* "Each of the bodies will be accounted for and returned to their loved ones. They'll bring in ground radar once they understand the scope of what they're looking at. We'll get them to open those clearings in Idaho again, somehow. You've got this. Okay? You're just the trail runner who stumbled onto a field, disoriented from dehydration so you'd strayed from the main trail. You found a woman and saved her. You got a text out to a friend who happens to be me, but that's all you know. I've pushed that text back to your phone, so you're covered if they want to look. You're making it so every one of his victims will be recovered. And one of them alive. That's a feat in and of itself. You're there and saved Nyla. There's nothing in the woods right now. He's long gone. Stay close to the woman, keep her calm, and she'll be okay."

"You're using the bioshit, aren't you? That's how you knew I was getting freaked?" He choked on a laugh as he finally holstered his gun, feeling somehow not right about laughing in what amounted to a cemetery. *A field of dead.* "Then you're using some serious psychobabble on me."

"It worked, didn't it? I always say to apply the appropriate tools to the job to get the best possible result." Alace sounded pleased with herself, and that did pull a chuckle from him, the humor slipping past his defenses.

"Quit preening. Is Eric there? Eric, can you make her quit now, man?"

"He's downstairs. Do you hear the helo yet? It should be there in minutes."

"Not yet." As he said so, the distinctive thudding sounds reached his ears from the distance, and he shook his head. "Ope, I'm wrong. There it is. Are you tracking the bird, too? I wouldn't put it past you. You're a woman on a mission now. Gonna build your network and then overlay maps and shit until you've got everything organized just how you like it."

"I might be tracking the bird, yes." Alace still sounded self-satisfied. He could hear the grin she wore in the tone she used.

"Well, I might be hearing it coming in from the north." He turned back to where Nyla still sat, face tilted to the side so she could keep him in view without looking directly at him. "You looking to keep the mic active?"

"From the north? That doesn't make sense. Do you want the mic live while you're talking to the rangers and other folks?"

"Yeah. It doesn't hurt for you to hear what goes down. They'll try to take me in with them, but I'm just a trail runner. I don't want nor do I need a rescue. Paperwork for the gun is in order and I don't have anything on me that's concerning. Rest of the tech will go into the hidden pocket of the bag, so no worries there, either. I just need a refill of water and I'll trot my happy ass back to the trailhead and my car. Then home." He tried not to wince at the thought.

No such luck when Alace had all his involuntary information at her disposal.

"What's wrong with your home? I thought you'd settled into the house in New Jersey, Owen. Are you still having problems staying in one place?" She was referring to a period a few months ago when he'd been between missions and had moved housing arrangements seven times in nine weeks.

"No. It's nothing like that." Each house had turned into a nightmare, walls closing in on him with every car door slam in an adjacent driveway. He'd stalked window to window for hours, keeping an eye on any vulnerable approach angles. The kicker had been when he lost his shit over a door-to-door salvation salesman who'd come knocking. That was when he shifted from the city with conveniently close stores and accessible entertainment, and rented a sprawling ranch along the edge of a forest just outside town. "These days my visitors are of the furry and four-footed kind, and the worst that happens is the squirrels running across the roof."

"Then what was that reaction to the idea of going home?"

"You're like a dog with a bone, Alace. Now's not the time to be digging deep." He looked over at the edge of the woods. "Anything on thermal?" The sound of the helicopter was louder now, and Nyla had already hunched her shoulders up around her ears. "They'll be here in minutes. I've got stuff to tuck away."

"Negative. Either he didn't see or hear you and has gone along his jolly way, or the sound of the gunshot scared him off entirely. Is it something you're worried about dealing with on your way back to the car?"

Owen stood and faced the aircraft, arms over his head as he waved widely. "No. I don't expect to run into him. And just sayin', we're both of the opinion that figure was male, right? Which means I was correct when I made my original assumptions." He waved again, turning to keep an eye on the bird as the helo circled their location, finally settling towards the ground a distance away. Even from there, the winds from the whirling blades were still enough to kick up a blinding blizzard of dust and foliage particles, and Owen tucked his face into the crook of his elbow, waiting for the engines to wind down.

"Alace, there's just one guy in this bird." It was a smaller craft, with barely enough room for a copilot seat in front and a narrow bench in the cargo area. "Unless they're lying like cordwood on the floor of the back section, he's all alone. I thought you said they were bringing in a bunch of folks."

"They are. They commandeered an S&R bird, holds like twelve." He could scarcely hear Alace over the noise of the helicopter, and he frowned deeper as he realized the pilot had opened an access port set into the larger side window, but the aircraft didn't seem to be settling in to stay.

Nyla shrieked, hunching forwards with her arms wrapped around her torso. Red bloomed in between her fingers, and he was on the move before the implications fully registered. Diving for the ground, Owen landed on his side, elbows tucked tight to his body, before rolling to his stomach and sighting down the barrel of the gun, not even aware of having pulled it from the holster. A puff of dust less than a foot from his face confirmed the intuitive reaction as the right one.

"What's going on?" Alace was screaming in his ear, but he didn't have time to talk to her. He didn't have time for anything as the man's hand appeared through the sliding window, a black pistol seemingly grafted to his fingers. The barrel turned towards Owen, and he rolled to evade the shot he was certain was coming. He didn't have time to sight or aim but took a shot on the move, his gun swinging from right to left as he pulled the trigger three times. One hit the window just over the man's hand, and the shrapnel from the implosion of the canopy made the man's gun useless. *It's hard to pull triggers without fingers*. His second shot impacted the canopy inches to the side of the first one, and a huge crack split up through the windscreen. His movement had slowed, the arc of the gun's trajectory perfectly lined up so his third shot entered through that crack and pierced the man's throat, a spray of blood and tissue covering the inside of the cabin.

The helicopter jerked and shuddered, then lifted a few inches from the ground before rotating swiftly. For a moment Owen was afraid his final shot hadn't sealed the deal; then the front of the bird dipped abruptly, nose digging into the ground. Angled away from him, the blades impacted yards ahead of the falling helicopter, their whipping motion tossing sod and debris through the air as the blades dug into a holding pen. The resistance was enough to cause the helo to twist to the side, slamming onto the pilot's side as the blades quickly tore themselves apart, now throwing dirt, grass, and bones in a broad circle around the dying aircraft.

The engine whined loudly, and then something gave way inside, because the blade assembly separated from the cabin, flinging to one side. In the sudden silence, Owen realized Nyla was now quiet. He looked to see her barely upright, body slumped to one side, her arms having fallen lax at her sides.

"No, no, no. Dammit." *Threat management first, triage second*. As much as it killed him to leave her as she'd fallen, he didn't hesitate. Couldn't, there wasn't enough time. Sprinting to the helicopter, he swung around the front to come face-to-face with what was left of the man's head, pressed against the only surviving piece of windscreen. No movement and no breathing confirmed the unknown man's change in status, and Owen turned to retrace his steps at a dead run, sliding to a stop on his knees next to the woman.

She'd been hit in the back by a bullet, and the exit wound was gory but placed in such a way he held out hope nothing vital had been hit. Blood pooled in Nyla's lap and was slowly soaking the earth around her as Owen carefully stretched her out flat on the ground.

"How long until the real bird gets here?" His ears were still ringing from the gunshots and the noise from the wreck, so the incoming helicopter might already be within hearing distance but would be undetectable for some time. "You seein' this, boss lady?" Owen stripped his backpack off and dug into it, pulling out a T-shirt that he efficiently cut into strips, using them to quickly bind Nyla's torso. "This is literally an *Old Yeller* bandage, dammit."

"It'll hold her together. See if you can get a pulse and respiration. The helicopter should already be there based on their last coordinates. I'll encourage them to unass and push things."

Owen gripped the woman's wrist in his hand, finger to the pulse point. "Slow, but steady. Respiration is way slow. If they know what they're coming into, it would help."

"I'm on it."

Silence battered at his nerves, and he found himself taking Nyla's pulse again, reciting the numbers to Alace. "That was a DNR-logoed helo. How the hell would the killer have access to a service bird?"

Her voice was calm, soothing as she helped piece the puzzle together. "Remember Nyla talking about the ground shaking? I bet that was how he transported them. It makes sense in all the worst ways. Remember we talked about how hard it would be to get all the shit we found actually through the forest and into the clearings?"

"He didn't go through; he went over. In and out, easy peasy." Owen sat back on his heels. "But what about the Temple chick? Why was she in the woods?"

"Remember how records showed Maddy had been volunteering for the forestry service for several years? Maybe her being on the trail was just a coincidence?" Even as she said the words, Alace laughed. "No, I don't believe in those kinds of coincidences. Or any."

"The setup at their house and these clearings—way too similar to be chance, either."

"Agreed." She cursed abruptly and fluently, and he grimaced at the sound, because Alace ruffled was a novelty he could have done without. "The idiots transposed two segments of the coordinates. They're within three minutes, though, so you'll have help soon."

"I killed the ranger."

"You saved Nyla." Alace huffed. "Self-defense all the way."

He couldn't keep the bitterness from his voice when he told her, "I'm not going to be running out of here today."

"Nope. But I've already got things rolling for you. I know where they'll take you, and in this case, it's actually good that the deputies are along for the ride. We'll set the tone we want from the beginning this way."

"You've got my back, right, boss lady?"

"I will always have your back, Owen Marcus. I will never, ever bail on you. It's you and me, and we're a team." Low and intense, Alace's voice soothed him, leaving behind a sense of belonging he hadn't felt since leaving the military. "Lose the tech. I've got their phones and radios. You are not alone. I've got you."

Before removing and hiding the rig, he responded in the only way that seemed appropriate, knowing she'd still hear him over the rotor wash from the approaching helicopter.

"Besties."

CHAPTER TWENTY-FOUR

Alace

Alace leaned away from her computer, arching and stretching the aching muscles in her back. Her palm found the upper curve of her stomach, fingers running along the outline of a foot pressed there. "Are you absolutely certain you have to do that?" As if in response, the foot flexed and pushed harder; then the shape of her belly changed, shifting, and now it was the larger bulge of a butt that pressed against her hand. "Okay, clearly you know what you're doing."

It had taken two different ultrasounds until her obstetrician was confident they had a good idea of when the baby would be born. Of course, it had taken three obstetricians before Alace was confident she had a doctor she could trust. Fortunately for everyone, this guy seemed to have staying power, because Eric had threatened to pick a doctor for her if she hadn't settled finally.

For dating the pregnancy, Alace's irregular cycles hadn't helped, but after the last test when the doc had finally announced she was eighteen weeks pregnant, the panic had set Alace's heart racing. Nearly halfway through a pregnancy without knowing about it didn't make it sound like she was as aware of everything as she wanted to be.

In the three months since finding out she was pregnant, Alace had experienced a continuing assault from a wide and confusing array of emotions. She pressed two fingers against each tear duct, holding back the stinging sensation that started whenever the baby interacted with her this way.

A glance at the clock in the corner of the monitor had her leaning forwards, hands extended, only to sit back abruptly when the baby shifted again, making her displeasure known. *Her.* Alace drifted her palms down both sides of her abdomen, fingers caressing the slope of her belly. Their daughter was only weeks away from making her entrance into the world, and that knowledge made Alace simultaneously ecstatic and terrified.

Instead of leaning, Alace grabbed the edge of the desk and tugged her chair close enough to reach the keyboard more easily. If her daughter wanted a little extra room in her belly while Mommy backed out of the servers and darknet, then her little girl could have it. She had timed her shut-down routine perfectly, it seemed, when she heard the downstairs door open and close. The monitors showed Eric, chin angled to the camera, flashing her a wide grin he knew she'd see.

She'd removed the battery and stowed it and the laptop in the safe inside the locking drawer by the time he walked through the door. Alace was on her feet and moving—well, waddling—in his direction so they met in the middle of the room, just beside the foot of the bed.

After the doctor lifted the bedrest restriction, it hadn't seemed worth the effort of moving her office again, so for the duration of the pregnancy, she had accepted Eric's proclamation that it remain where it was. Mostly because sharing the bedroom made it easy to nap between bouts of work. So much of what she did was during nighttime that it also made it simple for Eric to keep watch over her.

The final benefit was it made it easier to go from being Alace Sweets, criminal mastermind with one main hunter, to simply Eric's sweet Alace.

Lifting on her toes, she reached up and threaded her fingers through the hair on the back of his head, tugging him down until he covered her mouth with his. Heat coiled in her belly, and she moaned softly, knowing how much he liked to hear how he affected her.

"My baby need me?" His murmured question against her mouth had been a constant refrain over the past month or so. Once she'd settled into the pregnancy and her body had become accustomed to the hormones and physical changes, Alace found her internal engines were revved up. Not just in terms of heat, although Eric claimed she was now a furnace at night—but she was horny *all* the freaking time. "Baby."

That word. That fucking, fucking word, when spoken in that specific softly guttural tone, tore her breath from her throat.

Eric never feared showing her how he felt, what he wanted, how much she pleased him. The entire relationship thing had come so much easier to him than she could understand. Where she still fumbled and tried to interpret actions and words, he reacted immediately, seeming to simply know what came next. She fought against it, but at times, her terror over getting it wrong would freeze her in place. *If he said this, does he mean that and expect some other thing?*

Unlike her, Eric had patience in spades, and he never seemed flustered at having to help her along. Like a baby deer on a frozen pond, her efforts at moving them forwards sometimes sent her spinning out of control, and Eric was always there with a hand, ready to steady her. Alace thanked God every day that they had somehow beaten the odds, coming together in unforgettable ways.

"Yes." Her eventual response was breathless and needy, and Eric swept his arms around and under her, lifting and carrying her to the bed. He made it seem effortless, as if she drifted to land lightly on the center of the mattress, his long body stretched out beside her. One hand underneath her to unfasten her bra, his other shoved her shirt up and out of the way. Alace took over removing it completely as Eric's attention fastened to what had become arguably some of the more sensitive areas on her body.

His lips ghosted across one plump nipple, the edge of his teeth grazing the hardening nub. Palming her opposite breast, kneading it gently, he continued to tease the one with mouth, tongue, and teeth until she arched up against him. Eric responded by latching on and sucking, drawing her deep into his mouth, his tongue lashing across the nipple with each cheek-hollowing pull. Magical strings connected her breasts to her core, sparks erupting between her legs, and she pressed her thighs together.

"Eric." He read the urgency in her tone and shifted, changing sides to mouth at her other breast. One hand slipped down, and she felt the corners of her mouth curl up when his palm stopped on her rounded belly. While still worshiping her breasts, he drew his hand

and fingers over the swell that marked where she sheltered their child. He hooked a finger in the waistband of her pants and stretched the elastic out, pulling it down to expose her stomach. Protruding bellybutton, dark line extending down around the bottom half of the beachball-sized bulge, silver and purple stretchmarks—none of that mattered to Eric. She didn't have to hear him say it to know, either. He made it clear by how he turned what she'd originally seen as negatives into things he cherished. *Evidence of our love*, he'd said the one time she'd asked about his reaction.

Alace wiggled her hips and shoved at her remaining clothes, slipping them down her legs. She turned on her side, facing away from Eric as she gripped his hand and pulled it to cover the breast he'd been playing with. Face-to-face sex had become uncomfortable for her a couple of weeks ago, and he hadn't skipped a beat, switching to various positions until they found one she liked almost as well. Nothing matched having the chance to watch Eric's face as he fell apart, but she'd take the closeness of having him inside her any way she could.

His hand slipped between her legs and he groaned. "Always so wet for me, beloved. Always what I need."

With her heel curled around the back of his leg, the brush of skin against skin was drugging as he nestled himself closer and gave a lazy push of his hips. The heat from his hard cock branded her skin as it glided along her soaked entrance. "Don't tease."

"I'd never dare." The laughter rumbling through his words made her grin, face turned so she could see his expression. "My baby gets what she wants." Eric's blunt fingers dipped inside, and he thrust shallowly as Alace's breathing quickened. She'd been aching for his touch, and this was stoking the fire inside her. "And if my baby wants me." He held her open and she arched her back, ass eagerly angled for what was coming next. "Then my baby gets all of me." He filled her on a slow, controlled push, not stopping until he was buried deep inside her. His fingers retreated to nestle alongside her clit, trapping it with a firm twist, the pressure making Alace's hips writhe uncontrollably underneath his touch.

Eric eased into a gentle, deliberate tempo, his deep groans carried on the breaths gusting past her ear. His features carried a tension as his gaze stayed centered on her. The intent scrutiny would have bothered her a year ago, but now knowing she was his sole focus was a turn-on.

Everything's a turn-on.

"What's funny, baby?"

Alace didn't answer as she twisted her neck and rolled her shoulder against his chest in a silent demand. He captured her mouth with a hard kiss, one that ramped up immediately and bordered on inferno.

She lost his hand between her legs, but the attentive tweaks and twists his fingers gave her nipples were entirely worth it.

"Alace." Eric's mouth pressed against her ear, her name followed by a reverberating groan. "You shouldn't laugh at a man—" Eric pushed deep inside and held there, muscles of the arm underneath her touch strained and shaking. "—when he's about to lose himself to you." Muscles in his abdomen jerked and jumped behind her, and his hips shuddered forwards and back. "Jesus, baby."

When she nipped his bottom lip, his hips faltered with lost rhythm; then he redoubled his pace, the slapping of flesh against flesh now echoing around the room. His caresses changed, grew rougher, fingers teasing the nipples in between plumping strokes of her breasts.

The telltale uterine contractions started, and Alace huffed out a moan when the baby flipped and rolled inside her, glad the sensation didn't slow the rush of her body to orgasm. Alace gripped Eric's wrist and forearm, holding tight. The sensation built, pleasure stacking up in a towering structure that needed only the touch of Eric's mouth to the side of her face to topple it. Her body tensed and released, tensed and released as the sensation crashed over her, the wash of feelings and emotion burying her control and she wailed out Eric's name.

When she surfaced, it was to the indescribably beautiful sensation being tucked against his side, head on his shoulder as his hands glided across every inch of her flesh he could reach. Including the mound of her stomach. As his touch slowed, his hands returned to the baby belly repeatedly, until they came to rest protectively folded over her stomach.

"I luuuv you. Moar than ican explain." Her slurred words were hilarious, and one corner of Alace's mouth crooked up. She laughed and then complained, "I soun funny."

"Love drunk." Eric's quiet description was a chuckling murmur against the top of her head. She shivered and he shifted underneath her until she made a complaining noise, menacing his pec with the edge of her teeth. "Hey now, none of that. You're cold." A blanket drifted into place over her, edge drawn up to her shoulder. "I was getting my woman some covers." His hands returned to their previous position, cradling their baby. "I luuuv you, too."

Alace's eyes were closed and the covers cocooned her warmly where she lay pressed against his side. She turned her head aga n, but instead of threatening a bite, this time she pressed a kiss to his chest.

"I luuuv you moar."

CHAPTER TWENTY-FIVE

Owen

Hunkered over his camp stove, Owen found himself humming a classic arena anthem from one of his favorite bands. He glanced around the campsite. A thick screen of closely growing trees, ferns, and other undergrowth was doing a great job of blocking the wind, but unfortunately for his nerves, it was also cutting off any possible sightlines.

Nothing evil waited for him in these woods, though. He'd hiked them often enough to be able to say that with confidence.

Unlike what had happened out west.

Suppressing a shudder, he forced the image of a dead man from his mind. It had been three months since the serial killer no one had expected set his helicopter down only yards away from where Owen had stood, desperately signaling for rescue.

Holding Nyla together with what amounted to rope and hope wasn't something he'd soon forget. Her piteous cries, terror escalating when the second helicopter had swung in a tight circle over the clearing, wouldn't be easily forgotten, either. Owen had played the shell-shocked innocent well enough the deputies took his rendition of the events at face value. The ranger had been outed to the world as the Deep Woods Killer, as the tabloids had decided to call him. Owen and Alace thought his kill count was higher than the authorities would ever attribute to him, and the motives were murky as hell.

Or had been until Alace got Owen into the hospital to interview Mackie, posing as the research assistant to a well-known author.

Maddy had met Leon Bellowship first, and after a few coy encounters with the ranger, had shared about her activities during her previous year at camp, anger and pain over her mother's death expressed in a bloody fashion. Bellowship had already been angling down the same path, his kills restricted to more remote locations, targeting only isolated hikers, where the risk was minimal. Maddy had cultivated him as a partner, showing him the ins-and-outs of long-term imprisonment and how satisfying it could be to feed the brutal perversion in their souls.

Then she'd introduced Mackie to him, and her sister's self-destructive nature aligned even more perfectly with Bellowship's sadistic one.

When their original killing fields farther north had been discovered, suddenly the little trio of darkness had found themselves needing to relocate their activities. Mackie's supposed boyfriend in Utah had been a distraction, a way to throw any suspicion off the trail. The girls' public falling-out had been staged, all part of the overall plan to have better access. Alace groused about that information until Owen had finally dragged it out of her that she'd thought differently.

Bellowship was a helicopter pilot, flying both privately and for the forestry service. His skills made it simple to get the abducted women and girls into the deep woods, bringing the tools of their trade along with them. Then Mackie got lost inside her head, doggedly staying at the active killing field to watch her "guests" ever more closely. That had led to the boyfriend reporting her missing.

Maddy had been going back and forth often, caring for their grandfather, ensuring the pot was regularly stirred in regards to Mackie's "disappearance." Todd had been her way to keep tabs on what the authorities truly thought.

As Owen talked to Mackie, the medication he'd dosed her with started to wear off, and when he'd seen the bright interest in her gaze turned on him, he'd gotten up and walked out. Alace had captured ample footage to ensure the women would never be released. He shivered. The possibility of the twins one day walking the sidewalks gave him a chill.

That right there? He shook his head and used a short stick to position the fuel cube before he set his pan of water in place. *That's what's wrong with your shit these days, Marcus.*

That hadn't been the first time Owen had been betrayed during a supposed rescue, and the dreams he'd suffered with since that night continued to underscore how not "over" he was—with everything.

Between old dreams and new nightmares, he'd told Alace he was taking a couple of weeks for himself.

With Alace's reputation, he could stay as busy as he wanted. Not out of financial consideration, because he'd been set for money years ago with various accounts held in the stereotypical offshore banks. No, the reason he kept working was personal. Something he didn't think Alace even knew, and his boss lady knew so much more about him than he was comfortable with.

Since closing the books on Bellowship and the Temples, Owen had accepted and completed four more missions.

Each of them had surrounded his personal vendetta, sex trafficking.

Soul cleansing work.

He could eliminate the traffickers with prejudice, but while he'd gone into the secure ward of the hospital expecting to deliver a lethal dose of the drug he'd had with him, in the end he couldn't. In his mind, Mackie would forever be tied to that tiny girl who'd been so betrayed, and it didn't feel right to play at being her judge and jury.

So he'd done a one-eighty and dived deep into the underbelly of America instead.

Alace's darknet identities had vouchered him into a variety of different rings, and while the ease with which he was able to adopt the sick bastards' language always turned Owen's stomach, it was how you got in and stayed in.

Alace's personas were long-established and carried a lot of clout, so when he'd registered one of his deep-cover identities for a new forum dedicated to pedos bidding on sibling pairs, her sponsorship had gotten him into the inner ranks within hours.

Once in, he found he'd missed an auction by a couple of weeks, the winning bids showing underneath the pictures of the children who'd been bought and sold. Digging deeper, he'd uncovered plans for several additional upcoming auctions. The idea of not doing whatever he could to stop them wasn't something he could stomach.

Each sting had only been allowed around three weeks from inception to culmination, and as he'd walked out of the final riverfront warehouse leaving bloody boot prints behind, he'd told Alace he needed time. The memories of the children and young people locked behind wire fencing, in some cases electrified, made sleep a stranger if he allowed himself to dwell on them too much.

"Mister." The little boy who'd called out to Owen couldn't have been more than eight. He sat in the center of a tiny pen, his younger sister cradled in his lap.

"Grok, don't bother." That came from a pen across the aisle, just wide enough to move two abreast. "Don't matter he's new; he's shit just like the rest of 'em." The two boys in that holding pen were slightly older than the other pair, probably twelve and ten years old. It was the younger boy who'd spoken up. His older brother was curled on the cement floor, head resting on the younger sibling's lap. Fearing the worst, Owen stared hard, unable to tell if the boy's chest still rose and fell. If he were breathing, it was shallowly. "Don't look at my brother."

Owen lifted his gaze to the younger boy's face. Anger and resignation branded what should have been childish features, giving the child a mature cast to his expression Owen never wanted to see again. Softly he asked, "Is he okay? He looks sick."

"You're sick. You're one of them and you're all sickos." The boy's fingers patted the sleeping boy's hair, palm coming to rest on his forehead. "Leave us alone."

Owen swept the warehouse with his gaze, rage bubbling just underneath the surface. This ends tonight, he thought. Six rows wide by nearly thirty cages deep, the building could house more than three hundred children when paired two into an enclosure. It was currently about one-half full.

He was there under the guise of looking over the offerings. The murmuring wave of sound that followed the other men who were strolling around made him sick. Cries of pain and fear, some shouts of anger—it all pounded against the walls in impotent protest. Each of the men, including Owen, had their faces covered by cheap plastic masks, and every breath he exhaled washed back over his face, heating his skin. A precaution, just in case any of the children regained their freedom. A tenuous chance, if things were allowed to progress through the upcoming auction, but a chance nonetheless. These were buyers selecting stock for upcoming transactions.

Owen's cover was a party ring in Minnesota. Seventeen real men who had paid him exorbitant fees to acquire assets according to their tastes. Half up front, half upon delivery.

He let his lip curl in anger. The deliveries would be happening tomorrow, but instead of children inside the vans, there would be a much different cargo. Significantly hotter, and presented with force. He couldn't even consider the drivers he'd hired as collateral damage because they were involved with the ring, too, understanding very well what they helped facilitate. Looking the other way for a paycheck would become very expensive for them.

He'd placed the final bomb himself last weekend, and the proximity triggers attached to each of them were the best Alace could buy.

It didn't matter how good these motherfuckers thought they were.

I'm better.

"Mister." That was the little boy again, and Owen crouched next to the wire, careful not to touch it with any part of his body. The way the boy huddled in the center of the cage told him all he needed to know.

"Yeah, buddy?" Owen wanted to push up the mask, wanted to pull off the hood covering his hair and neck. Wanted to show the boy not everyone in this building was a monster. Not yet. *He had two goals tonight, neither of which would be achieved by tipping his hand too soon. "You need something?"*

"Natalie is awful quiet." The boy's hand trembled as he stroked his little sister's hair. "I can't wake her up."

"Owen." He closed his eyes when he heard the pain in Alace's voice. "He's just a...she's so small."

"Mmhmm." The boy was staring at him, a single tear tracking down his cheek. Owen leaped to a decision. "I'm going to help your...Natalie?" The boy nodded. He restated the promise, hoping the boy heard the truth in his words. "I'm going to help Natalie."

"No you won't." It was the naysayer from behind him, and Owen tried to ignore that bare thread of hope he heard in the boy's voice. Hope that he was wrong and maybe Owen wouldn't turn out to be one of the bad guys after all. "You're a sicko liar."

He shifted and stared out at the sea of cages. Color and movement marked the occupied ones. Way too many for what he had planned, and even with changes in the scale of the plan, it was a slim chance of success.

"Plans have changed, boss lady." He'd gotten better at the subvocal aspect of the com unit Alace preferred. The active mic was woven in the gold thread along the edge of one pocket of his current costume while the subvocal mic had been placed on his skin, covered by a thin prosthetic to hide it from view. The rest of his jaw and throat were covered by a different set of foam and latex appliances that aged him and provided a scar-riddled disguise. "I need a high hide."

"It's a fucking warehouse, Owen."

He pushed to his feet and stared down at the little boy. "What's your name?" Natalie's brother stared at him, bottom lip quivering. "I'm going to do my best, okay?"

"Are you for real?" Owen swung to look down at the other pair of children. The older was still sleeping—or unconscious, he thought—while the younger one was glaring up, his ferocious gaze piercing.

"Yeah. I'm for real." To prove it, he tipped the mask up, giving the boy a glimpse of his face. He wouldn't know it wasn't really Owen's face, but it might give him the courage to survive the next thirty minutes. "I'm very for real."

"He's Tony." The boy tipped his head towards the still little boy seated with his sister. "I'm Nate and this is Walt, my brother."

"Nate, Walt, Tony, Natalie." He was glad the subvocal utility recognized each of the names, a downfall of the software which he and Alace had tried to train out of it. As they'd gone through and added words to the database, the incidents of "translation not available" had virtually dried up.

"Got it." Alace huffed out a sigh, the sound she made when she'd found something that pleased her. Hopefully it meant she had a place for him to get to where he could familiarize himself with the weaponry he'd be taking off a guard in about two minutes. "Hallway to the south of the entrance you used coming

in, there's a set of stairs that leads to what's probably an observation area."

Owen kept his attention focused on Nate, not looking for the viewing ports that had to be located above him. "Hang in there, buddy." He settled the mask back into place and reminded him, "I'm for real."

Turning on his heel, he stalked back along the aisle, chin angled down as if studying the floor while his eyes tracked up.

"I can't see anything." Alace's complaint wasn't rhetorical. The camera they'd selected was built into the prosthetics overlying the shell of one of his ears. With his hood up and head down, she probably had a very limited field of view. "I'm going to have to take out their drones so I can put mine in place. I think you need to know how many people are upstairs."

"Body heat from the prisoners will mask everything. Do not do anything to alert them yet." He reached the end of the aisle and turned towards the front of the building, coming to an abrupt halt when a beefy man stepped in front of him. "Get out of my way." He'd found the men wealthy enough to be able to afford to pander to their depravity were not the kind who would tolerate being stymied, by anything. He stepped to the side and shoved past the man, ignoring the grasping fingers that plucked at his clothing. Another three strides and he was through the door. He heard the rustling movement of the guard he'd brushed off and

knew he would have to deal with the threat before moving towards his destination. "Positive note," he added via the subvocal, "he has what I need." The man had been armed with what looked to be standard issue semiautomatic weaponry.

"Small favors." Alace gave another of those tiny huffs. "Found their subnet and I am in." That was good news, because when he'd made it past the initial wand sweep and pat-down area into the warehouse itself, she'd been still trying to determine if what they'd found earlier encompassed their entire computer network. She already controlled their cameras and alarms, but this would probably give her access to the data behind the group. "Downloading everything I find. They don't have even the most basic of safeguards in place."

"Stupid bad guys." He swung left into the partially hidden hallway and stepped into the first doorway he found. He reached behind himself and groped for the doorknob, gripping and turning it to push the door ajar. The guard bustled through the entryway and put on a burst of speed upon spying the apparently empty hall. It was the work of moments to grab him as he was running past and use the momentum to dent the man's temple against the doorframe. Owen altered the falling man's trajectory towards the open door, catching him under the shoulders to drag the body into the darkened room. He glanced at the closed head wound and used his thumb to peel up first one eyelid then the other. The satisfaction he felt at the unevenly

dilating pupils would bother him later. The trauma would be enough to guarantee this guard was eliminated from any upcoming fight, and without medical intervention, probably wouldn't survive. Efficiently stripping the man of the weapon he'd been cradling, as well as a heavy revolver strapped to his waist, Owen ducked out of the room, pulling the door closed behind him.

"You're quick." Owen allowed himself a tiny grin at the honest praise from Alace. "I've got their drone cams now, too. I don't have to disable them after all, looks like they've got pretty decent thermal. I can count three guards in that whole upper room, which looks to span the length of the building. There are internal walls, though, so someone could be masked by something as stupid as a furnace vent, Owen. I can't give you specifics, not enough. Not like I want to."

"We got this, boss lady." He took the steps two at a time, pausing at the top of the stairs. "Anyone close?"

"Ten feet to your left. Not distinct enough to tell what direction they're facing. Maybe my drones would have been better." He grinned at her tech-disparaging sigh. He suspected that while Alace would have rather had her own tools, she could have taken a paper towel roll and some tinfoil and made something happen.

Easing the door open a crack gave him a decent enough view of the dimly lit room. As Alace had already noted, it was long and narrow, with a low ledge running along the wall that faced the main floor. Openings appeared at intervals, disguised from the outside by fabric that waved gently in the breeze from the climate control. He saw three guards, all facing away from him, which accounted for the bodies Alace had seen.

Creeping along the edge of the room, he took advantage of a deeply shadowed angle of the wall to handle his first target. The man went down without a sound, the heavy thud of pistol butt against skull a quiet, hollow noise. bones just behind his ear fragmenting and piercing the brain matter easily. Owen folded him into a nearby chair, hoping if one of the other guards turned around the man would simply appear to be taking a break.

Neither of the two remaining men moved, which allowed Owen to slip up behind the second guard unseen. Thinner and shorter, he was a good candidate for a rear chokehold, which was what Owen did. Applying downward pressure to the top of the man's head, he held the guard's feet off the ground until the kicking stopped. Knowing he'd been incapacitated for only a brief time, he settled that man's back against the outer wall as he kept his gaze on the third man.

It wasn't until he was right upon him that Owen realized what had so distracted the men. A computer monitor showed live video of a small room with a handful of armchairs scattered across the floor. There was a slim platform ct one end of the room, and upon that stood the man Owen had identified as the mastermind behind the entire organization. Shit. The bidding had begun. That was why the guard downstairs had tried to stop Owen from leaving and why the warehouse had become so unexpectedly quiet. Each chair shown in the broadcast held a man with a differently colored paddle, a way to identify the identically masked individuals. His breath caught when he realized there were children chained to the leg of each chair. Owen's heart dropped as he saw the way the men were using what was intended as the entertainment. His cover identity was expected to be in that room, but none of the chairs stood empty, which could mean only one of two things. Either they only seated the buyers anticipating bidding on the next few lots, or they'd pulled a chair, which would mean they knew he was missing.

Alone in this room with the single guard, he no longer had to worry about making noise, so he shoved the pistol against the back of the man's neck. The guy froze at the touch, which was the reaction Owen had hoped for.

"Wanna live?" The question earned him a silent nod, and he wondered how the people who ran this organization couldn't see that money alone didn't earn loyalty. "How many guards total?"

"Twelve on each shift." That number matched what Owen knew, which was good. Meant the guy wasn't lying in an effort to lull him into a sense of

complacency. "Nerds have their own guard." He made an aborted move to jerk his head back towards the stairs, stopping when it pressed the muzzle deeper into his flesh. "Just one needed there. Three up here. Four for the floor and four for the events."

"Cool." Owen plucked a wide-bladed knife from a sheath at the man's hip. "You get that, boss lady?" He grunted with the effort as, using a smooth motion of thrust-and-twist, he severed the man's spinal cord, allowing the weight of the body to drag it off the knife.

"Roger. Are you headed down now?"

"Gotta clean up after myself first." Retracing his steps, he used the knife to end the other two guards, the slick sound of the wet blade sliding through flesh loud in the quiet room.

"Anything else on this level I need to know about, boss lady?" Owen pushed the mask on top of his head and reached out to brush the fabric covering one of the slit windows slightly aside. From here he could see the entire warehouse floor. "Four on the floor, that's stupid." Alace snort-laughed in his ear. "Stop it, boss lady. Tell me what I need to worry about."

"Nothing up there. The nerds, as he so elegantly put it, have been isolated, and I've disabled the lock on their door. They don't know it yet, of course." Silence on the open line was interrupted by her keyboard clacking and clicking. "Owen, I found schematics for what looks like a secondary suppression system, but

it's not rated for the kind of water pressure a building that size would need."

"You think they've got a termination plan in play." He went back and cut a shoelace free from a guard's boot, then used that to secure the fabric in a makeshift drape. It would be less obvious from the floor if the fabric was still in place, but he didn't want to be fighting to see around it. The two inches he'd created at the bottom would be all the space he'd need. He ejected the magazine from the rifle and checked it, pushing down on the top cartridge to find the container full. Perfect. "Makes sense. None of the guards or other employees have their faces covered. The kids would be able to identify them."

"If they got out." Alace's voice had turned cold, steady as steel. "What's the plan?"

"The plan is I kill these motherfuckers." The running narration stumbled and inserted, "Translation not available." His laugh almost escaped and he barely choked it back. "Okay, that was hilarious. We need to teach the system swears." He propped the barrel of the rifle on the window ledge and knelt behind it. "I am using an unfamiliar weapon, so there might be a moment or two of adjustment. I got this, Alace. The sound will bounce off the walls and by the time they locate me, they will be dead."

"The auction room is through that wall opposite where you are."

Owen paused. "The walls are not thick." She made a sound. "There are kids in that room, Alace. Did you see the monitor they were watching?"

"I've got the stream, yes."

Owen chewed on his bottom lip, thinking. "Can you get into their radios? Do we know the frequency? What if you bring one or two of those guards back into the main room of the building? That would leave only two for the auction and they would be more cautious about coming out and leaving the event exposed. Make them slower to react."

"Lemme see what I can do." A moment later, a radio crackled to life behind him and he grinned. "...us a hand." Alace was in stereo, with one version female, the real one in his head, and one a muffled male voice, the one coming from the radio unit in the room.

"Say again?"

Owen studied the guards below him, convinced none of them was the speaker. Which was good, because just those two words screamed military, which was a complication he didn't want or need.

"Say again control. Did not copy."

"...with the door. Give us a..." The crackling static that broke up her words was genius. Instead of using a name or phrase that might be a hint it wasn't one of the actual guards speaking, interjecting static provided a fill-in-the-blank communication that

sounded plausible. If they weren't on high alert—which they weren't but should be due to buyers being on site, just saying—then the guards would simply hear what they expected to hear.

"Jesu—" The muttered transmission was cut off in mid-word and Owen settled himself. There was a door in the opposite wall. Aiming his confiscated rifle at the bottom of the door, he pulled in a slow, deep breath. It opened and he fired. The trigger never came to rest, already being depressed even as the hot cartridge was ejected, shiny cylinder flying through the air. The second man fell on top of the first and Owen slid to the side, pressure applied to the trigger again as his next target came into view. He kept a mental tally as he went. Three. The silence was so profound he didn't know if it was a result of the gunfire or his focus. Didn't matter right now. The next target was on the move, but it was an easy adjustment to nail him from the back. He fell and the barrel of the rifle moved again, lining up precisely as Owen's finger depressed the trigger a fifth time. Four. He missed, grunting in disappointment as he adjusted and fired again. He didn't watch the man fall, looking for the final guard. Five. He saw a rifle pointed his direction but didn't flinch as the wood and metal above his head took a hit, shards and splinters flying. He released the last of his initial breath as the man fell, blood spraying in a wide arc behind him.

Six.

He shifted back to the entrance that had been his initial target, pleased to see the two men had fallen far enough inside the room that the door had closed fully.

"What the hell's going on?" That was definitely not military guy on the radio, and Owen had a moment to relish the panic in this man's tone.

Alace responded to the question with a blatant downplaying of what had transpired. "...still having trouble. Nothing to worr—" The radio cut off, and in Owen's ear, she said, "Two more targets coming your way. Not guards. The last two are staying put in the auction room."

The door opened and he saw two men in white button-down shirts standing and gawping at the bodies lying on the floor in front of them. Three shots later their bodies had wedged the door open. Seven, eight.

"Time to go on the offensive." He collected the magazines from the three guards in the room with him and went down the stairs the same way he'd come up them, his pace fast but controlled. As he crossed the room, Owen glanced up the aisle he'd been walking earlier and saw Nate's gaze fixed on him. The boy fucking dipped his chin at him, granting Owen a single nod as if in approval. Owen gestured, making a motion for the boy to get down, and Nate ducked; then Owen saw the other boy, Tony, duck too. Nate, Walt, Tony, Natalie. *They were as protected as he could make*

them until he finished clearing those involved with the warehouse and auction. Everything for the kids. *"Got anything for me, boss lady?"*

"No change in the targets' behavior. I don't think the sound was truly audible in the auction room after all. They're carrying on like nothing's happened." He heard a soft sound that lifted into a tune and realized Alace was humming. A lullaby. Surreal didn't cover how bizarre this moment felt. *"There."* Pipes rattled overhead and he glanced up. *"Just in the auction room, and only enough to put them all to sleep. The kids don't need to have these memories."*

"How did you know to trust what was in their system?"

"Delivery receipts. They have everything digitized, so it wasn't hard to find." Alace cleared her throat. *"What's the plan?"*

Speaking plainly, leaving nothing to chance, he told her, "None of those bastards walks out of here alive. If I let them live, they will get off on a technicality." He knew that for a fact, because half the buyers he had paper on so far had been busted for pedophilia before, with none of them serving any time. A combination of corrupt officials and skilled lawyers, paired with unlimited funds, had bought their freedom. *"They stay here and get made official, names splashed in the news as they are identified, or—better yet—disappear entirely, and you can assume their identities, help us flush out even more bastards like them." He paused in front of the door he knew led into the auction room. "Am I good to enter?"*

The pipes rattled again, and he saw the door settle more firmly into the frame, as if something had pushed against it. "Yeah, I just cleared the gas to be sure."

He steadied his breathing, slowing his heartrate and dialing in the focus he'd need for the next few minutes.

"Owen?" Alace sounded pensive, almost as if she needed reassurance.

He gave it to her. Trust in a word, knowing she'd understand. They were partners, in this together, and he needed to hear her thoughts on how to proceed. Sure he had his preferences, but friends didn't ride roughshod over their allies. "Yeah?"

When she spoke again, it was no surprise the steel was back in her voice as she echoed his own words back to him in affirmation. "Kill the motherfuckers."

That was an order he would be happy to act upon. Still, he needed to tweak Alace just the tiniest amount. He gave it a two-beat pause, then sang out, loud and clear, "Yes, ma'am."

Owen shook himself free from the memories. After first removing the unconscious children from the auction room, he'd left behind an abattoir. It had taken him nearly five hours to organize and carry out the release of the other children and young adults who had been kidnapped and kept for sale. Turning off the fence charges, locating all the necessary keys, digging into storerooms for clothing for the kids—it all took time. Some of them had been in their cages at that location for weeks, and some had been taken months ago and only moved to the warehouse recently. He'd seen at least two pairs that looked shellshocked, and when he asked found out they'd been kidnapped the previous evening.

Nate had been the first child he'd released. Tony right after. Then he'd watched as those resilient eight- and ten-year-old boys had organized the kids closest to them, keeping everyone calm until he could get them outside.

Only once they were safely installed in a nearby church gymnasium—door efficiently jimmied open for access—had Owen gone back and made five dead men vanish forever. Then he'd torched the warehouse and attached buildings. He and Alace had agreed at every step along the way, and it was freeing to not be the sole decision-maker on the mission. *Another thing to make sure I tell Alace.*

Finally satisfied the kids were safe and the bad guys dispatched—nerds included—he'd been walking away when he dialed the cops, staying on the line long enough to ensure the dispatcher had their priorities straight: kids over property. That burner had been one he'd tossed into a river five miles away.

Owen rocked back on his heels and lifted his head, staring into the darkness overhead. Stars flickered, showing themselves between the sweeping branches of the pine trees. The weather was perfect, the location even more so, and he didn't have anything on his schedule for a minimum of eight days.

His time to regroup and recharge and put the scenes from the past few months behind him.

After that, he'd be back out into civilization and would reach out to Alace.

She'd line him up with another mission and he'd gladly go.

Owen closed his eyes, relying on memory to draw in the details of the child's face. Natalie had been so little. Her brother fierce in his protection of her. Tiny defender of a tinier fighter.

They were both so fragile.

So easily damaged.

Just like his Emma had been.

EPILOGUE

The old man climbed slowly from the cab of his truck, arching his back as he stretched out from the hours-long drive just concluded. Shame he had to live so far from his playground. He grinned down at the pack flowing around his legs as he walked to the rundown shack straight ahead. The stairs creaked and groaned, and the pack's feet scuffed across the wood of the porch, nails clicking as they surged forwards when he opened the door.

Inside, he steadied the lantern as he opened the access to the wick. A quick flick of his wrist and a sputtering flame appeared at the end of the wooden match held between thumb and finger. Held to the oil-saturated fabric, the wick greedily accepted the flame as it spread across the top edge. He trimmed it, rolling the wick to a height that cast a steady glow around the single room.

Boots toed off, he scolded one of the pack when they threatened to abscond with his footwear. In an instant, the animal's head dropped low, neck plunging from between slumped shoulders.

"Oh, here now. No need for that." He crouched and held out a hand, letting the animal approach, claws scraping the wood as it came close. He ran his fingers through the tangled hair on top of its head, smoothing it to one side as the animal leaned into the touch, a seldom-experienced pleasure.

He pushed upright and drew his glance across the pack, seeing a couple that were in poorer physical condition than he liked to keep them. He made a mental reminder to set their food aside, giving them a chance to eat without dealing with the normal scrapping and fighting the pack did at mealtime. They were a sibling pair, and the most recent addition to the pack, something he suspected played into their challenges.

"It takes a while to get used to it, but you'll be fine." He bent over and snapped his fingers, frowning when the male locked gazes aggressively. "Get over here now." Another snap of his fingers called them to him, and he used both hands to smooth and scratch, cradling the female underneath her jaw, holding her in place as he looked her over.

The skin along her back and sides was marred with scrapes from claws, and he saw the distinct marks of teeth imprinted in her flesh. "Oh, honey. You gotta stop fighting." She looked up at him, watery eyes blinking as she trembled in his grip. Her brother shoved between them, pushing her to the side and taking her place at the man's feet. With his square, blunt teeth bared, the male's lips were pulled back in a quiet snarl, his emerald green eyes flashing angrily. He snapped at the man's fingers, coming close to connecting and received a solid thump on his nose for his trouble. The male's mouth opened wide, and he sucked in a shocked breath.

"Don't touch my sister."

The shout rocked the air in the cabin, casting silence onto the rest of the pack, each of the mix of children and dogs pulling away from the pair, not wanting to get caught up in the confrontation.

"Boy." The man's mouth twisted to the side, his contorted expression revealing the endless pit of rage that always simmered just under the surface, something he never could completely quell. "You shouldn't oughta done that."

~

THANK YOU SO MUCH FOR READING
Seeking Worthy Pursuits!

This story is the second in what will be at least a three book series. I'm so pleased you've taken this journey with me and my dark characters, and I hope you enjoyed and rooted for Alace and Owen as much as I did.

ABOUT THE AUTHOR

Raised in the south, *Wall Street Journal* & *USA TODAY* bestselling author MariaLisa learned about the magic of books at an early age. Every summer, she would spend hours in the local library, devouring books of every genre. Self-described as a book-a-holic, she says "I've always loved to read, but then I discovered writing, and found I adored that, too. For reading...if nothing else is available, I've been known to read the back of the cereal box."

Want sneak peeks into what she's working on, or to chat with other readers about her books? Join the Facebook group! **bit.ly/deMora-FB-group**

deMora's got a spam-free newsletter list she'd love to have you join, too: **bit.ly/mldemora-newsletter**

~~~~~
~~~~~

Also by MariaLisa deMora

Please note that books in a series frequently feature characters from additional books within that series. If series books are read out of order, readers will twig to spoilers for the other books, so going back to read the skipped titles won't have the same angsty reveals.

Rebel Wayfarers MC series:

Mica, #1
A Sweet & Merry Christmas, #1.5
Slate, #2
Bear, #3
Jase, #4
Gunny, #5
Mason, #6
Hoss, #7
Harddrive Holidays, #7.5
Duck, #8
Biker Chick Campout, #8.5
Watcher, #9
A Kiss to Keep You, #9.25
Gun Totin' Annie, #9.5
Secret Santa, #9.75
Bones, #10
Gunny's Pups, #10.25
Never Settle, #10.5
Not Even A Mouse, #10.75
Fury, #11

Christmas Doings, #11.25
Gypsy's Lady, #11.5
Cassie, #12
Road Runner's Ride, #12.5

Occupy Yourself band series:

Born Into Trouble, #1
Grace In Motion, #2 (TBD)
What They Say, #3 (TBD)

Neither This, Nor That MC series:

This Is the Route Of Twisted Pain, #1
Treading the Traitor's Path: Out Bad, #2
Shelter My Heart, #3
Trapped by Fate on Reckless Roads, #4
Thunderstruck, #5

**Rebel Wayfarers & Incoherent MC
(NTNT) crossover stories:**

Going Down Easy
No Man's Land

Mayhan Bucklers MC series:

Most Rikki-Tik, #1
Mad Minute, #2
Pucker Factor, #3
Boocoo Dinky Dau, #4 (TBD)

Borderline Freaks MC series:

Service and Sacrifice, #1
More Than Enough, #2
Lack of In-between, #3
See You in Valhalla, #4

If You Could Change One Thing:
Tangled Fates Stories

There Are Limits, #1
Rules Are Rules, #2
The Gray Zone, #3

With My Whole Heart series

With My Whole Heart, #1
Bet On Us, #2

Alace Sweets series

Alace Sweets, #1
Seeking Worthy Pursuits, #2
An Embarrassment of Monsters, #3

Other Books:

Hard Focus
Dirty Bitches MC: Season 3

More information available at **mldemora.com**.